Dead Girl

A Romantic Zombie
Tale of Revenge

Written by Stavros
Illustrated by Aaron Alfeche

Edited by Tara Lindsay Hall

CRAZY DUCK PRESS

Library of Congress Catalog Number: 2011913419

ISBN: 978-0-9828121-9-8

Published by Crazy Duck Press
www.crazyduckpress.com

Layout & Graphic Design by Stavros
Illustrations by Aaron Alfeche
Copyright ©2015 Crazy Duck Press

Typeset in Garamond, Traveling Typewriter, and Typist.
Printed in the United States of America

Praise for Dead Girl

"It's so good I had a hard time putting it down."
-*Alethea Devary, Book Nerds Unite!*

"Wow. I just loved this story. This book is unlike any I've read before... The author paints such a great picture for the reader to imagine... Highly recommend! If you are looking for a unique Zombie book, then check this book out, you wont be disappointed!"
-*5 Out of 5 Star Amazon Review by Jessica Figueroa*

"Loved it! Once I picked it up I didn't want to put it down. I wanted to find out what happened to Jamie, well I was going to say just as much as she did, but I don't think that could be possible since I have never been there. But you did feel like you were right there beside her trying to help her find her killer." -*5 Out of 5 Star Amazon Review, The Avid Reader, Nancy Allen*

"Right from the beginning, I was pulled into the book and couldn't put it down. Jamie and her ex still have a bond, and you can see that from both of them... Kuddos to Stavros for making a dark subject that much more appealing!!" -*4 Out of 5 Star Amazon Review, B. Johnson*

"Dead Girl is creative, funny, and sad. I especially liked the ending. It was perfect. I recommend Dead Girl to zombie fans, and those who like some humor, some 'get what's comin' to ya', and some gore with their love story."
-*5 out of 5 Star Amazon.com Review by Laura Thomas*

"Just wanted you to know...I was about to wrap Dead Girl in festive Christmas paper but decided to read the first page...now I'm on page 88 and I'm keeping the book...and I'm not going to bed anytime soon."
-*Sabrina Buckman, a Facebook Post on Dec 21, 2011*

"WOW! Holy shit...Thank you for this. Thank you for bringing forth a story that more than restores my faith in a type that has gnawed at my entrails for over a decade. It was different, it was refreshing, it was a damn awesome break from the "same old, same old" crap this genre is filled with. It's so hard to find an original zombie tale any more. And even harder to find someone who can make an old story their own in some personal way. But this? Definitely not the same old crap." -*C. Dulaney, author of the Roads Less Traveled series*

"OMZG! (*Oh My Zombie Goodness*) I absolutely Loved this book. Dead Girl is not the conventional zombie book, but a great one! It's a book of mystery and revenge with Egyptian influence felt within the pages... I love this book and highly recommend it to anyone who loves a good revenge tale. Plus, I couldn't put the book down!"
-*Sunshine Rose, a Facebook Post, April 2013*

With Love & Admiration To
Jacquie Cote'

*Without whose belief in me
and stalwart nature
there would be no Jamie.*

I.

Jamie didn't hear the splash when her body hit the water. She didn't feel the cold grip of swirling liquid engulf her or lift her back up to the surface minutes later. She never noticed a murder of crows perched on the railings of the dilapidated concrete bridge. Or the way moonlight reflected off their coal black wings, shimmered in the rippling river and her wet hair. Jamie didn't see, feel, or hear much of anything anymore. Because at twenty-two... Jamie Lund was dead.

The water carried her like a baby and birthed her to the grassy bank on the other side of the bridge. A branch grabbed the black mini-skirt that she had worn that night and held it against the tug. A thousand ebon eyes watched her body drift and moor like a boat. A cold wind bent the tall grass on the river's edge and filled the night with wings. Against the churning bubble and the damp lights of the city in the distance, a cacophony of beaks erupted. Caws like locusts fell from the sky.

As if struck by a hammer to the chest, breath fueled Jamie's lungs. An awakening gasp burst through icy, cold lips and teeth that were filled with muddy leaves and liquid. Jamie's back arched and her head rose from the water with a jolt. Her eyes were milky white and distant. She sucked in a gulp of air with the grate of a straw searching for that last drop of soda under the ice; raspy like thorns – broken as the wind in the hollow of a tree. Her arms pushed up and drove her hands deep into riverbank mud. The chips and cracks in her red-polished nails were covered with dirt. Crows swarmed above her as a single mood. She coughed the river from her throat and pulled her shaking body from the frigid wet.

Ebon eyes glared at the wretched girl from the sky, from the trees, and their concrete perch on the dilapidated bridge as she struggled with stiff limbs to drag her sore and aching body through the tall weeds to the road. Jamie sat at the edge of the busted tarmac and looked around as her vision slowly tuned into her surroundings. The moon smiled down on her, a faint yellow, illuminating a patch of earth that she had never been to before. Nothing was familiar. Everything felt wrong. Fog peeled back from her memory like Russian nesting dolls, opening into themselves, getting smaller and smaller with the same effect, revealing nothing. She didn't know how or why she was here. Worry blossomed inside her chest like a fruit basket.

She tried to call out. To simply speak, to utter a sound, to work her feeble voice, but her throat burned hot nails all the way down her windpipe. A tiny squeak parted from her icy blue lips and she placed a hand to her throat. It was fraught with pain. She struggled. She worked her jaw to loosen her voice box, wind the organ up to play, but a flash of memory slammed into the back of her skull. It shook her shoulders awake, repeating on a loop. Scorching Jamie's cerebral cortex, her eyelids fluttered.

She was looking at herself in a freestanding mirror - getting dressed. A column of jet-black hair fell past bare shoulders, framing her pretty face. She had a lithe, curvy shape, sensual lips, and thin fingers that pulled the zipper of her skirt up the side of her hip. She turned the cute little black number around so that the fastener was in the back. She straightened her black lace bra, smiled, and then did her make up. She was going out...

But, where?

Suddenly, Jamie felt wet and shivered. Fear crept past her damp clothes and crawled under her skin as she lifted herself onto the road. Every muscle rebelled. Her knees argued at the thought of bending. The joints in her fingers and elbows ached, popping with movement. Her back felt as if someone had surgically implanted a slab of concrete, and a blinding pain ran from her neck down her spine. Her shoes were missing, toes numb, the sides of her feet scrapped along the busted edge of the tarmac as she rose crooked and wobbly onto two weak legs. It was a horrible dream, unspooling limbs for the audience of the blackbirds. Nothing was clear, nothing was familiar. A dull ringing

filled Jamie's ears and she felt cold. Bitter and deep, that sprang from her center. Jamie Lund felt the cold that no one ever feels but which we're all made to visit. Somewhere vaguely in the coils of her mind the little lost dead girl was reminded that it was July. *Its not supposed to be this cold out!* Slowly, Jamie wrapped her arms across her chest and lumbered toward the distant lights of the city.

II.

There is always something beautiful about a city at dawn. Something strange and inspiring - surreal and often telling. Something genteel and forgivable that can climb inside of your spirit, and is a wonder to behold. The soul of architecture can open like a rose and secrets are revealed to prying eyes as simply as a blushing prostitute. In the twilight all the hardness of the city seemed soft, spilling light across acres of rooftops. Automated memory, buried deep in the mesh fibers of muscle had brought Jamie to the apartment building on East 21st Street as night faded. Walking up the small flight of steps to the stoop, the poor girl pulled at the locked door with an earnest desire to finally be inside. Out of the cold. Out of the cold, hazy-blue, July morning.

"Shit," Jamie mumbled with a scratchy voice.

Only now did it occur to her that she was without her purse. That somewhere in the tumbling odd occurrences of her evening, from where she'd gotten dressed in the mirror to waking up on the bank of the river, that she had inadvertently lost her purse and everything in it. No keys. No credit cards, pictures, lipstick, or cell phone. The river could have carried it to its murky depths. Or it could have been lost elsewhere.

Jamie looked up and down the street. A single piece of paper fluttered on a breeze past her. Thoughts came slow and languid, a huge puzzle, spread out over the course of a single evening. It felt as if someone had shaken her mind and poured it back into her skull. Only they had left pieces out. The puzzle wasn't complete. Her joints ached worse now than when she had awakened on the riverbank. Jamie attributed it to the long walk into the city. As the closing Cyclops-eye of the moon spied her moving down corridors of streets, she kept telling herself that she'd feel better once she got home, got a shower, and got some sleep.

But now the door won't even open. And those damn birds again! At first, Jamie denied the thought because it was just too creepy, but here they were, following her. She was sure of it now. The crows from the river had followed her all the way to her apartment. They were perched on the lip of the building across the street. They collected on telephone and electric wires. The little tenebrous towers glared down at her from on high. The new light rising up through the city spires illumined their winged features. It was just the dead girl and the awful blackbirds. It wasn't something that she could easily dismiss now. The whole block was filled with the filthy little buggers. A shiver raced from the tips of Jamie's shoulders and down her arms. Cautiously, suspiciously, Jamie Lund watched them as she solemnly climbed down the steps and headed for the alley.

She couldn't recall knowing anybody else in the apartment building and didn't think it would go over all that well if she began ringing buzzers, waking her neighbors up, as a way of introduction. She knew that she had only moved into the building about two months ago. Her flat was on the first floor and she hoped that she'd left a window unlocked around back. As bad as that would be in this city, to leave one's window accessible to the criminal element, Jamie prayed that she had been that stupid. She needed a shower. She wanted the nightmare of these past few hours to end and simply…go to bed.

In the alley, a stray cat hissed at her, raising its fur and tensing up. The other strays just ran away, bounding into dark holes, hiding under an old tire and behind trashcans.

"Well, good morning to you too," Jamie sarcastically muttered.

She'd taken to feeding them, and thought they were getting along much better than this harsh reception. A few mornings ago, she was even able to pet the Tabby stray and it had come by the window a couple of times, meowing for her. She considered it the beginning of a beautiful friendship. *Oh, well. Little traitors.* There were better things on her mind to worry about than whether or not the alley cats liked her. Jamie sighed harshly. *It's a sad state of affairs when I get upset at the lack of their rancid love in the first place.* Jamie turned sharply to the tiny fur-covered heads that poked out at her from the odd places in the alley and hissed. The sandy Tab barely touched any ground, it fled so fast.

The delicate beating of wings clamored softly around her and Jamie looked up. *These things aren't afraid of me.* The base of the window was just out of reach. Her shoulders slumped. It was all beginning to be too much. Jamie looked for something to stand on and spied a couple beat-up, plastic milk crates. She stacked them under the window and climbed up. Her legs were really sore - *worse than any time after the gym.* She reached up to the window, but it was locked. Cursing herself for having done the right thing, Jamie almost tumbled off the crates. The girl was getting flustered now. Anger was a heat that warmed her insides. *It's too much for a single gal to handle for just a night out!*

Jamie looked around the alley again, and walking over to the far fence she picked up a stone and threw it through her window. The crashing glass was louder than what she thought it would be. It made a jagged hole in the pane's center. Grabbing a mangled trashcan lid, the dead girl climbed up her makeshift steps and cleared the remaining glass with the metal shield. She tossed the wrinkled disc back at the cans, but it skidded off the alley floor with a loud clanging, dislodging cats that fled from the narrow causeway. Jamie just didn't care anymore about waking up her neighbors. She wanted to be inside. Nothing else mattered. Pulling herself up, her arms strained and a small glass shard dug into the flesh along her ulna bone, but she didn't feel it. She scraped her shins as she crashed onto the glassy floor. And she was in. She was home. *Finally!*

Outside, the veil of day awakened further and the caw of crows echoed in the alley. Outside, there was worry and doubt, fear of never being safe, and the drama of bodies crushing one another. Outside was cold and vacant. It pulled through the broken window. Outside, something mean and nasty had happened and Jamie Lund didn't know what it was.

The light above the bathroom sink flickered and spat, arriving to the point where it splashed Jamie with a soothing 75-watt glow. Instinctively, she grabbed a handful of toilet paper and looked herself over, examining her pale extremities for any cuts that she'd received from dragging her tired body over broken glass. But all she spied was a cut along the length of her forearm. It wasn't bleeding. She looked at the scrapes on her legs too. They weren't bleeding either. It was the first time that night that Jamie thought something was going right. An unrecognizable face stared back at her in the mirror. Tiny spots of hemorrhaged blood dotted her pale, enormous eyes.

"Did someone slip me something?" she muttered to the porcelain face staring back at her.

Thoughts of date rape fueled her imagination as she ran her fingers through her knotted and matted hair. She removed a leaf and twig from a thick tangle, along with a few strands of grass, and noticed the pallor of her hands. They were dark white with a tinge of blue, caked with river mud. She lifted the other one to her face. Her nails were chipped and cracked - dirt-laden. Several of her painted fingernails were broken and split, but Jamie didn't feel any pain from them. Nor could she remember how they had gotten into such a sorry state. Jamie stared at the front and backs of her hands trying to grasp the pieces of what had happened to her during the night. It was elusive and blank. Theives of time. There was a hole the size of Texas in her memory. She compared the color of her hands to the tone in her cheeks. It was the same. It was the same deathly pallor.

Her eyes went wide, staring through the cleave of her fingers to the bruising around her neck. She tilted her head up, touching her skin delicately with dirty fingertips on the purplish and brown blotches that circumvented the globe of her throat. Her hands navigated the course brutality she witnessed and her breathing became erratic. Panicking, Jamie swore the indentations looked like thick fingers and the press of palms.

"What the hell happened to me last night?" Frantically, she tried to remember.

She closed her eyes and forced her will to recall: *A flash of dancing and bright lights. Blurry faces at a party. Thudding bass.* Jamie's chest violently moved up and down as if her breath were hot, a steam engine pumping raw images from her wounded parietal lobe. The torn ligaments and muscles in her throat spat like a fiery spike. She felt dizzy and grabbed the sink with both hands to keep from crashing to the floor. Club music reverberated through her head. It bubbled like ginger ale and laughter. Her body swooned, dipping sideways. She gripped the argillaceous bowl tighter. She felt pushed and her body jolted as a dark stranger filled her mind towering over her. She felt his press against her ribs and a sharp pain digging in her back. Her dirty little fingers dug into the unyielding sink. Splintered nails broke from her body and fell down the drain.

Her voice snapped; an erupting spasm shot out from her cold, hollow belly. Jamie's demure frame shook against a maelstrom of sensations as vague images beat lively against her skull. Finally, she pushed herself away from the porcelain comfort of the sink. Head tilting, Jamie felt as if she were falling. Her equilibrium was off. Balance was an odd concept. Abstract. She opened her eyes for support and saw an unfamiliar face. It stared at her from the silver sheen of the bathroom mirror. Ugly. Strange. *I'd never allow something like this to happen to me. I'mma smart girl. A decent girl. Dear God…what happened?*

Jamie had never been so upset without tears. Her universe was cracking. Her eyes were swollen. She wanted tears, sobbing, and all the natural sounds of sadness and falling apart that traditionally flailed her senses with ordinary hurt. But there was no water. She wasn't crying. She didn't know it yet, but she couldn't relieve her pain with tears.

Jamie straightened up with purpose. Removing her blouse, she tossed it to the floor and unsnapped her bra, laying it on top of the grimy shirt. She twisted around to look at her back in the mirror where she'd recalled the sharp pain. There was a bruise. Daintily, her hand outlined its oval shape, but she couldn't figure out what had caused it. Slowly, Jamie backed away from the mirror, encircling her arms over her breasts, pulling herself inward.

The plastic shower curtain folded at her touch. The knobs turned and jets of hot water pounded the tub's basin. Her fingers fumbled with the zipper on her skirt, frantic and nervous. Jamie couldn't remove the garment fast enough. Salvation waited in that shower. The rising steam was a baptism of hope. Mechanized rain washed all the horror away.

Hot. Jamie didn't even turn on the cold tap. It should have been scalding as it pounded life into her dull skin. But the heat still felt so far, far away. She dipped her head under. Jets of cascading liquid danced on her skull. *I woke in a river.* Jamie remembered the taste of murky water in her mouth. *Did I jump into it? Was I…pushed?*

If tears could have bled from her eyes they would have done so by now. Every other trait of crying gripped her body except liquid. Jamie Lund stood there with the shower's heated water throbbing over her and it became her tears. In the cascade of running water it wasn't obvious that her tear ducts had stopped functioning. For all she knew or wanted to know tears had finally found her and flowed with swirls of mud around her white feet, traveling down the drain.

Jamie washed herself with a bar of soap until the water became frigid. Shutting off the taps, a few drops beaded the porcelain basin and Jamie waited for their soft patter to stop before she climbed out. Wrapping herself in a towel, she patted the moisture and dried her hair with another strap of bathing cloth. The bathroom light cut through the short recessed hall into the living room. Jamie stepped into the hard glow, pressing strands of hair with the towel, until she heard a crow's caw and the flapping of wings. Turning to face the second bedroom, where she had climbed through, Jamie saw one of the blackbirds perched on the windowsill. It was huge and foreboding. Its coal eyes pierced hers and she felt a strange stirring rustle around inside.

Watching the bird, an odd sensation overcame her and she swore that the thing's ebony eyes reminder her of someone. She tilted her head and the crow tilted its head. Each looked at the other and for a brief moment Jaime saw herself, in her mind's eye, standing in the hard glow of the bathroom light as if she were the bird sitting in the broken window. The vision was strained, elliptical, and she never noticed that she had stopped breathing. For the first time in this horrid chain of events Jamie felt calm, centered, and a face began to form from the fog of her memory. But it wouldn't rise to the surface. It stayed buried within her. A sudden burst of anger seized her ribcage and she threw the towel that she had used to dry her hair at the flighty beast.

The bird cackled and cawed, lifting its wings, and flew from the window. Jamie entered the room in a huff and began riffling through the junk that was piled on the desk. She still hadn't completely unpacked from when she had moved in. Having found the tape, she picked up the damp towel off the floor and used it to cover the gaping hole that led into the apartment. Jamie didn't have to look. She knew they were out there. The sky was gray this morning and the alley behind her apartment was filled with a murder of crows.

III.

Douglas Rand had waited all morning for her. He checked
with the temporary Secretary twice to make sure that Jamie had not
scheduled the day off or called in. In the two and a half years that
Ms. Lund had been with the firm she had only taken one sick day.
And even then she called it in. Douglas couldn't help but worry that
something might be wrong, even though he had no tolerance for
tardiness. And refusing to call the office, if indeed something was
wrong, was inexcusable. He loathed the idea of firing Ms. Lund. She
did her job well, was pretty to look at, and never once cluttered her
desk with family photos of cats or husbands. She had a pleasant
demeanor. But as the little hand raced around the big hand, falling
from the noon hour, and she still hadn't arrived, he toyed with the idea
of firing Ms. Lund more and more.

Though when the day tilted towards quitting time, Douglas
Rand took it upon himself to call the winsome gal and discover why
she had not shown up for work. Jamie listened to her boss's agitated
voice as he left a message on the answering machine. His brawn was
terse, denoting a hint of concern. But Jamie was unable to make it to
the phone, pick it up, and explain to him why she'd been absent. In
fact, since Jamie Lund had lain down on her bed to get some sleep
she'd been unable to do anything at all. Movement, it seemed, was
something she had no control over.

The weight of the blanket and sheets on top of her held like
a vice. Her eyes had been fixed to a spot on the ceiling for hours now
and any recognizable detail in the plaster had grown stale eons ago.

She did try to move. She tried to call out. But nothing happened. She was stiff as a board, unable to break the invisible bonds that kept her in place. Panic gripped her caged mind, swirling in abject confusion. Her thoughts screamed in terror, an inconsolable traffic jam. It was all so desperately wrong! So unbelievably awful!

Every simple daily action that Jamie took for granted was impossible to perform, and immeasurable to the ache and want to rise. She couldn't wiggle her toes. She couldn't lift a finger. Her chest did not pump air into her body. Her limbs were prison gates, her flesh hell! Even if she was capable of answering the telephone, how would she be able to explain this to her boss? She didn't want to believe it herself. And it was happening to her. Since she'd crawled from the tumble and turn of the river, nothing was making any logical sense.

Her body was an uncompromising shell and the ceiling was cold and unyielding. After a time, though, her thoughts relaxed and she began to deal with it. She didn't have any other choice. It wasn't a thing one could sweep under the carpet and forget about. Her muscles and bones had rebelled against her will and she was immovable – a statue that couldn't raise a faint whisper in the back of her own bruised throat.

Slowly, it became increasingly obvious. Death was a dream of sleep where the eternally dying dream the sleep of death. The undeniable evidence in the stillness of her being, the stark paleness of her complexion, and the lack of blood pooling from her cuts after climbing through the window whispered dark truths in her ears. *Rigor Mortis*. There was nothing familiar to Jamie about her skin. Time and time again, she found herself asking what had happened, only to arrive at the hard won conclusion that she, Jamie Lund, wasn't alive anymore. Somehow in the foolhardy night, she'd been a dumb girl. She'd gotten herself killed. The handprints around her neck were more than enough to convince her, but she didn't want to go there earlier. It was too bizarre. Too horror show. Too ungodly to consider. But confined against her will, mind freaking out, all the crazy notions began to make perfect, practical sense.

She lay like a boulder in her bed. Incapable of speech, incapable of motion! Awake, not dreaming – watching tender shadow play on the ceiling. Millions of nerve endings reported nothingness back at her. It was an odd sensation – *nothingness*. Warm like mother's milk. Calm as a placid sea. After awhile, her fear fell away to sluggish acceptance and the scared little girl felt an eerie calm like nothing she had ever felt or dreamed before. It was as immovable as her limbs, as stoic as a towering tree. The roots of it dug deep. Her mind branched and splintered and came back on itself with definite possibility, and the idea of her being a living dead girl made sense – *perfect, ludicrous sense!*

As if on cue with Jamie's acceptance of her fate, the eyes of an olive skinned man flitted across her mind and she remembered him following her into a room at a party. His pupils were bold, large and black. His hair was the color of raven wings, cut spiky and short. His chiseled jaw was set like a king. He was devilishly handsome, smelled like a crisp desert and sex, and when he looked at Jamie she felt her form, weightless. Her body was a feather on his fingers, but she walked around the room to another man. She nestled up to *his* side, but she couldn't see him, couldn't make out who he was. She felt him there, but his features were lost to her. All that was visible was the radiant stare of the gorgeous stranger.

Then, his breath whispered in her ears, as if it were he at her side, and his tongue was hot and moist in her mind as he spoke the name, Horus. The sky rumbled overhead like the wheels of a huge train on rusted tracks. Clouds tumbled over thunderheads as lightning lit the universe, a pantheon of unending stars. It ignited the soul of the sun and the sign of the eye of the ancient Egyptian God glowed, as if a dream. All of a sudden, feelings of nothingness were replaced by burning, like a brand was being forged to the temples of her dead flesh. When that ceased, Jamie felt as if she was flying, like she had wings and was one of those filthy blackbirds that had followed her from the riverbank. She felt like she was flying until the deadness of her flesh pulled her down. She was a stone – *falling!*

The bed caught her and Jamie looked up at the ceiling. She felt her eyes blink. A cool breeze brushed against her exposed cheeks. She knew it was night. She listened to the quiet and the distant murmur of a city beyond the walls and thought the horribleness was finally over. That was until she tried to get up. Like so many times before, her muscles reneged on their promise of motion. She was still a cripple to her unnatural death. The germane recollections and alien sensations walled up around her so high that Jamie began to hate herself. The vermin in her blood and stillness of her frame made her seasick. If she could have moved she would have puked!

Jamie longed for the taste of bile in the back of her throat and the quaking spasms of flesh, a heaving stomach, lungs ripped by air. It would have made her feel alive! But that was the thing that was missing, that was the thing that was missing all along. She felt it in the shower and during the long walk home. She saw it in the face in the mirror, in her hands and hemorrhaged eyes. The missing puzzle piece that rattled through the fog of her lazy memory was the fact that she had died. Someone had murdered her. She felt his frame against her, felt his force upon her flesh, but she could not will his name or face to mind. The unbearable finality of it broke upon her jailed gait with the coming of another dawn and there was nothing she could do except lie, like a log, and wait.

But her eyes lurched in their sockets! Looking down, straining over the bridge of her nose, Jamie saw the mountain of her feet sticking up like bandits. It had seemed like forever since she had last been able to rotate her pupils. *It was a blessing! And a curse...*the dead girl noticed that the sheets above her breasts did not rise or fall gracefully. It was exactly as she had thought. Her brow furled into a worried knot, but she didn't notice.

A slump in her waist was the first movement she recognized in God knew how long. She tried to move her arm and only found it difficult. But not impossible as before! Pain ripped through every joint and tether of flesh like an electrical current. Jamie pushed past it, pushed into the marrow of her bones, reclaiming ownership of her vessel. She was the Captain of her cruise ship, the Admiral of her body of water, and she'd be damned if she wasn't going to climb out of this bed and find the filthy bastard that had murdered her!

Once Jamie had lifted her arm enough to pry her shoulder from the mattress, the dead girl let out a wail so frightening and shrill that it tore the blackbirds outside from their perch. The sky above the apartment complex had become a torrent of dark feathers and wings encircling the place like a dower mood. Her blood-curdling scream was the first time since yesterday that Jamie had heard her own voice. It didn't phase her. It had been too much already. A hot plate of hate filled her gullet and there would be hell to pay once she'd regained all the ranges of motion that she'd once been accustomed to perform.

Now, bodily gestures were a luxury. The Eye of Horus had made that clear. She was on borrowed time. Jamie's spine arched like a wave. The pain was intense. The stiff road of her structure bent, pulled, and cracked. Each limb was a delight of ache and utter anguish. Movement, was her joy and wellspring as she broke the mooring of her body from the anchor of the bed. She was no longer paralyzed and caged, freedom loomed across the folded corners of her dust ruffle. Jamie pushed hard and rolled onto her side. The momentum sent her careening off the bed and she fell to the floor as the covers tumbled on top of her.

She stayed there on all fours for a moment, summoning the power to rise and noticed the pure absence of color in her hands. They were bone white. Inhuman. Turning her head, she looked up the course of her arm to the socket. Her limb was the same ghostly pale until her eyes strained on the ball of her shoulder. The stark contrast made her eyes go wide, and through the crease of a dangling breast and her forearm, she saw the two-toned nature of her hip and legs. Running down the length of her, where her body had touched the bed, was a ghastly buffet of purple, burgundy, and brown blotches, as if her blood had congealed to the lowest point. If there were any doubts lingering in Jamie's mind about her unnatural condition then seeing this gruesome sight dispelled them. She was cut in half, a living cadaver, and then the smell began to take effect.

The bedding was all tasseled and strewn around her. She couldn't see it, of course, but by the unbelievable stench she knew that at some point during her intense ordeal her bowels had relieved themselves against her knowledge. Trapped under the covers, her senses abandoning her, Jamie never knew that she wallowed in her own muck. Now, more than ever she wanted to vomit, spew the contents of her last meal into the fray and have all the nastiness of living done with!

As if climbing a rope to nowhere, the dead girl forced her fickle limbs to remove the sullied sheets. The cold feces stuck to her frame like a sickness. Urine stained the mattress, and as she peeled the yuck off the smell of the dark mixture sent bile racing to the back of her teeth. Her stomach jammed up into her lungs and the remaining matter of that forgotten last meal dirtied the coffin of her bed even further. The violent up-chuck riveted her corpse like a striking bell.

In the shower, she removed her soiled undies, and for the second time in as many days, Jamie lathered her flesh with soap and rinsed off with the hottest water she could muster. She felt the blood in her veins soften and noticed that with time a little color began

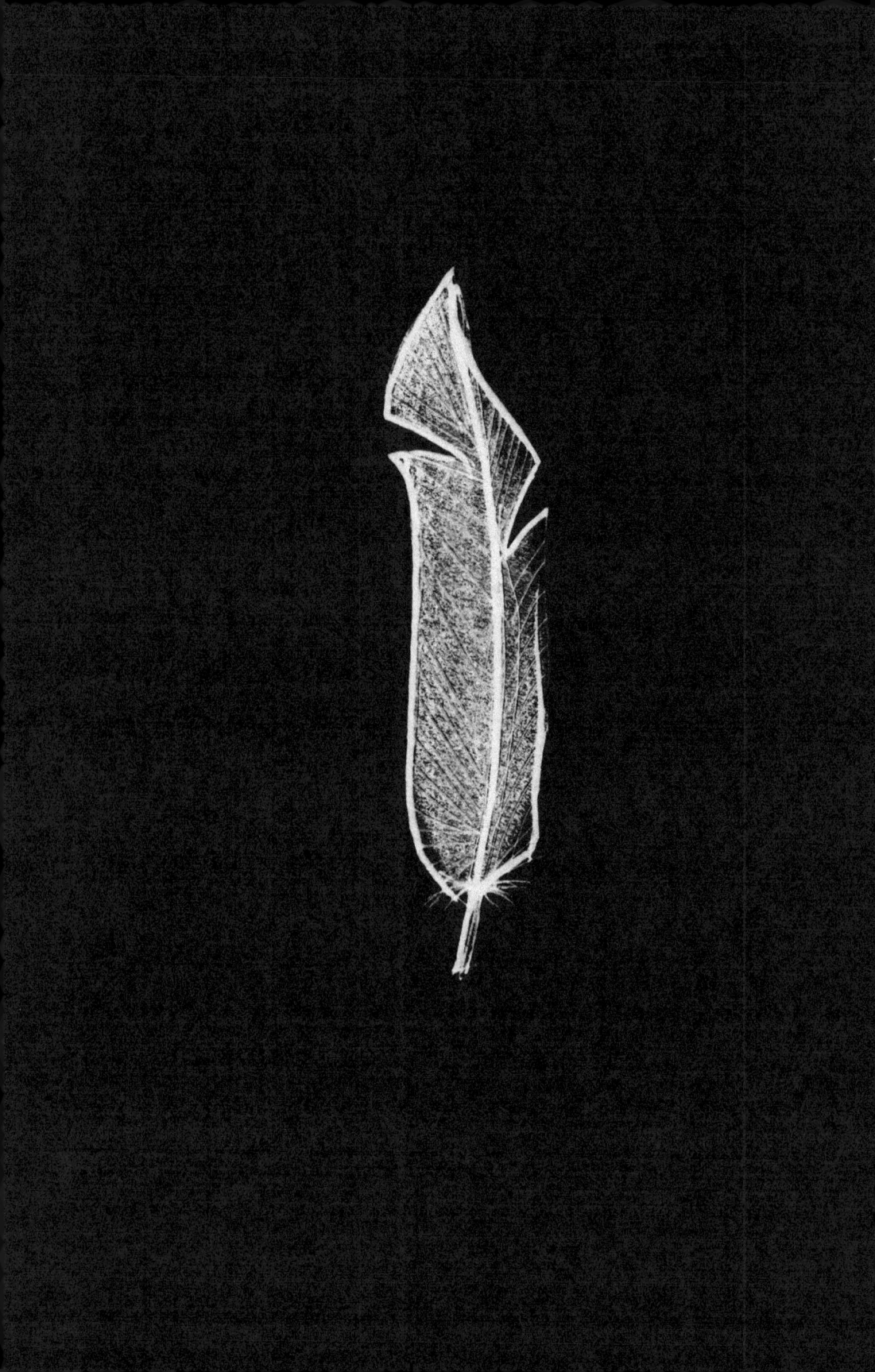

reclaiming her surface to a fine, lightly pale pink. As if by compulsion, she washed over and over again until the soap disappeared in her hands and the water ran cold, feeling distant to the emptiness that housed her core. Jamie Lund crumbled like a molding piece of paper to the tub's basin and cried her tearless sobs, weeping with her shoulders, cradling herself like a fetus.

IV.

The ratchet whirl-clicked and turned, tightening the bolt. Billy Kimmel was under the hood of a yellow body, black racing striped 68 El Camino with a 350 small block, dual headers and an aluminum intake manifold, when Hector told him he had a visitor. He grabbed a rag from his toolbox, pulled the grease from his fingers, and headed into the office. Through the windows he spied the small frame of a woman dressed in sweats, wearing a hoodie pulled down over her brow. Tufts of dark hair poked out through the hood and she wore sunglasses. The way she stood, outside the office door, slightly turned toward the street made it impossible for him to see her face.

"Yeah," he said to the unfamiliar figure, "can I help you?"

"I hope so."

Turning around, Jamie kept her head low and it took Billy a moment to realize that his ex-girlfriend was standing in front of him. He had always thought that he would relish her return in a more humbled form than the less than perfect little Ms. Thang that she used to be. Perfect hair. Perfect manicured nails. Always the trendiest nightspots and fancy restaurants. He watched her forget about who she was right before his eyes. As she bled his wallet dry he watched her quickly forgot about him as well. Now, the prim diva was looking haggard as hell and he actually felt sorry for her. He never expected to see her again – *Ever!* And he especially never thought he'd see her in anything less than a brand new sports convertible and a Gucci bag; definitely not wearing a pair of aged baggy sweats and his old Varsity pullover. The sight of her made his voice stumble and it took him a minute to respond.

"Jamie?" The question lingered between them. "What the hell are you doing here?"

"Ahhh," Jamie stuttered. "Who...who's party did we go to this weekend?"

"What?" Billy blurted out the word with a wrinkled face. His mouth hung open like the dot on a question mark.

"Who's party did we go to?" repeated Jamie nervously, fidgeting with the hood, and looking toward the traffic on the street. "Did you leave me there? Did we have a fight? Where did we go?"

Billy was too awestruck for words. It was like a dream. She wasn't really here looking like shit, asking him a bunch of stupid questions like they were still going out. It was a mirage; an apparition of his broken heart playing tricks on him.

"Jamie," he slowly said. "I haven't seen you in over six weeks."

Jamie tore off her sunglasses. She wasn't sure if she had heard him right. *Did he say 6 weeks?* "What?" she exclaimed, and the word dangled from her gaping jowls with callous fear.

Earlier, Jamie felt a dreadful urgency. There were holes the size of Texas in her memory, and as she climbed out of the tub she was determined to find out who had murdered her. She didn't know how she could accomplish such a feat. It loomed in front of her with crushing impossibility, yet she had to be here for a purpose. Somehow, someway she'd crossed over from where no one returns and came back to the world with a vengeance. And just like that, she felt another puzzle piece click into place.

Jamie stared at the strange wet face in the mirror and knew it as her own. There was no getting around that now. Death wore her like a cloak. *What am I? A ghost? But I have a reflection. A walking corpse? Zombie?* She had heard of vengeful spirits from some A&E TV Special on the paranormal, but didn't pay too much mind to it when it was on. She used to laugh, and scoffed at that kind of nonsense. Now as a ghost hunter's wet dream, Jamie didn't know what she was. *Perhaps there's a book or website online?* Jamie's mind struggled with it all, so huge and compact in her five foot, three inch frame, where all the logic blocks had been thrown out the window. Yet, there was a cohesive sense at work here, under the skein of the world, a larger machination was playing her like a doll, as she waded deeply into uncharted waters.

"Who are you?" she had said to her cadaverous reflection in the bathroom mirror. "Where are you now? And why did you kill me?"

He wasn't lounging around her sock drawer, that much she knew. It had happened out there in the city, among the river and the birds, at the club, and at that party. Somewhere someone had seen her with him. Somewhere someone had spoken to her! That olive skinned man and the faceless stranger from her tattered memory were the only leads she had. All she had to do now was find them. In a city of nearly twenty million screaming souls, all she had to do was reach out and… *find them!?!* Jamie's shoulders slumped with a penetrating sigh. Looking down, she noticed the small, yellow rug was soaked. Her feet and bony ankles were ghastly. She'd really banged up her shins climbing through the window. The rudeness of her knees were gangly and sallow. Her pubic hair jumped away from her flesh. And dark blue rings had formed around her toenails and fingernails.

This curse…or gift…nightmare! – whatever it was – it was all the evidence she needed. Her body was his downfall. Out there, her killer was on the loose, and Jamie Lund couldn't let that stand. Out there, he gloated, thinking himself invincible; that he had gotten away with murder. The thought of there being another victim, another dead girl like herself, but perhaps not as fortunate as she had been, riveted her to the bone. *That can't be, that just can't be!*

Getting dressed, Jamie wanted this maniac, this destroyer of youth, this bandit of darkened light to taste the river as she had, and feel death's cold embrace as she had – *slow and sinking.* Jamie wanted him to feel all of it. She wanted him to choke on it as he had choked her. There was only one person now who came to mind who could help her with this dilemma. One person, out of everyone she knew and could remember that would aid her to find justice. But he was staring at her like she was a mad woman.

"Six weeks…" she mumbled.

Billy leaned in close and whispered. "Are you fucked up right now?"

Jamie was aghast at the question. Her shoulders rocked with tension as she slammed her eyewear back into place. "How can you even ask such a thing!"

"How?" Billy's blue eyes were raised on pause. His brow formed three thick, wavy lines. "Have you looked in a mirror lately? You look like ass and you're asking me what party we went to." He shook his head like a rattle. "I haven't seen you since you broke up with me."

"It's not funny, Billy. I'm not in the mood for this right now."

He threw up his hands. "Oh, I'm sorry. *You're* not in the mood, right now." He leaned forward and tapped his chest. "I'm at work. And I haven't seen you since you walked out on me, saying you can do better."

Billy nodded his head, slowly, as he pulled back, and thrust his hands toward her, indicting that she clearly wasn't doing all that well since she'd left him. He turned to leave. Jamie bit her upper lip, feeling panic watching him go. The parking lot of Hector's Garage was turning into quicksand and the horror of her most recent immobility was fresh on her thighs. She didn't know how long she had before something even worse happened.

"I'm not high, Billy," she said as his fingers touched the door handle.

"You sure?" He didn't bother to turn around, but he didn't go inside either.

"Yes, I'm sure," she exclaimed heatedly. *Drugs are the least of my concerns!*

Jamie felt wired — *ready to snap.* She was clearly missing more than a few hours from over the weekend. Six whole weeks and her entire break up with Billy had been wiped clean from her memory by the cruelest maid to ever crawl through her ears! He stared at her, and she felt meek. It irked her to be so helpless and uninformed. Pride kept poking her in the side like a knife. She stared up at him, watching the colors around his head and shoulders fluctuate and ripple with pink and yellow spikes. Jamie wasn't sure what it was or what it meant, but everyone she saw along her walk to the garage this morning had a faint glow surrounding them. It was beautiful and scary. Some people glowed orange or red. Some people glowed a dark yellow, like sulfur. A few people even radiated brown, pink, or white. Billy's dominant color was blue. Jamie wondered what the purpose of each hue was and why all of a sudden she could see it.

Though, deep down Jamie knew why it was suddenly visible. She didn't really have to ponder too deeply. It wasn't every day a girl wakes up dead! *Maybe this is really hell?* Usually, death went unnoticed by the ones it claimed. It couldn't be looked at for what it was or appreciated by the dead. The dead were just that…*dead*. Jamie kept telling herself that she was a lucky one. That it could've been worse. That it could've been a whole lot worse. She was dead. She didn't have to wake up at all.

"I need your help."

"I don't have any money for drugs," he said.

"Jesus, Billy!" Her Irish rose up as she stomped the ground with a foot and clenched her fists. "Come off it already. I'm in real trouble here."

Billy didn't notice, but the canopy of the garage behind him had taken flight. Jamie had riled her travelling companions and they beat the air.

"Like what?"

Jamie exhaled and shook her head. "I can't say."

"Then I can't help you."

He turned to leave for real this time and Jamie's whole body tensed.

"I didn't say I wasn't going to tell you. I just can't do it here, ok? Look, dammit…" she reached out and grabbed him by the arm. "I'm asking you…" Her eyes were a havoc-crash of panic behind dark spectacles, pleading for him to not make it anymore difficult than it already was.

"Asking me what?" he voiced as he pulled away from her tiny grasp.

"Will you help me?"

It practically sounded like begging to Billy's ears. He'd never heard such desperation in Jamie's voice before. It had to be something serious. He was angry with her for the way she dumped him, but he wasn't an asshole. *A sucker, maybe.* He had always had a soft spot for Jamie, ever since they were kids. So, he couldn't leave her in the lurch if she needed him, and besides…she had asked for him. She had asked for him, specifically. She could've just said, *I need help*, and not indicated him at all. But she used the word, *you* – making it personal. She didn't want just anybody's help; she wanted his. And that made all the difference. It tugged at his gut.

"Meet me here at five and I'll see what I can do."

Jamie scraped her top teeth across her bottom lip. She hated to ask. "Can we go someplace to talk…*now?*"

He raised his voice. "I'm working."

Jamie squished her face, titled her head like a puppy, and simply said, "please?"

Billy sighed bitterly and shook his head from side to side, thinking himself a sucker. He knew Hector didn't mind so much if he, or the other fellas, took an extended lunch just as long as the work got done. It was more about quality than quantity at the garage. That's why people came to ole' Hec in the first place. The man treated cars like an art and he distilled that appreciation throughout the whole crew.

"You wanna go over to the shop?" Billy asked, indicating the coffeehouse across the street with a nod of his head that used to be their frequent hang out when they were dating.

"Can we…" Jamie fidgeted with her fingers, spying the blackbirds perched above his head. "Can we just go to your place?"

Billy looked down at her with a scowl. *Nothing but drama.* "Wait here. I'll ask Hector."

Billy entered the garage and she watched him disappear into the back of the building as the murder of crows watched their wounded guest stand alone in the parking lot. Jamie felt caged and had no idea how she was going to tell him or *if* she should even tell him that she was the walking dead. *But how can he help me to catch my killer if I don't?*

Leaving her apartment this morning to come to Hector's Garage, Jamie was reminded again about the vacancy of her purse. She had no keys for her front door or car. Her cell phone was missing, all her credit cards, and IDs. She couldn't access any of her money in the bank. She was fucked. Royally fucked. And it wasn't in a good way. She was a defacto nobody with no ties to the world anymore and no way to get around. It was a big city, and she couldn't even afford bus fare.

Jamie clenched her teeth and scanned the parking lot, noticing the tail end of Billy's burgundy Chevelle. *He still has that car.* The dead girl cracked a smile, remembering its smell and the way it shook when the engine roared to life. She'd lost her virginity to him on its leather bucket seats when he first got it seven years ago. She recalled the way the belt buckle had dug into her back and Jamie's thoughts turned to the bruise she wore now, just below the rib line. She remembered feeling that she was being pressed against something firm as it dug into her flesh. Hard, but not piercing.

The sun beat down on top of her head and shoulders. It shimmered off a thousand feathers. She was covered in layers from the sweltering summer heat. Clothed to hide from everyone. Though inside, Jamie still felt cold. She heard the soles of Billy's boots on the tarmac before she turned around. Cleaned up and out of his work overalls, he looked rather nice. Handsome, even. And for the life of her, Jamie Lund couldn't remember why she had dumped him.

They had known each other since high school, and began dating their Sophomore year. They were on again off again, but they made a real try of it after community college. Had even lived together. She remembered that much. But she didn't recollect what went wrong or why they had broken up. From her rancid, Swiss cheese perspective they were doing alright. Things were good between them. But he had seemed annoyed at the mere sight of her and Jamie wondered what she could have done to make him hate her so. She made a mental note to find what had happened between them when the time came.

Now, she was being led to his Chevelle, tossing a glance back at the flighty audience. She hoped that they would finally leave her be. Billy held the door open for her like a gentleman as she slid inside. Bucket seat anamnesis, the metal ride framed her thoughts. Billy didn't say much as he climbed in, turned the key, and that familiar quake shook Jamie by the belly. The sound of the engine should have been comforting. But the Chevelle was nothing more than a museum

36

now. *Dead things filled museums. Memories filled homes.* She had no home anymore. People with homes had keys. She didn't have anything. She was just the dead thing sitting in the car, on display, and she felt fucked. Royally fucked. Unsure as to how she was going to break the news to him that she had died.

V.

Blue carpeting. Billy still had that ratty ole blue shag covering the floor on his half of the duplex. Jamie smiled when she saw it. She used to hate that carpet with a passion, now it was simply nostalgic. Who had blue carpet in their house, she'd ask, and he'd shrug, and they'd screw on it for hours after falling off the bed. Life was good then. Life was...well...*life*. Jamie was alive. She sucked down air like the rest of the people on the planet. Worried about the rent, paid car payments, taxes, and painted her nails. But since the blue rings had formed around her cuticles, Jamie hadn't thought much about what was considered normal. Normal was simply a town in Illinois and not the state of things with her flesh.

Billy was dying to know what all the fuss was about. He had asked her what was going on a couple of times while they were in the car. Jamie didn't think blurting it out casually as he drove down the street was the smartest thing to do. Might make him crash. Better to wait until they were safely indoors, less chance of an accident.

"Still have those boxes you never picked up," he said as he hung his keys on a hook by the kitchen door. "Take 'em when you leave or I'm gonna toss 'em."

"Ok," replied Jamie not remembering any boxes, packing, or that she had moved out.

The reliability of her memory was as accurate as a weather forecast. Chunks of her life were missing. Gone, leaving a hard wake for her to surf. Though, little things seemed relevant and held purchase in her soul. Like the way he kept a box of tools by the back door and the sound of the bubbler in the fish tank, it reminded her of home despite the fact that she had her own apartment.

"Hi, Oscar," Jamie said to the tropical fish in the tank, gently tapping the glass.

"That's not Oscar," informed Billy, passing her to turn on the air conditioner. "Oscar died just about the same time you left."

The pirate treasure chest gurgled air and the fish that wasn't Oscar swam to the corner of the tank.

"He looks the same."

"Yeah," Billy mumbled. "Thought about getting a different fish, but I just couldn't decide. So, I got another one that looked just like him. Two in fact." Billy pulled along side of her by the tank, grabbed the can of fish food, opened the lid, and began sprinkling some flakes into the water. "Thought the company might make 'em stick around longer, you know. But he ate her in about a week."

"Oh," uttered Jamie, peering at the fish more closely to discern its differences.

The fish that wasn't Oscar swam upward to the sinking flakes and slurped them up. Jamie felt Billy's presence, his heat, next to her and moved away.

"This one's Merlin," he informed.

Jamie waved and said, "Hi, Merlin."

She wandered into the livingroom, noticing immediately the dust outlines of pictures on the vacant walls. "What happened to all your photos?" She turned toward him. "You redecorating?

Billy just gave her that same awful stare that he had given her at the garage and walked into the kitchen. "You thirsty?" He didn't give her time to respond. "Mostly have water, a few beers, and a swig of OJ left."

Jamie listened to the sounds of the refrigerator opening and closing, questioning if she could even eat or drink. She hadn't felt the slightest bit of hunger since climbing out of the river. She spied those blank, square portraits not hanging on the wall and wondered that if she unpacked her boxes, back at her apartment, would she find them there? Each wrapped up in newspaper? Their dirty white absence stared at her and she felt wretched.

Stepping into the doorway, between the two rooms looking at her, Billy popped the cap on a bottle of Killians. Jamie felt the weight of his stare and wandered over to the firm island of the couch. She knew he was waiting. She knew what he wanted. He took a slow sip of the beer. Its soft red malt treaded over his tongue and fell down his gullet to dull bliss. There was a long moment of awkward silence in which Jamie could have started talking. She could have said anything to get the motor of her mouth moving, rev it up to tell him the truth. But telling him the truth seemed as hard as nails when she didn't even know what the truth really was: A gaggle of stalking birds that followed her around, a lack of breathing, and one crazy weekend that she couldn't remember. Not much of a bucket list.

Jamie avoided the obvious carcass in room, noticing instead how Billy's T-shirt fit his slender frame and accentuated the muscles in his chest and arms. The way that the bottom of the shirt tucked into the top of his jeans made his long legs ride, and in spite of her erratic memory, Jamie couldn't forget about how he felt inside of her. Billy leaned against the doorjamb, cradling his bottle of beer. Jamie sighed, thinking that he looked as languid as a model.

"You know," he stated, "it's hot as hell outside. You don't have to keep all bundled up like that." He pointed at her attire with the top of the open bottle, and then took another swig.

Jamie's brow furled. "I'm just a little cold right now."

"Suit yourself."

Merlin swam to the bottom of the tank, around the pirate treasure chest, and back up to the top of the water, where he crapped a thin, two-inch strand. The A.C. hummed. The bubbler gurgled. If Jamie weren't here, Billy would have taken off his shirt and jeans by now, lounging around the house in his underwear. His place never really got all that comfortable in the summer. It was something he complained to the landlord about in between bouts of trying to fix it himself.

"You still have your father's old stethoscope? Jamie asked.

Billy's face curled with bewilderment. "Yeah?"

"Could you get it for me?"

He considered asking her why, but figured it was useless. He shrugged, went into his bedroom, and turned on the closet light. Soft illumination spilled onto the blue shag and from her perch on the couch Jamie spied the tip of it. The top of Billy's closet was a topple of collected boxes. Most of which had momentos of the girl in the next room. Photos that they had intended to put into albums, dried carnations from their high school prom, yearbooks, ticket stubs, and about two hundred Chinese fortunes, cracked opened and saved from those little yellow cookies. He dug around a bit until he found the item and brought it out to her.

Jamie didn't see the years of memories he also carried with him from the bedroom and Billy was too wrapped up in being annoyed with her to notice the hesitation with how she received his father's old medical instrument. Nor did Billy notice how nervous she became as she finally removed her sunglasses and unzipped her jacket. He didn't know that the way he stood over her made her feel caged and confined on the couch.

He watched her as she put the two ends of the stethoscope into her ears and placed that cold, round metal piece to her chest. He truly thought she was on drugs. Her eyes looked bloodshot, her skin was pasty and pale, and she was acting weird. Puzzled, he sipped his beer, noticing how her shoulders slunk and that she wouldn't look at him as she handed the instrument back, saying "Here."

Billy walked around the coffee table. "Look Jamie, enough of the games. Tell me whatchya got to tell me so I can get back to work."

"Just listen."

Billy sighed heavily and rubbed his eye. "You wanna play doctor?"

His tone was droll and there was nothing about the energy in the room that was remotely sexual. Yet, here she was asking him to put the device to her chest, like he had done so many times before.

"Just listen," she urged.

Begrudgingly, Billy padded the length of carpet back to her, grabbed his father's old tool, placed it to his ear, and put the tip to her chest. The roundness of her breasts pressed upon the sides of his hand as he tried to position himself so that he wouldn't feel anything softly luscious.

A few seconds passed. "What?" he asked irritated.

Jamie's eyes flared in annoyance. She grabbed the tip of the stethoscope, jamming it against Billy's chest. The grate of her fingers on the instrument's mouth and the sheer force of movement sounded like cannons in Billy's ears. He tore the ear-pieces away and glared angrily at the girl.

"Sorry," she muttered, humbly falling from her rash burst of anger.

Lightly, she held the stethoscope to his chest. His warmth pushed into her hand, driving his heartbeat through her palm. She felt it knock within her like a bell. Then Jamie gently pulled the tip of the medical tool to her own chest as her shoulders sighed in the wake of his thriving echo. Billy listened for a few seconds before he shook his head.

"I don't hear anything."

"Exactly," replied Jamie.

Billy removed the metal tubes from his ears. "Just tell me what ya got say and let's get this over with."

"That was it, Billy," Jamie shouted. Furious.

"What's it?"

Jamie stared at him hard. He was being thick. "My heart's not making any noise! Doesn't that strike you as a bit odd?"

"Your heart's not...what?" He paused and scrunched up his face, smiling against the thought, because it was absurd. "Wait a minute, how's…" He shook his head from side to side. "Naw." She was messing with him. His high school jersey was too thick. It had blocked the sound.

Turning toward her again, he put the tubes back in his ears, stuck the round metal end of the stethoscope up her shirt, and placed it to her chest. He listened intently. The shifting crinkles of his brow told a story. He opened his mouth to say something, but stopped. His eyes landed on her and bored like a drill.

"How's…How's that…" He stepped away from her quiet shell, removing his father's old tool, and absentmindedly set it on the coffee table. "How's that even possible?" He pulled at the dollop of hair under his lower lip, looked at her, and then turned away. "There was aahhh…"

Jamie sat on the couch, watching him pull the pieces together, before she blurted out the obvious. "There's no heartbeat."

He turned toward her as if she'd found the answer to the Holy Grail. "There's no heartbeat."

"Yup," uttered Jamie with a long slow drawl, bobbing her head up and down, as she leaned back against the cushions and folded her hands in her lap.

A strange silence descended on the room. Billy just didn't know how to respond to such a thing. Slowly, he paced, thinking. He ran a hand through his hair, feeling that he should be saying something, or doing something, though he didn't know what. He turned toward her again, searching for answers, but only shrugged. After a few solitary moments, in which Merlin swam the length of the tank a couple of times and his own heart knocked repeatedly against the bone of his breastplate, he politely asked, "Should I take you to the hospital?"

"It's a little late for that, don'tchya think?"

"Yeah," Billy uttered, shaking his head in agreement and continued to pace.

He was earnest and confounded. The gravity of what it meant to be up and walking around and have no heartbeat hadn't fully unloaded on him yet. He'd seen Night of the Living Dead, but he wasn't a horror buff. Billy preferred action movies, but things were beginning to feel more like a creeped-out feature than a shoot 'em up. Jamie leaned forwarded, placing her elbows on her knees, and watched Billy as his mental cogs aligned with the unreal and the impossible.

"You're not suggesting that you're..."

Jamie smiled and sat erect.

"No," he added.

Jamie shook her head up and down, lifting her eyebrows.

"No," he refuted again, drawing the word out. "You're fucking with me."

"Sorry."

"This ain't the Twilight Zone, Jay. There's a logical reason…"

Jamie's chuckling derailed his denial. He felt a shortness of breath. He wandered over to the wall and leaned on it for support. His knees felt weak. His chest was a numb hammer. It pained him to think of her in that way. Placing a hand to his chest, it felt like a thousand bee stings. The pain had its own gravitational pull that plucked all of the light from the room. He exhaled slow and deliberate.

"There's simply no way you could be, ah…"

Jamie eased back on the couch, outstretching her arms. "That's me…" Her grin was a sad monster. "The dead girl."

There was a musical lilt to her sarcasm that bent Billy's afternoon to a surreal evening. He pressed his back against the wall and stared at the shag blue carpeting for awhile, becoming seasick. Then he took a swig from his beer and wrung its long neck with both hands.

"Are you here to haunt me or somethin'?"

Jamie burst out laughing. Billy didn't find it funny. His eyes darted from the specter on the couch to the front door. Subconsciously, he was analyzing the space between him and it, calculating the distance between him and her. He couldn't decide if this was an occasion for flowers or if he should call the cops. His carpet was a vast sea. His legs were concrete. The reality of what she was saying began to gnaw at his ankles.

"I'm not a ghost, silly," replied Jamie. Then she thought about it. "At least I don't think I am."

"Then what are ya, huh?" His tone was loud and abrasive. His voice raised. "Christ, Jay!" He peeled himself off the wall. "I haven't seen you in almost two months and you come back here...to me...like this?"

His face was torn and frantic. Jamie was stunned to a simper. "If you're not haunting me then what are you doing here? What is this?" His breath was a heavy pant, small torrents of frustration. "You're tellin' me you're....you're..."

He choked on the unsaid word. It felt like a bad seed in his mouth. He couldn't spit it out. He grit his teeth and clenched his fist tighter around the neck of the beer bottle as Jamie watched tears begin to stream down his face.

She hadn't considered the impact that her news would have on him. She didn't think it through. Jamie stood and took a few steps toward her ex-lover, moved by the passion and love he displayed. But he threw up a taught hand.

"Don't," he warned. "Just don't."

Wandering to the opened entrance of the kitchen, he stood at a great distance from her. Jamie felt locked in place, relegated to the awful position she was in and glared at him hard. That tender moment was gone. Fear made him look small. It changed the color of his aura and Jamie didn't like it. She didn't like it one bit.

The ceiling pressed down on his back as he cradled his near-empty beer. His eyes held blame. His brow wrinkled with worry. His shoulders pulled in on themselves. It made Jamie hate. So in one huge gruff, the dead girl stomped toward the coward. Billy backed away from her into the kitchen. Jamie reached out toward him and he cringed. Stopping in front of him, she grabbed the beer out of his frightened, loose fingers. The look on his face was disaster. She stole a swig of the fermented hops and wiped the wetness from her mouth.

"Get a grip," she said and emptied the rest of his beer in a single pull. "I'm the one who's dead," she complained and burped as she crossed to the refrigerator, the liquid had gone down hard. Tossing the empty container into the trash, it landed with a loud clink. She opened the freeze box and retrieved two more cold ones, walked back to him, popped their caps, and handed him a beer. "Not you!"

Billy was stunned, quietly staring at her in disbelief. He held the fresh drink gingerly as he watched her return to the couch. The two of them had carried it up the front steps and into the apartment together when they moved in. They banged the doorjamb a few times. Though once inside, they set the couch against the wall and plopped down. There was nothing else in the room at the time and they shared a single bottle of beer before moving the rest of their stuff in.

She lay across his lap then. With her head resting comfortably, her hair fell past his knees. He had to bend over to kiss her. She was alive and they were in love. Billy thought they were going to be together forever. Grow old. Have kids. The duplex was supposed to be the beginning of their life. But it turned out to be the end.

Jamie sucked down her beer, eyeing the cannibal fish. It swam lazily back and forth. It's beady little eyes poked past the glass at the dead girl. The bubbler gurgled through the long silence that engulfed the room and she decided that she hated that fish. It had killed Oscar. They had bought Oscar together. He was their first pet because the owner of the duplex wouldn't let them have a dog.

Moments later, Billy sauntered back into the livingroom. The light around his body crackled with more blue and he eyed her with one hand halfway stuck in a pocket as he sipped his beer. She turned toward him and he looked sad. She was the dead thing, and *he* looked sad?

"Ok" he said, calm and controlled. "What can I do?"

VI.

"I think that was it!" Jamie said, careening her neck backward to peer out the window at a passing intersection.

"That's what you said last time," returned Billy, tired and sarcastic. He pulled the Chevelle to the side of the narrow, two-lane street and waited for a car to pass.

"I'm sure this time," assured Jamie as she straightened herself in the seat.

Billy pulled down on the steering wheel, cutting a U-Turn through the county road. His tires chirped across the asphalt, crunching loose stones. The sign at the intersection was mangled. Its paint chipped. It read, *Copperdale St.* It was the closest they'd come to yet.

Jamie said that it had "something with some kind of metal in it." She was vague. Not on purpose, she explained. She just wasn't paying too much attention when she woke up in the river and was forced to walk all the way home alone.

The sky above the Chevelle was a teetering black, widening with soft blue as the crows landed on familiar branches. Billy didn't push the issue that she didn't really know where to go. He liked to drive. It calmed his nerves. And after what he'd just been told, he needed a good, long drive. It was strange having Jamie in the front seat again. It oddly felt like old times, except this time he'd just been told she was dead. *Dead and talking to him. Dead and sitting in the car. Dead and still giving bad directions.* All of it smacked as unrealistic and felt ironic in that kind of way that just wasn't funny. So, Billy drove around looking for roads near a river, listening to her tell him things that he wished he never would have heard.

Pulling the car onto Copperdale, tires ate dilapidated tarmac. Pebbles sounded like chewing crackers. Jamie scrutinized the surrounding landscape. Everything always looked different in the daylight compared to night. The great gas giant was waning in the sky. They'd been driving for hours. Twilight approached and the place glowed orange.

"This is it," she stated with acute firmness, turning to the driver. "Just up ahead is a bridge."

Billy lightly depressed the gas pedal. They both sat in silence. He looked to her demure, folded hands sitting calmly in her lap. It was still hard to believe. *What would she be doing all the way out here in the first place?* Jamie hadn't mentioned what she hoped to find by returning to the spot where she woke up dead. Yet, the road felt as if it unfolded with purpose. Billy wasn't convinced if this was all just a waste of time, a fool's errand, because he felt the fool. But he also needed to see for himself. Billy needed to understand why she had come back.

Up ahead, past a low-lying field of green, where the setting sun gathered in stark luminescent brilliance, was a thin row of trees. The timbers stretched out from the street on both sides. Swarming above the trees, gathered in their branches, shimmering in the sun like black leaves, were the iridescent shapes of crows. Thousands of them circled like vultures. Billy looked from the windshield to the dead girl as nudging misgivings formed within.

Jamie's grim countenance announced that they had finally found the right place. He swallowed hard as he pulled the car to the side of the road. The bird's caws and the flaps of their wings sounded above the finely tuned engine. He saw the small, concrete bridge arching over the river. He shut the engine off and the din grew louder. Leaning over the steering wheel, Billy gazed up at the sable mass of living feathers, swarming above the car and the brook. Jamie opened the door. It creaked softly, and she got out.

She peered up at the waiting flock. There were more here, gathered at this location, than what had followed her around the city. The sky was massive. Dark. The line of trees was thick with them.

Deep down she knew why they had gathered here. Deep down she knew that they had come for her. The sky was alive and it was all for her. She didn't know how to accept that. It was huge, like learning that Santa Claus was your Daddy as a child. She didn't know why she knew what she did and other things remained hidden, but she felt the tiny creatures' expectation and thrill at her finally returning to them. It was unmistakable. It was as thick as old milk. Palpable. Raw.

Billy joined her outside the car as she began to wander toward the edge of the riverbank. "Have you ever seen so many of them?"

She didn't respond.

Cascading shadows beat the slow moving crawl of the tiny river. Down-a-ways, Jamie spied where the grass was flattened along its bank. Walking around, the perched birds eyed the dead girl and it began to grow quiet. Billy turned toward the heavens as the crows took roosts. Jamie felt their stare and it pressed as thick and as warm as hands around her throat.

"It might help if I knew what you were looking for?" asked Billy as he caught up with her.

She turned toward him. "I don't really know." Stepping through the grass to the edge of the riverbank, her memory flashed to the rush of breath that filled her dormant lungs. "Anything, really," she uttered and shrugged. Stopping, Jamie caught the bridge over Billy's shoulder. "Anything that could..."

Her words fell onto the dead flat grass as she walked past him. His eyes darted to the strange council that glared down at them from the trees. They made him feel uncomfortable, raising the hairs along the nape of his neck. It was ominous. He followed her toward the bridge. It had been an uncanny day, for sure. With so many blackbirds gathered in one spot, Billy felt that they should leave, come back when they were gone.

When the dead girl stepped onto the dilapidated bridge, the heavens erupted in a violent shudder. It caused Billy to jump. Tree limbs shook with the weight missing from their branches as the sky swirled into a great black sea. Jamie appeared not to notice or care that the birds had left their purchase. She victimized every inch of that bridge with her eyes, scanning for some rancid clue as to who it was that had killed her. But nothing seemed amiss or out of place.

Then peering up at the onyx swarm, Jamie briefly caught a glimpse of herself standing on the bridge looking up. It reminded her of when she was staring at that crow in the broken window. She felt like she could see herself through its eyes. She wondered...*Can I really?* Bracing herself, she widened her stance and the dark birds began circling directly above her head. Billy stopped, drawn by the spectacle he witnessed. He had never seen anything like it before. An inky, thick scribble of blackbirds swooped over Jamie's crown. It was scary and awesome at the same time.

Jamie felt the eyes of her winged adventurers on her dead flesh, and she looked at Billy near the mouth of the bridge. He wore a fearful gaze, stalled by the massive swarm that congregated above her. She wanted to tell him that it was all right, that he shouldn't worry, but instead she smirked and closed her eyes, feeling the pull from so many winged creatures.

Once more a powerful breath entered her body. Jamie felt as if she was lifted off the ground. Her back arched and she rose to her tippy-toes as her arms reached out from her sides, limply pulled upward by the magnitude of the circling throng. From a bird's eye view, she could see herself on the bridge and Billy. She could see his car and the long straight road that she had walked. She could see the river and the shadows of thousands of tiny bodies breaking upon the water and the grounds.

Caws charged from the bevy of birds and the sound was deafening. They began flying faster, fluttering in wide mad elliptic arches. Jamie looked as if she was suspended in the turbulence, a marionette under the moving mass shadow. In the dying daylight Jamie saw night. A pregnant moon lit the place where she and Billy now stood. The river tumbled gently over rocks and Billy was gone. The late evening was peaceful until distant headlights disturbed the shoal of the riverbank. Watching, as if from a roost within the trees, Jamie spied a black car driving down the road to the bridge, where it stopped. Headlights faded to moonlit darkness. A man exited the vehicle and walked around to the trunk. She couldn't make out his face. Shadows from the trees cut across the bridge. His walk was heavy – casual and confident.

He looked around before he opened the trunk. The suit he

wore was an Italian cut. His gold watch glittered in the nightlight like a moonstone as he moved around, rustling something big out of the trunk. Jamie tried to see his face. She wanted to know. More than anything, she wanted to see the man and what he carried. Fortunately, she didn't have long to wait.

He stepped away from the rear of the car holding a body. It's bulk obscured his face. The person was limp and unconscious. Jamie recognized it immediately as her own and realized that she was seeing the memories of the crows. The man carried her to the edge of the bridge and tossed her body over. There was a loud splash and then Jamie was flying with the other crows. She felt weightless, buoyant on the cushions of air under her wings. She soared higher, away from the bridge, but she wanted to know who the man was. She wanted to see his face, discern his identity once and for all! She tried to steer the flighty creature, but it ignored her, climbing higher. Then of its own accord the tiny being turned around. Jamie felt gravity on her small, feathered frame as she fell toward the horrific scene. She hoped to glimpse the man's features then, but all she saw was him climbing back into the car. Headlights pierced the night and he drove off. Red taillights echoed shimmering trails. She looked down as she joined the flight-path of the flock and saw the vehicle's license plate. Jamie began to caw.

Suddenly, she was falling. There was no night. There was no day. She was formless and plummeting deeper. She screamed because the wind that ripped passed her ears burned. The sound drilled into her skull and there was a great pressure at her temples until Jamie opened her eyes. Billy's smile and elated joy at seeing her wake from the trance was a beautiful sight.

"Are you alright?" he asked.

She looked around. She had fallen and he had caught her.

"I saw it," she whispered. "I saw it."

"You saw what?" he asked as he helped her to stand.

"I saw the man who did this to me." She walked to the other side of the bridge and laid her hands on the broken, concrete railing. Bits of Rebar poked through. "I wasn't killed here. He threw me off." She turned to Billy. "He threw me off right here."

She stepped away from the railing, taking a few steps across the bridge. "And then he drove off. That way." Jamie pointed in the direction that they had come, turning to look back at Billy.

"What do mean you saw it?"

He was confused. One minute the sky was a swell of thunderous dark, beating wings circling above his ex-girlfriend, and the next, Jamie was crashing to the road. He had barely caught her before her head cracked the ground as the thick horde dispersed.

"They showed me." She looked up at her sentinels as they returned to their roosts.

"The birds?" The height of his eyebrows tasted altitude. He didn't even know how to respond. *Of course…it makes sense. Jamie is dead and she can talk to the animals.* Billy scratched his head. Who was he to argue? If the dead girl said that several thousand swooping crows showed her being dumped off a bridge by some stranger, then why argue. *Really?* It had been just that kind of day!

"His license plate was Z, something, X246."

Billy decided that he wasn't going to argue with that either. At least, it was something he could wrap his brain around. Digits to a license plate number were solid. He didn't have to like or even understand how she had arrived at such hard evidence, because it was more than what they had before. His eyes darted to the haunting blackbirds and knew he was out of his league.

"Come on," Jamie said, tapping his arm, walking at a brisk pace to the car. "We need to find a party."

Billy started to ask, but gave up. He shook his head and followed the dead girl. It didn't appear that he was going to be able to land on any sane ground anytime soon, so he figured that it was best if he just went with it. Above them the din calmed. A few lone caws ripped the twilight as Jamie and Billy climbed into the waiting Chevelle. Over ten thousand ebon eyes watched the vengeful soul and her champion as they sped away.

VII.

Jamie watched Billy chow down on the burger. His teeth tore chunks of bread and meat out of the circular dish. She should have felt hungry by now, but she didn't. He had asked her, an annoying number of times, if she wanted something. He even offered to pay for it. Jamie kept telling him no. Each insistence of his to procure her a menu item was simply a gnawing reminder that things weren't right. It had been a couple of days. She should have been hungry.

She was glad that they decided to sit outside, instead of inside the restaurant. She could barely handle watching Billy eat, let alone everyone else. Hearing his teeth gnash and pull and chew, as it rent the cooked flesh, was more than enough anguish to bare. Each bite had a wetness and a sticky tape pluck to it that crept down her thighs. It made her ankles twitch. Several times she thought she was going to shove the thing down his damned throat. Eating was just disgusting.

Outside, away from the people and their families, the dead girl could try to enjoy the evening. At least outside she didn't have to deal with all those auras cluttering around their heads and shoulders as they mashed foodstuff with their incisors. The lights were more pronounced at night than during the day, and Jamie simply didn't want to see the sparkling colors anymore. The sky was vast, warm and clear. She opened another sugar packet and poured it into the glass of water that she'd been given.

"Everyone looks like streetlights after a rain," announced Jamie as she watched the granules of sugar float down to the pile at the bottom of the glass.

"What?"

"Everybody has it." She looked up at him. Billy was shrouded in a blue veil.

He turned around and scoped out the scene. Everything looked the same. *Normal.*

"Everybody has what?"

Jamie shrugged. "I don't know. They just glow."

Billy looked around again as Jamie opened and emptied yet another packet of sugar into her water. She lay her chin on her hands in front of the glass, watching the sweet descent. Billy took another bite of this burger. He chewed it more quietly now, slower, though he didn't realize it. People went in and out of the restaurant's front door and he wondered what she saw.

"Do I have it?" he asked as he engulfed the last bite of his sandwich.

"Yeah," she answered, not even looking at him

"Hhmm." He swallowed and took a sip of his soda. "Maybe it's like an aura or something."

Jamie made fish sounds at her reflection in the water. "What's an aura?"

"It's supposed to be a person's energy signature, or something like that."

Jamie sat up. "Are there colors to it?"

Billy thought about it and shrugged. "Yeah, I guess," he said, watching Jamie's eyes outline him as if they were crayons. He couldn't help but ask.

"You're mostly blue," she answered, standing. "There are some orange spikes, though." She placed a hand over his head, gently grabbing and pulling the air, and chuckled.

"What?"

"It tickles," she giggled. "There's a purple rim, very faint. Ahhaa..." She smiled. "Now some green is entering into it. It is very warm." She pulled her hand back and looked intently at him. "What are you thinking about?"

The question knocked him off guard. "Don't know really." Though, he knew perfectly well what he was thinking about.

"C'mon, what was it?" She sat back down.

Billy hid behind his soda and bit the end of the straw. She stared at him, waiting.

"I like your laugh." He sucked down on the drink, but it had run out, slurping around the ice for syrupy pockets of goodness. He set it down. "It's nice to hear you laugh, is all."

Jamie avoided his eyes. She wanted to reach across the table and grab his hands, but instead fidgeted with her own. "Maybe that's what they are. Auras. I don't know. I see it around everyone, though."

"That's kind of cool," decided Billy. "Able to check out people's personal energy in a single bound. It's kind of like Superman's X-Ray Vision."

Jamie peered up at him, crinkling her forehead. He smiled and they laughed.

"Hey," he said. "What's that guy's look like?" And pointed.

"Green and pink mostly. A little blue and yellow."

"Wow." His grin spread across his face. "That's pretty cool."

"Yeah, I guess." Her voice was heavy and melancholy.

He looked at her before asking. Her eyes hung to the pavement. "What's yours look like?"

She stood and thrust her hands in her pocket. "You ready to go yet?"

Billy just peered at her and then slowly shook his head. "Sure. We can go."

He balled up the paper bag, sandwich wrappers, and the 'lil box that the fries came in and Jamie sat back down.

"I don't have one," she announced, staring at the awkward position of her shoes.

Neither said anything for awhile after that. Billy sat quietly with her until he carried the refuse to the trashcan. He stood a distance away from the receptacle and sunk the garbage ball like Magic Johnson. Tucking his hands in his pockets, he sauntered back to Jamie at the table.

"What's this about a party?"

"I remember being at a house before..." She kicked a small stone. It skirted into the grass. "There was this guy there with heavy black eyes." She turned toward him. "I keep seeing his face. He knows something." She exhaled slowly and sat up. "I think he's responsible for me being here. And I was there with that guy who drove the car to the bridge."

"Ok then." Billy pondered. "We need to locate a party at someone's house that took place over the weekend. Somewhere in the city?"

Jamie nodded and Billy sat back down.

"Did you know the host?"

"No, I don't think so."

"Ok. So...this guy that took you to the party probably knew the host. And this other guy, the one with the eyes, he was probably a guest."

Jamie squished her face. "Yeah, that feels right."

"Do you remember anybody else who was there? Any land marks?"

Jamie thought on it, but all she could recall was the interior of the house, a bunch of blurry faces, and the two men. "Not really. They had some tacky statues like they were trying to look richer than they really were. And a pool. But nothing else stands out. Sorry."

"Sounds like half the houses along the shore."

"If I knew I'd tell you," blurted Jamie in frustration. "It's not like I'm not trying."

It's ok," he reassured. "We'll find it. There only has to be about a few hundred houses with tacky poser statues. We'll just comb the city until we find the right one."

He smiled at her and Jamie wondered why she ever left him. He was positive, confident, good-looking, and genuinely cared. He didn't have to be out here. He didn't have to drive her around looking for a needle in a haystack. *He's living. Has a job. Probably a girlfriend. What do I have?*

Just then Billy's cell phone rang. He pulled it out of his pocket and looked at the little window on the front of it. Opening its face, he placed it to his ear and said, "Hello?" He mouthed the word *work* to Jamie, rose, and took a few steps away from the table. She listened as he informed Hector that he needed to take the next few days off to help a sick friend. Jamie felt bad. She was making a mess of his life again. Despite the dry, hot July night Jamie felt coldness against her covered arms. She tucked her elbows closer to her torso. *He didn't have to do any of this. He didn't have to do anything at all. I'm a dead girl. Toast.* He flipped his cell phone closed with a soft click as he wandered back to the table, and sat. He didn't return the device to his pocket.

"Hey? You still have the same number?"

Hesitation jump-started the words from Jamie's blue-tinted lips. "I think so."

He started dialing, bit his lower lip in a cute sort-of way, and lifted the phone to the delicate curves of his ear. She could hear it ringing. She wondered if it made any sound at the bottom of the river or was it still in the trunk of *that man's* car. She didn't remember seeing him throw it off the bridge after he tossed her in. Billy hung up once Jamie's answering message came on.

"Well," he added, "it was worth a try."

He pocketed the cell, stretching his leg under the table.

"Thank you," said Jamie shyly and stood.

Billy just smiled and rose. "C'mon. We have a city to comb."

Jamie followed him to the car. It was easier to be about business. All the quiet moments were eating at her. She didn't know they were eating at Billy too. He wanted to reach out and pull her close. Hold her in his arms and tell her that everything was going to be all right, that he could fix it. But deep down he knew he couldn't. It wasn't going to be all right. Things were screwed. His ex-girlfriend had climbed out of a watery grave to seek him out and find the bastard that had murdered her. And then there was the constant flapping of wings above his head in the night sky that made him shiver.

Jamie had waited for Billy to pass her to the car for fear that she would fall against his chest. She wanted to be enveloped in his arms. Swallowed in his warmth and strength; feel his charisma wash over her, and make all the silent pain go away. She wanted to feel her heartbeat against his, and find the creep that had killed her. And find the man with the dark eyes so that she could make him make her whole again. *Alive and normal.* Jamie prayed that it was still possible, because she wanted to apologize to Billy for breaking his heart with her body. But the only thing to envelop her outside the restaurant was the same stark bitterness and the sounds of their shoes as they walked to his car; the hammer of the doors as they closed themselves in and the purr of the automobile's engine.

VIII.

Somewhere in the city, in a darkened room cut by a slender shaft of light, Jamie's cell phone rang. It erupted from its spot on the desk like a baby's cry. It jarred the man's attention as he was heading out the door. He stopped. He turned in the direction of the familiar ringtone as did the other man at his side. The other man was huge, a hulking figure, with brow beat eyes and a scar on his left cheek. He had come to fetch the younger man for their boss.

"You gonna git that?" asked the brute.

The young man didn't answer. He was drawn by the sound like a deer caught in headlights, standing on the precipice of his great evening. Everything else faded against the phone's shrill pitch and the man hadn't even realized that he had stopped breathing. The brute opened the door.

"C'mon, Tony. We gotta go."

The cell's last ring chirped and twittered, annoyingly bleeding through the rooms. Tony shook his head and walked through the opened portal as the hulking man shut the door behind him. He should've gotten rid of the phone by now, and her purse. But he just couldn't bring himself to part with them yet. Silently, he chided himself for keeping them. He should have dumped them that night with the body. It was stupid to keep things like that around. He knew it. He wasn't dumb. And he wasn't going to go down for killing that bitch, either. She didn't listen. Got him in trouble and left him no other choice.

Tony chewed the inside of his lower lip as he entered the elevator and depressed the white button for the parking garage. He had kept the purse and Jamie's cell phone for a reason. He hated to admit it, because it made him look weak, but he liked the girl. He couldn't show any weakness now. *Not now!* It was all just an unfortunate mistake that he needed to put out of his mind. The elevator lurched, setting in place, and the doors opened with a gentle hiss. He stepped from the lift, straightening his tie.

For weeks, he'd been waiting for this meet. He'd been the lackey long enough. Now was his time to shine. He felt it. This was his moment. He wasn't going to let anything stand in the way of what was going to happen tonight. He proved that. Ironic, that it was her cell that had lit up, reminding him of what he had done to secure this sit-down. He chuckled sardonically. *She's a blessing beyond the grave. Pity,* he snickered. *She had a lovely ass.*

Entering the backseat of the black sedan, Tony watched the passing city through the window. The brute was chewing his ears off as they drove down the road, but Tony wasn't listening. He was thinking big. Tony always thought big. Things were finally happening for him, like he always knew they would. After awhile he leaned back against the polished leather, closed his eyes, and pictured Jamie. He had liked her alright, but he had to do what he had to do. There was no getting around it. One had to be a shark when they swam with lions. So he decided to discard her affects once he returned home. He didn't need that sort of thing lying around, waiting for some flatfoot to find it. There were plenty of fish in the sea and tonight, he thought, tonight he was the damn king of the ocean!

IX.

By midnight, Billy was tired even though he said he wasn't. They'd been driving for hours blacking out squares on a map with a newly worn out Sharpie. The map just seemed to grow larger with each square cordoned off and filled in by the slow ebb of time and distance. The task appeared daunting. Jamie struggled with going about finding the house this way. Black spots littered the ends of her fingertips from coloring the map. There was also an indentation of the marker in her middle finger that she feared would never go away.

By 2 a.m., she had Billy take her back to his place. The thought of being left alone at her apartment wasn't appealing and she simply couldn't stand seeing his head nod south with sleep any longer. She explained that it was just easier that way. Despite the fact that they were closer to her place than his, he didn't argue.

Like a gentleman, he offered her his bed, reasoning to take the couch. But she wouldn't have it. She knew she wasn't going to fall asleep. That necessity was over. His kindness would be wasted. So, he laid out blankets and a pillow on the couch, rendering the furniture for a sojourn to dream, and went to bed. Once he was asleep, Jamie lay her blanket over him. The July night air carried a small chill through the opened windows and she didn't want him to catch his death.

The moon was fat and high in the sky. Its light filled Billy's room as Jamie watched him sleep. His breath was gentle and deep. The sound reminded her of waves and being at Coney Island with her father. The memory was an old one. She could feel the ocean breeze on her cheeks and smell the wet crest of the sea as it wafted across the beach. She remembered the grit of sand between her toes and the taste of hot dogs. Jamie wanted to curl up inside of Billy's breath just like her tiny hands balled into the palms of her father's. She was thankful that both her parents were dead. Jamie had no idea how she would've been able to tell them the gruesome news of her passing.

Even as a child, death seemed to ride her coat tails. Her mother passed away when she was very young and she recalled how her father looked thin and yellow after the cancer and Chemotherapy had their way with him. He was a shell of his former self. Billy took her to her father's funeral. He wore a blue suit. It was his color. Only now did Jamie understand why. Her father was the only one left of her family and disease had destroyed him. Once he was gone all Jamie had was Billy, and she left him long before he could ever leave her.

Billy rolled over. His reposed face stared closed eyed at the dead girl. She remembered watching him sleep when they first moved in together, and instantly, she knew why she had dumped him. She had thought that he would have out grown his fascination with automobiles and gotten a real job where he could have made some real money, so they could've moved out of the city. Instead, working at the garage turned out to be exactly what Billy wanted to do. He was happy and Jamie just considered him a fool with no ambition. She thought his life wasn't going anywhere. She wanted more than what he was able to provide. So, she left.

Knowing it now made her feel foolish. Not even six months out on her own and she'd gotten herself bumped off. Pride sunk to the bottom of her gut. It festered its own slow decay. *This is what hell must feel like. To witness the sum total of all your mistakes and realize so clearly the path you should have taken!*

The curtains fluttered. Billy turned again and spread out across the bed. Jamie's eyes traced the lines of his form tucked neatly under the covers. Her gaze traveled up his legs, curved around his waist, and slid across his chest. She yearned and sighed heavily, falling backwards on the floor. *Stupid. Stupid. Stupid, girl.* She rolled her head to the side and spied the opened door to the balcony, got up, and walked over to it.

Black eyes spied the dead girl in the unlit room from their perch of wires and rooftops. She stepped out onto the small terrace with a crow's caw welcoming her. In the full glare of the moon, Jamie could make out their small foreboding shapes against the night as a cool breeze washed over her like a baptism.

X.

Jamie stood on the balcony, watching the sunrise. The city was lit like a matchbook. Radiantly beautiful! If her tear ducts had worked, tears would've streaked down her face in the glorious light. Never, in all her life, had she seen a sunrise more elegant and majestic than the one she witnessed this morning since her death. Such profound meaning and natural poetry swelled within her from the simple act of pushing night back into star pockets, under blue sleeves. Her deathly witness held exquisite and painful truths, which she bore on her conscious, vowing to never again miss the morning spectacle.

For too long, pride and arrogance guarded sway over the course of her existence. She delighted in distraction. She didn't know her real heart. Every second the sun touched her face was a blessing. She understood that now. Simple actions, daily actions – *life is a wonder of small gifts*. And nothing seemed so joyous a gift than her being present, on the balcony of her old home, with a man she once loved, simply watching the wooden mechanics of heaven turn darkness into light. Jamie knew that by all logic and reason she should not have been here. This dawn was not meant for her, but yet...*it was*. It was her calling. She was an exception to the natural order, taking place beyond her window. This morning, this resplendent, fantastic morning was an extended prayer over the bounty of her life.

Not even the thousand black, thankless eyes of her feathery watchers could darken this sentinel moment with the sun. She had peered into the souls of the blackbirds too, digging deep to find the purpose of their constant visitation. Apollo's chariot rode higher through the sky above the elevated steel and concrete of the city, awakening delicate clatter, and releasing the manacles of mortal coil from Jamie's chalice-ribs. This was a new earth that she witnessed. One where the dead claimed all the beauty that the living yearned to know, missed daily, and sought to hold. She was the piper at the gates of dawn.

Billy groggily stepped onto the porch, yawning. His hair was a chestnut tussle and the worn faded gray sweatpants he wore last night to bed tugged loosely at his hips. He stretched under Jamie's new dawn. The dead girl turned in his direction.

"Morning sleepy," she said, beaming.

His aura was a deep royal, brimming with purple and white. Spikes of yellow and green danced around his head. He looked knightly.

"You're up early," he noticed.

"Yeah," she lied.

Overlooking the sparkling dawn, he said, "You still got that license plate number from yesterday?"

"It's inside."

"Cool." He moved to the railing and turned, leaning the small of his back against it. "I should've thought of it yesterday. I have a friend who works at the DMV." He yawned. "She might be able to helps us out and find the missing letters."

Jamie beamed. Her smile was a lighthouse. Billy squeaked a glance at her.

"Did I miss something this morning?"

"No," she revealed. "Everything is here."

He turned his head in the direction of the telephone and electrical cables that hung to the alley. "I see your flock is still in attendance."

"They're going to help us out," informed Jamie raising a single eyebrow.

"Yeah, well..." Billy didn't buy it. He separated from the wood railing. "Maybe they can pay the rent."

Jamie laughed at his wry joke and Billy thought it odd. She had never found his sense of humor all that pleasing. As he moved to go back inside, Jamie reached out and hugged him. Wrapping her thin arms around his waste, she flattened her face against his lively, hot chest. The coolness of her skin made the embrace alarming. His breath lodged in the back of his throat and it took him a second to respond. Slowly, he placed his arms around the dead girl and pulled her closer. After a minute or two, he did not count, Jamie thanked him, but he hadn't a clue as to why or what for.

"I'mma..." he said as they parted, "I'm gonna go take a shower." He looked at her and she was smiling. It was a happiness he didn't understand, but was glad to see. "You're welcomed to one. You know, just... Just make yourself at home."

Surprising! The word, home, didn't burn in his mouth or in her ears. The sting of their break up had faded. It was simply nice to have her around. He returned the girl's wild grin, feeling a little uneasy, and disappeared behind the curtains. Jamie, alone once more on her perch, gazed at the skyline of the city. Soon, the sounds of water beating the tube basin and the scent of wintergreen soap flitted out through the opened doorway to her joy. She felt contented, naked, and ready for the charity that life bestowed upon her, until her eyes fell on a black-clad figure, standing in the alley.

He stared up at her from a distance, but his eyes seemed to penetrate right through her, as if he was only inches away. He felt familiar and Jamie was drawn to him like a magnet. The city dwarfed by his presence and the sun glared off his dark sheen as if he were a mirage, or someone standing on the peripheral, in the corner of her eye.

Jamie feared that she would lose him if she did not hurry, so without thinking she tore through the curtains with purpose, crossed the rooms, and exited the apartment, via the kitchen door. Its wooden frame bounced in the jamb, but it did not close, and the soothing sounds of the shower filled an empty space, spilling onto the front porch and steps.

Her sock-covered feet padded the hard concrete to the alley, hoping to find the man still there. He was a striking figure, dressed in black denim jeans and a tight fitting black silk shirt. He had olive-tan skin, green eyes, high cheekbones, and a rich dark mane. Jamie slowed her pace, feeling trepidation flit through her belly. He was the one from her dreams. His aura burned golden, a bright majestic sun that danced in a ring of fire around his body. He seemed of-this-world and not-of-this-world. Jamie was awestruck. The closer she approached the more powerful his soul glistened. It eclipsed the brick and mortar of the buildings that lined the small street.

"It's you…" she began, squinting from the light that only she could see.

"Silence child," boomed his voice in her head, for his lips did not move. "Do not squander the gift that I have given you. Even the Lilly fades. Know this…that you walk with a piece of me inside of you and will outlast the greatest of these earthly things. Take care of it, child. For I shall want it back, when the time is right."

"What piece are you talking about?" blurted out Jamie in a rush. "Am I here because of you?"

"It was a moment of weakness when I saw you last," continued the voice in her head. "I held pity for you. But in my pity there is a price."

"What price?" She screamed, stepping closer to the man. "What do you want from me?"

The magnificence of his aura grew brighter, and Jamie reared back from its blinding glare.

"Pay it with the heart, young one, pay it with the heart. Heed not the flesh."

As he spoke, he started to fade into the ether between worlds. Jamie raced over to where his presence ignited the dingy alley like an angel of the sun.

"Wait!" she cried, running toward him. "Wait!"

Reaching out to touch the familiar stranger, her fingers grazed his vanishing form. Instantly, he scattered into a thousand coal-black

feathers. The air around the dead girl pulled violently into a cold vacuum as the jigsaw pieces of his bodily essence swarmed around her in a fiery gale of beating wings.

Jamie was lost in the chaos of feathers and sharp talons. Under the swirl of quickening heat, her eyes went belly up, rolling to the top of her skull, white. Jamie never felt the tug and release of the marionette strings as her weight sent her body crashing to the rough pavement. She didn't hear the echo of wings vanish from the causeway into the vast morning. Nor did she witness the corpse of a young girl lying prone and still in the alley.

XI.

Billy turned the shower knob to the right. The water ceased and residual drips thumbed from the spout, clanging against the porcelain basin. He sucked the air in slow and heavy, stretched his neck, and pulled the shower curtain back. Stepping naked from the tub, his feet landed on an old tattered rug that was squished up against it. Cool air washed over him as he grabbed an olive-green towel off the rack. Its fibers were made from Egyptian cotton. He had paid a pretty penny for it. It wasn't rough or abrasive against his skin as he exited the shower. It felt smooth and nice, pampering and warm.

It took a while for Billy to notice how quiet the apartment had become. Stepping from the bathroom, he half expected to find Jamie asleep in his bed. But she wasn't. He pulled the lush towel off his waist, laying it on the floor, as he slipped into a pair of jeans. Eyeing the gentle sway of the curtains, he figured that she was still on the balcony. He called to her. But there was no response.

He walked into the living room, tossing a glance to the couch. The bedding was still neatly folded from the night before. Moving through the kitchen, Billy noticed the door was ajar. He chided the girl and curiously strode outside. He looked around. From the front porch he shared with his neighbor, Billy saw a police car turn down the alley. An awful, sinking feeling clenched his gut.

Briskly, he flew through the house to the balcony out back. Pulling the curtain aside, he hoped to find her there, exactly where he had left her. But the empty three-walled slab of raised concrete was nothing short of a rude awakening. He looked out across the fenced-in yard to the open alley. A battalion of flashing red and blue lights lit the place up like a circus. He saw an officer cordoning off a section of the causeway with yellow tape. All the beady little eyes from those annoying blackbirds were oppressively missing. Rooftops and wires were suspiciously absent of their gloomy shapes. And lying in the center of the activity and chaos was the placid body of Jamie Lund.

Billy felt his knees buckle. He grabbed the wood railing tightly with both hands to keep himself from going down. He thought he would never miss those pesky little creatures. Not ever! But he did. Billy wanted those crows back now more than ever. He didn't know what had happened in the brief expanse from when he'd last seen her, but everything was horribly wrong. The universe was tilting. Things were askew and Billy wasn't sure what to do.

XII.

Special Investigator James Riley didn't like early morning homicides. They crapped all over his twilight with ugly, destroying the serenity of what could otherwise be a peaceful scene. He observed the body of a girl stretched out in the center of the causeway. Her arms and legs were akimbo. She looked flung. A disposed flower.

Passing behind a police officer stringing yellow Caution Tape, the Special Investigator neared the corpse, surveying the site. White concrete road; one side was walled by bricks and buildings the other side was lined with a fence. *Fairly clean.* James Riley surmised that the body was visible to the duplex beyond the fence and yard. He looked toward the sky. Slow moving clouds. Empty telephone and electric wires.

A lone crow's caw pulled his attention to the big, black bird. It tilted its head at him, glaring with beady, coal pitch eyes. It flapped its wings and danced on the ledge of a building as it spoke to him again. The Special Investigator grinned satisfied that he kept the fowl from its carrion.

Kneeling beside the deceased, he noticed the pallor of her complexion. Marred by death as she was, she did not reek. He sniffed the concrete closest to the cadaver and found no odor embedded within it.

"Hhmm," he emoted, rising. *Dumped.*

Slowly, he walked around Jamie. *Old high school pull-over. Sweat pants. Socks. Black hair. She was pretty once.* He snapped into a pair of white rubber gloves and kneeled near her head. Taking his pen from his jacket's breast pocket, he pushed on the garment that was bunched around her neck and noticed ligature marks. He peeled an eyelid back to verify hemorrhaging and groaned.

"I see you're up early," announced the Medical Examiner as he approached.

"Claire wanted bagels, so I was already out when I got the call."

Stan chuckled as he set his toolbox down. "She's going to be pissed. To miss breakfast over this."

Special Investigator James Riley shrugged as he stood. Stan Hamerstien was over weight. Not fat, but he had put on a few extra pounds as he aged. Nearly fifty-five, he had most of his hair, a salt and peppered beard, and wore wire-rimmed glasses. He slid on some gloves and popped the lock on the top of his toolbox.

"Now what do we have?" Stan pulled the bottom of Jamie's shirt up a little and stabbed her side with a thermometer. He gazed upon her face. "Always the young ones, isn't it?"

"Seems that way."

Special Investigator Riley was eyeing Jamie's socks. Traversing the length of her slowly, he drew a small plastic bag from his pocket and a pair of tweezers. He knelt by the corpse's feet. There were faint impressions of her soles, lightly soiled on the bottom of her footwear. A tiny, blue spec came into sharp focus and he smiled. Plucking the fiber from the wooly fabric, Riley held it close to his face. *A carpet grain.* He opened the small evidence bag and placed the thread inside.

He held the sealed material up to the early morning light. It was such an odd color. Blue shag – *Not too many of those around.* He removed the bag from his line of sight and the anguished face of a young man staring at the body of the dead girl grabbed his attention. Special Investigator James Riley rose, taking a few steps forward. He was vaguely aware that Stan was talking at his back. His focus was set on the young man.

The boy looked distraught, anxious. He pressed upon the police line to where Officer Langford had to keep instructing him to step back. Riley swept the rest of the crowd. People had gathered to see the morning's main attraction. *Nosy busy-bodies. Some concerned. Better than a cup of coffee and the daily news. At best it was entertainment, but him... Him?*

Riley crossed to the line that Officer Langford held as the young man stepped back again. His expression was a crash site. His breathing was erratic.

"Excuse me," Riley asked. "Do you know this woman?"

He motioned to the deceased with a wide arm. It grabbed Billy's awareness.

"What? Uh, me? No." He slightly shook his head to affirm the negative.

Riley regarded him and stepped closer. "You seem upset. Is there—"

"Is she," Billy muttered. "Is she dead?"

Riley turned to view the corpse. He felt a mean streak shoot up his spine, turning toward the nervous kid he let it go. "You've never seen a dead body before?"

"What?" Billy didn't understand the question. "No. Why would I?"

Riley grinned. "Of course. Why would you."

The Special Investigator stepped toward the Officer, leaned in, and asked him to procure Billy's contact information. He headed toward the body as the wheels of his mind turned. Officer Langford approached the young man. Riley turned back and thanked Billy for his help. It sounded polite and sincere, innocuous and innocent, but it was far from that. Something wasn't right about the boy and Riley made plans to figure out what it was.

Stan was removing his rubbers and packing up when the Special Investigator returned. The old man wore an odd expression. One the seasoned detective hadn't seen before.

"Lividity is inconsistent with temperature," reported the Medical Examiner. "So I can't render an approximate time of death. But I'll know more once I'm back at the lab."

Riley nodded, his mind stuck on the quirky stranger. "I look forward to your report."

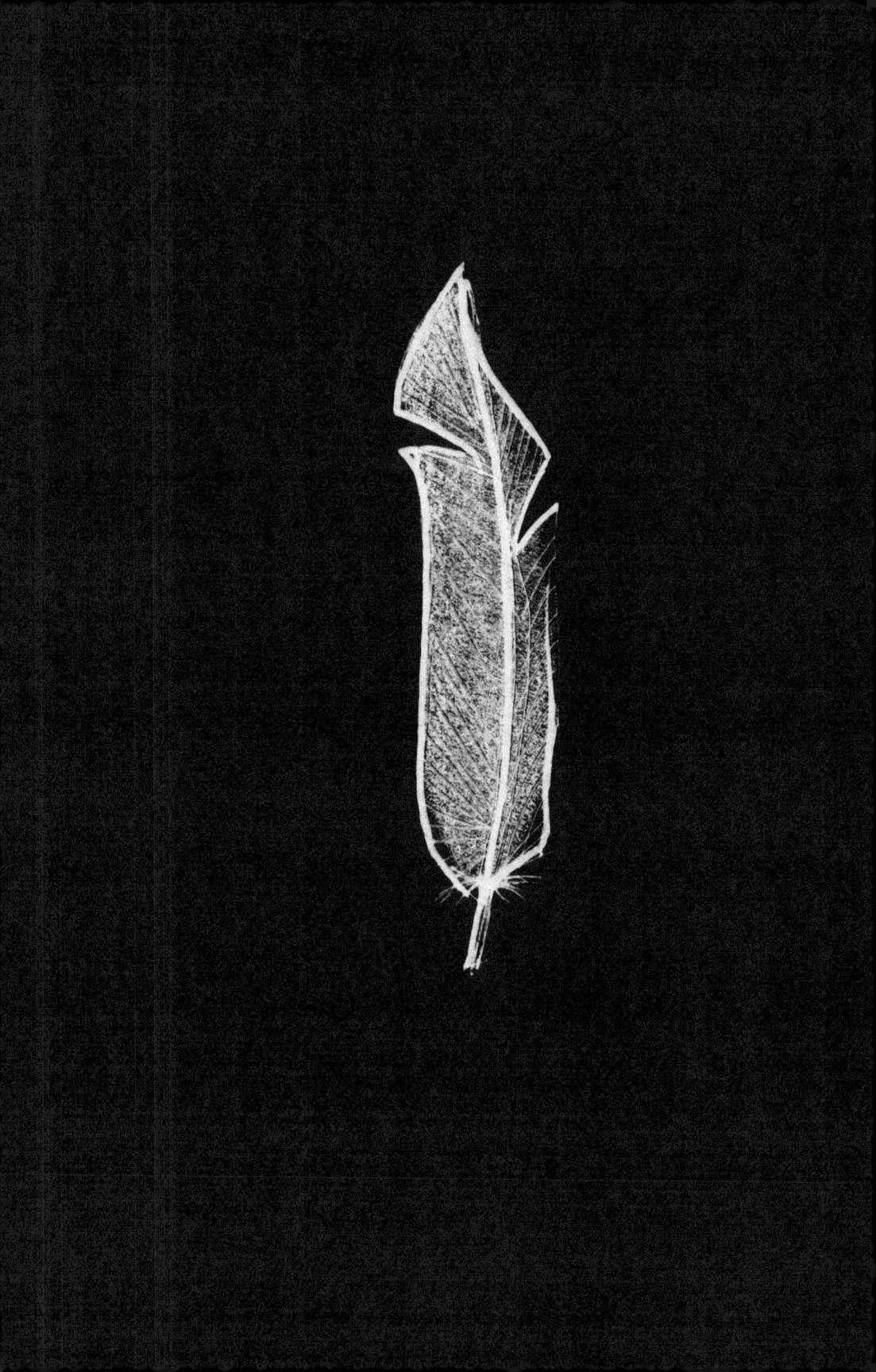

"Huh?" the old man scoffed. "Something strange about this one." His eyes fell on the inert shape until he snapped out of it, shifting his attention to Riley. "Got a double homicide over on Chesterfield, so don't wait up."

He clicked his toolbox shut. "Think you've seen it all." He tossed his head from side to side. "City is crazy this time of year."

"Don't I know it," replied the Special Investigator, eyeing the dead girl, so sweet and innocent looking.

"I'll call a ride for our new guest en route," added the M.E. as he bade Riley farewell.

But Riley wasn't listening. The dead girl appeared normal by his accounts – just another statistic. An average gal. *Twenty-two to twenty-four. Not married. Kept in shape, by the look of it.* Someone had done her wrong and dumped her along the side of the road like garbage. Riley hated early morning homicides. *The traffic of human life is meaningless to this scum.* It gnawed at his gut. Early morning site's just lingered throughout the day – sticky and irritating. *Coulda had bagels with Claire. Coulda slept in.* Riley's face twisted into a scowl as the annoying blurts from a blackbird cut through the ruined dawn.

XIII.

It hurt as if someone had hit him in the chest. Billy sat. He stood. He muttered and paced. Yet still, all his fury did not change the fact that Jamie was lying dead in the alley behind his duplex surrounded by cops. They had seen his face. They took his name, address, and phone number. *They could be coming here next!*

Billy raced through the small three-room tenement looking for anything that belonged to Jamie. He found her shoes next to the couch and threw them away. Standing over the trashcan, looking down. The heels of her old tennis shoes poked out from the bin like two sad eyes. He felt bad about tossing them away – *like she was going to use them again!* Jamie was dead. A corpse! No longer living. The dead didn't have a need for shoes. He exhaled and groaned. He had no idea what was going on. The universe was tilting; laughing at him. He imagined CSI Agents combing through his apartment, rummaging through his garbage, and took the shoes out.

He held them close to his chest, thinking. *Was she really here?* He gazed down at her footwear, pressing her rubber soles against his chest and sighed. He opened the kitchen door and stepped out. Spying his neighbor's bin, he quietly opened the lid and buried Jamie's sneakers under a bag of his neighbor's trash. He glared at the mouth of the alley with disdain. It was rife with all his confusion and doubt. Billy felt suffocated. He went back inside and closed the door to the outside world, and was alone.

Standing in his small half house, the one that used to belong to the two of them, Billy felt sick. Queasy. *I had to toss them away; just had to.* He needed a sit and wandered over to the couch. Looking at the bedding was a dull reminder that something unusual was afoot. Jamie had been here. He was sure of it. He had set out sheets for her to use. She'd come and found him at work. They drove around the city. He'd seen her engulfed in a cone of crows.

Ah, fuck. His shoulders slumped and he crashed backwards.

"Jesus Christ," he moaned and got up.

Pacing frantically, he nearly wore a hole in the blue shag. They'd been together for a day or two. They were in his car. They drove around. Ate at a restaurant. They had been seen together in public. She had spent the night. She came to his workplace. He took off work to be with her, to be with a....*dead girl.*

Billy stopped pacing and just stood there. He eyed his apartment like an advancing army. Dust fell through the air, ignited by the sunlight that streamed through the windows, and he knew how this was going to play out. She'd been there - dead alive and talking. It wouldn't take a crime lab geek too long to place Jamie in the apartment. Every speck of dust was working against him on that. No one was ever going to believe that his ex-girlfriend had risen from a watery grave to come find him so he could help her solve her murder.

Just thinking it aloud sounded like nonsense. They were going to ship him off to a nutty farm in a straight jacket as they pinned her death on him. He pictured himself sitting in a psycho ward with drool dripping off of his chin, eyes vacant from all the pills that they kept thumbing down his throat. He was fucked. Utterly fucked, and he knew it.

All the evidence pointed to him feeding a sick fetish. Who was there to say that he hadn't been dragging around a cadaver for the passed few days, imagining it all in some grand delusion? The mind was a tricky thing. Sure, he'd been upset by their breakup. A sleazy lawyer would twist that inside and out to make a jury view him as a love-struck lunatic. It was easier to believe than the truth. The truth was impossible. The truth was...

Billy chuckled nervously. He could almost believe the lie too. It sounded saner than what he'd been dealing with. *But I'm not a lunatic. I'm not crazy. Jamie was here.*

Billy's gaze craned upward to the kitchen again and he

wandered back over to the trashcan. He began digging through it until he found what he was looking for and pulled out the empty beer bottles that they had drunk the other night. There, along the outer rim of the bottle's spout, was a thin smudged line of rouge. Lipstick. *Sure, a lawyer would say that I merely placed the bottle to her dead lips. But I'm Not Crazy!*

"I'm not a killer."

He tossed the bottles in the trash again. They clanked and rattled as he scooped up the half-filled plastic bag, strode to the couch, and stuffed the bedding inside that he had laid out for her. *No*, he thought as he tied the bag off; *something strange and unique had happened.* He'd been touched by God's hand just as Jamie had been touched. Her rebirth and those damned crows were a miracle. *Had to be.*

Though only now something else, something even darker and stranger had happened to Jamie for her to become a grotesque centerpiece in the roadside freak show that was the alley. The circus of police noise was going to be methodical and logical – *Systematic to a fault.* All their little pieces working, independently, like one giant engine – *A detecting machine.* Billy understood machines. He worked on them everyday. The whole situation he was entangled in was irregular, lopsided, and illogical. It was his edge. It gave him time. He needed to play to the strengths of Jamie's truth and not focus on the drama. The drama was the sludge. It'd choke him up. *Sure, they're gonna come knockin' on that door. I left a deposit of personal information. It's just how they think. They gotta play it by the numbers.*

He unlocked the trunk to the Chevelle and threw the bag of trash in and remembered Jamie's shoes. *She's going to need those again.* He strode back up the steps, crossed to his neighbor's side of the porch, and retrieved the dead girl's sneakers from the sealed trashcan. Billy heard the click of a lock and the pop of a doorjamb releasing and he stopped. His breath was anchored to his chest, but he started moving again and raced down the steps before his neighbor could talk to him.

Billy had things to do. He couldn't wait for the system to fall on his head. He needed to shake things up a little; keep the advantage on his unbalanced side of the table. He made a beeline to the opened trunk, tossed in the footwear, and slammed the lid shut. He walked around to the side of his automobile and climbed in. Pulling the seatbelt strap across his chest he locked it in place, and jabbed the keys into the ignition. The finely tuned machine roared to life. Billy hoped that he knew what he was doing. It was a hard gamble. But she had come to him for a reason. He had to believe in that reason or else he was nothing more than a sick pervert.

As Billy pulled the Chevelle away from the curb, he spied his neighbor poking a nose at the commotion down the street. Billy was nervous. His palms were sweaty and his breathing wavered against his tongue as he prayed it wouldn't become a decision he later regretted.

XIV.

Ambulance attendants exited the large, square vehicle with no hurry. The driver put out a cigarette under the heel of his shoe before disappearing into the back of the medical truck after the other guy, an older, bearded fellow, had opened the doors. It was another minute or two before the two of them emerged, carrying a filled black plastic bag on a metal gurney. For the twentieth time today, Billy's stomach lurched like an Olympic diver and he felt sick.

He hadn't eaten. Hunger banged in his belly, saddled up next to his queasiness, but he did not want to eat. Once he had taken his position on the opposite side of the road near the alley's other entrance Billy was locked to the spot and didn't move. He wanted a clear shot to see when the Ambulance was going to pull out and carry Jamie's body away. He waited hours for the scene in the alley to break up, debating his sanity.

Four times that day he was approached by either local pushers or prostitutes - offering him an escape. A distraction from the mind clatter and all the worry that knuckled his fingers around the steering wheel. Billy's presence didn't make sense to the street merchants. Without an interest in their goods they called him a putah, pendejo, pervert, or worse yet, they labeled him a cop. When Billy wouldn't buy this one prostitute a lunch after her kindly offer of a blow-job she fired a volley of torrid adjectives and colorful colloquialisms at him that were meant to hurt his manhood and stain his pride. It was too surreal for Billy to take in, on the heels of such a lovely morning with his dead ex-girlfriend, being bound to the causeway with uncertain fate, the young man simply shook his head, dumbfounded at the difference that a single block made in this city.

The large green and white Mercy General logo plastered to the side of the Ambulance did not help to make the vehicle inconspicuous. It was easy to track. Billy kept at a distance and the vehicle never appeared to be in any real emergency. Its lights weren't on. The siren wasn't being used to push its way through streetlights and traffic. The Ambulance followed the normal ease and flow of the street as Billy trailed it to the backside of the hospital. He pulled into a free parking space and turned his engine off.

It would be hours before he had the cover of darkness. Mercy was a big place. People were constantly moving in and out of it. At least that afforded him with enough cover to blend in. Billy sighed. The last time that he'd been to this hospital was when Jamie's father was dying of cancer. It was a virtual labyrinth inside and the two of them had a hard enough time finding his room. Billy rested his head on the steering wheel and bounced it a few times calling himself an idiot. He'd never been to this side of the place before. He saw a sign for the Medical Examiner's Office and the mini-diver in his belly drowned. Jamie's impending autopsy was looming like an impossible mountain.

He didn't even have a plan. He wasn't even sure about his motives. *She was dead, right?* All the waiting in the Chevelle just made him more anxious and nervous. He needed a plan. He had a vague idea that he'd stolen from a couple of movies, but an actual plan? *God No*, and Billy was certain he was going to land himself in jail before it was all said and done. If it weren't for the nagging feeling that somehow, someway, Jamie was a real live dead girl, and that she was going to wake up and come back to him, he'd just go to work and wait for the cops to come collect him and toss him in a padded cell.

He waited for the Ambulance attendants to climb back in their vehicle and drive off before he crept out of his car. His body felt like a rusted lawn chair unfolding after a cold dormant winter. He crossed to the outside of the Intake entrance of the Medical Examiner's department and peered through the tinted glass doors that were distinctly lettered: *Medical Personnel Only*. A nurse passed his vision, so Billy pulled his head back beyond the entrance's line of sight. He gave it a minute before peering around the side again. The nurse was walking down a long hall away from him. He looked for Jamie's body bag anywhere inside, but only succeeded in finding another nurse perched at the front desk, just inside the door of the lobby. *There's no going in here.*

Billy walked the edge of this side of the hospital looking for any way into the building that was closer than the main entrance. *An opened window? A side door? Anything would do.* But the building was tight, secure against his intrusion, and the farther he wandered from his car the more ridiculous he felt his chances were at sneaking in and absconding with his unnatural haunt.

As Billy neared yet another grim edge of the building's blocky exterior he heard voices and saw tiny white puffs of smoke flitting away in the gentle wind. He stopped and listened. Casual stuff mostly, plays and scores from the game, a nurse on the fifth floor that had rejected another date, and comments about obstinate patients; Billy could tell they worked at the hospital. He wanted to peer around the corner and see if they were close to an entrance to formulate some sort of action plan. If he had been a smoker he would have thought to walk up on them and ask for a light or bum a cigarette, but as it was, Billy did not smoke, so he eavesdropped and waited for them to go back inside.

He was trembling and nervous as he heard one of them unlock a side door. He hoped his timing was right and turned the corner. Thankfully, they were gone. A half-extinguished butt still fluttered for life in the sand of a cigarette trashcan as a spring-loaded maintenance door slowly closed. Billy ran for it. The distance was short, but the door was nearly shut. He looked at the outer flank of the metal door. It did not have a knob, just a keyhole. He had passed several types of these doorways on his hike around Mercy General. The door was only inches now from closing and locking him out. He leapt and jammed his fingertips between the hard door and its unyielding jamb.

Steel made a firm impression upon him. His fingers felt as if they were going to snap. Mechanics against biology: the hardened compressed spring pushed against soft flesh and subtle bone. Billy gritted his teeth and swallowed a yelp. Frantically, he pried the fingers of his other hand into the tiny crack to relieve his little digits of the agony they endured. He had to put his back into it. When he'd pried the door opened, just enough, he slipped inside and looked around.

He was at the end of a long, dimly lit hallway with many doors – some opened some not. Large medical equipment and rolling racks filled with linen and materials lined the walls of the hall. Disinfectant filled his breath as tiny motors pulsed, beeps and clicks spouted in regular intervals, and occasionally an announcement drifted down from speakers in the ceiling. The hospital was a noisy place. Billy's crushed fingers throbbed. He squeezed them and shook out the pain, feeling lucky that no one had seen him sneak in. *But luck never lasts.* He had to find a place to hide before somebody noticed him and threw him out. He needed to get his bearings and find the morgue. Figure out what he was going to do next. So Billy did what appeared only obvious, he walked down the long hall searching for an unoccupied room to hole up and take stock.

Passing rooms with wheezing patients, an old woman asked if he was a doctor. Office doors were locked. The janitor's closet was locked. He spied an Orderly turning down the bed where someone had recently died. The man was humming along to the song that played through his headphones, so he never saw or heard Billy pass. One door had a little glass window embedded into it. Billy peered inside. The lights were off and the room appeared empty. He checked the handle and it pushed downward, opening.

Billy ducked into the room. He moved to the far side of the door and gave himself a minute to catch his breath. It was just in time. The click clack steady walk of someone in heels clanged in his direction. Billy looked down at the doorknob and waited for it to move. But it didn't. The crisp clack of shoes passed him by, going into another room further down the hall. By the look of the one he occupied, it was a Records Room. Through a valley of shelves, he saw another door on the opposite side of the expanse and made his way toward it. He moved slowly through the space, looking around, to make sure that he was alone and that no one was in here with him, off in a small corner somewhere, buried deep in thought or mischief, ready to surprise or pounce.

He was alone. He half-expected to find a lab coat, some scrubs, or a white doctor's coat with a stethoscope tucked neatly into a pocket – *somewhere in the room* – just like he had seen in the movies, but there was nothing of the kind cooped up with him. And without some sort of camouflage or disguise Billy didn't think he was going to last that long tooling around a wing of the hospital that was clearly marked for restricted access. He poked his nose at the small window of the other door. It presented only minimal visibility. It, like the other tiny, square pane of glass, was semi-opaque, tinted with a frost coating. Everything outside of it was mutated shapes, so he opened the door, just a crack, to see what he could see.

Luckily for the reluctant hero there weren't too many people milling about in the hall when he poked his head out. He didn't notice anything that he thought would help him until he was closing the door and drawing his head back inside. It was a small sign with white lettering above a wide green door that read: *Morgue.* Billy grinned an Irish grin, feeling ease and a nervous calm descending over him. He paused and just as he was about to make a mad dash to the green hatch conversations from medical staff barked behind him. So he closed the door, ducking back inside the Records Room.

The other side of the doorway was more active and brightly lit than the hallway where he had entered the wing. He needed to find a way to blend in, if only for a moment. He had to walk the distance to that green door as if he belonged there, as if he worked at the hospital. He needed that doctor's coat that was always there on TV. He needed fortune's smile on the foolhardy, but Billy wasn't feeling too bright about being in this type of situation. It was not like dismantling and reinstalling a carburetor. Billy poked through the aisles, searching for anything that would assist him to reach that door intact, but all he discovered was a clipboard lying on the desk and a laminated ID badge with a picture of a young East Indian-looking man.

Billy was, by and large, Caucasian. White Bread. The picture on the ID looked like a transfer student – skinny, brown skinned, short trimmed black hair, a faint wisp of a moustache, and he wore glasses. It was going to be glaringly obvious to anybody with only one eye and half a brain that he wasn't the person that owned the identification card. Though upon consideration, it was glaringly obvious that Billy didn't belong on this side of the hospital anyway, so what did it really matter? The name on the laminated badge read, Mehal Priyaranjan.

"That's a mouthful," he spoke aloud after butchering the man's name. "Hope you don't mind if I borrow this, Mehal."

He hung the chain around his neck so that the ID fell across his chest and picked up the clipboard. It wasn't a white lab coat, but it was better than nothing. He did his best to muster up an official looking face before he crossed to the Records Room door, but he just felt stupid, lacking the confidence to pull it off. He placed an ear to its cold surface, listened to the traffic on the other side, and waited until it had quieted down a bit. Billy took a deep breath and opened the door with authority, praying that it would work. With Mehal Priyaranjan bouncing around his neck he crossed to the wide green door, opened it nervously, and descended down the steps.

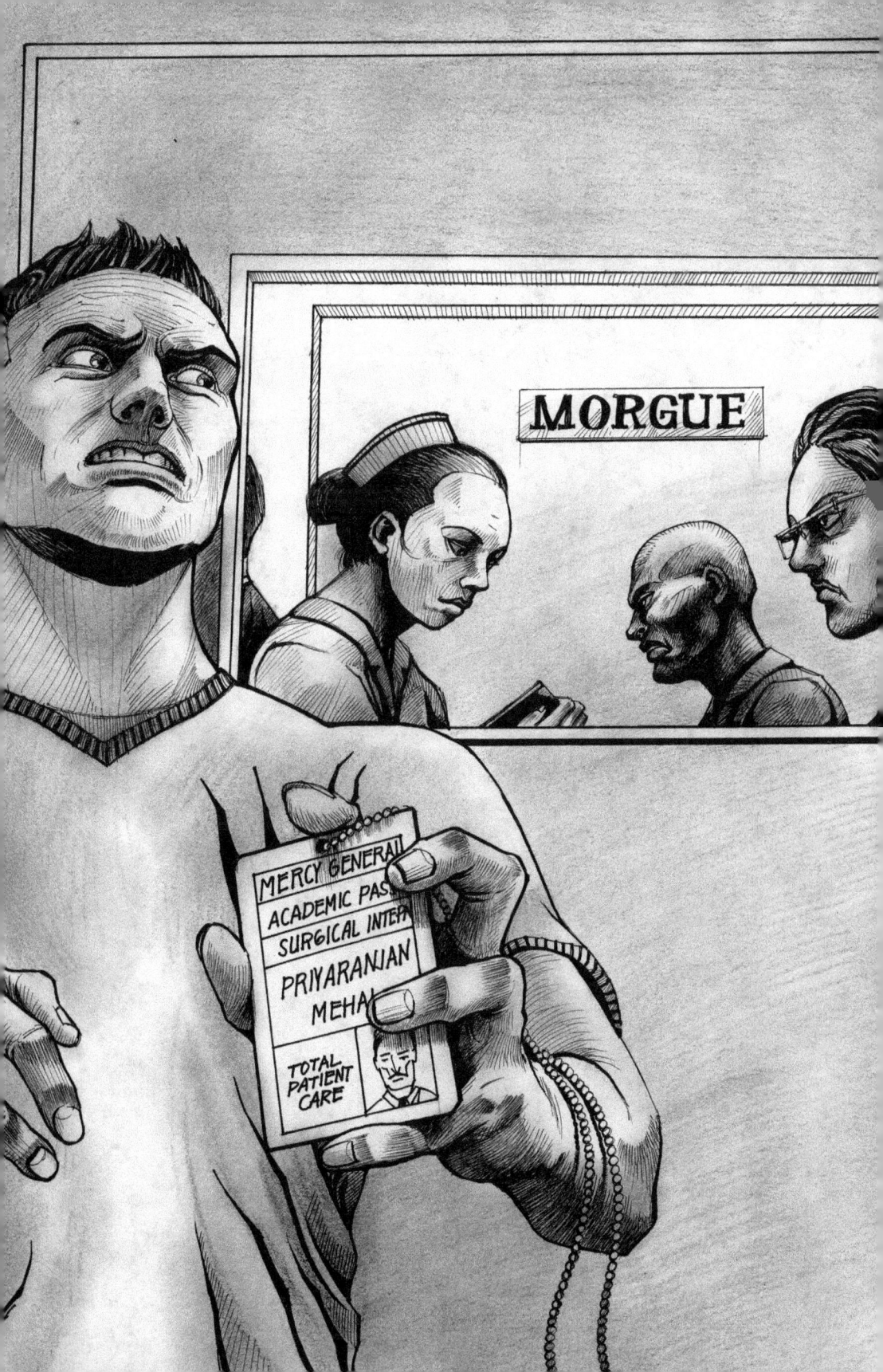

XV.

There was a soft click behind him as the green door closed on a dull, cool scent in the stairwell. His mind churned that, so far, it had been easy. He shivered like a frightened rabbit in a farmer's field. As he climbed down the flight of stairs voices below grew louder. He applied caution to each step. There was nowhere to go, if suddenly, an owner of one of the voices came clattering up the stairs. He was blocked by the openness of the utility corridor. He could go back or rush forward, but either way suggested that he was going to run into somebody unexpectedly.

At the bottom of the stairwell was an opened door propped with a bantam rubber wedge. A short hallway sprang out from the stairwell cubicle and led to an elevator. Between the unlit area where Billy now stood and the doors to the electric lift there were only two points of access. A single closed door that looked like it opened into a small maintenance room, which was closer to the elevator, and a pair of wide swinging doors with metal curtains and a tiny curving rectangle window. He was closer to the service doors, and one of them was also propped open with a bantam wedge.

He had a hard time seeing who was in the room without venturing further. Though now, he could hear her quite well. Her voice echoed through the stairwell. Billy surmised that it must have been the echo off the concrete that made him think there was more than one person talking. In due course a young woman did come into view. Black, average build, she had her hair pulled back and wore long rubber gloves tied at the biceps and a smock. She was talking into a recorder. Billy's heart sank as he imaged Jamie on her table being cut opened and dissected. His knees felt weak after such an adventure to discover the prize of his folly ruined.

He pulled behind the propped door and sat, resting his back against the cold painted brick, fretting about what to do next. He was not at all listening when he overheard the young woman describe attributes about her deceased patient that did not coincide with Jamie Lund. To this, Billy breathed a sigh of relief and summoned up the courage to venture a little further into the unlit hall and peer into the morgue. He was wide open. It wouldn't take much to flush him out. The elevator doors could open or somebody could come down the stairs. There really wasn't anywhere to hide, except of course, behind the propped door to the stairwell. *But what good would such a hiding place be if someone where to remove the rubber wedge?*

Inside, Billy saw the young woman wheeling a dead man to the far wall, which was comprised of a series of rows of tiny, square metal doors. There he watched her as she packed the man onto a long tray and pushed him into the tube. It was the first time that Billy had ever seen a real dead body. It struck him numb. Everything down here in this tank of hallways, stairwells, and rooms was making him numb. He had to press upon his fingertips to revive the life within them again, as they were growing cold and unfeeling.

Two more bodies, covered in clear plastic were stretched out on gurneys in the back of the room. There was an office off to his right with the lights on and two centralized tables bolted to the tile floor in the middle of the room. A sink. A small work desk. A tray of instruments. But Billy did not see the body bag that he witnessed the Ambulance attendants stuffing Jamie into. He wished he had. His stomach began to rumble. More from its lack of food than the unsettling thought that Jamie wasn't where he believed she should be. He tried to quiet his organ down, lest it draw attention to his peeping.

When the morgue attendant's back was to him, packing up the dead man, Billy stuck his head completely in the room and looked to the contents of the wall closest to him. There, he saw two filled black plastic bags on gurneys resting next to each other. But before he could dare to inspect either one of them more closely there was a ding from the elevator. Billy hastened to his perch behind the propped stairwell door just as the lift doors opened with a soft metallic hiss. He could not readily tell if anyone had disembarked until they neared the morgue, and only then Billy guessed that it was one person by the muted flapping of the individual's shoes on the linoleum.

"Hey beautiful," came the voice from a young man. "You ready for lunch?"

Billy crept out from behind the door.

"I can't," replied the female attendant. "The old man wants me to catalog these new arrivals and get one prepped before he returns."

"So whatchya got? Anything gruesome?"

"Derrick, stop that."

"She looks pretty. What happened to her?"

"You're sick, you know that. Close that up. Are you trying to get me fired?"

"Relax," coaxed Derrick. "Doctor Frankenstein won't—"

"It's Hamerstien. You know he hates that."

"Whatever. He isn't here and I want to take my gal to lunch. So, what's it going to be?"

There was a long pause. Billy hoped that she was going to say yes. He mouthed the word "c'mon" repeatedly like a magic chant, but it had little effect.

"I've two bodies going up to Student Studies that I still need to process and he was very adamant about wanting to get started right away with that girl when he returned." Billy could hear the sigh in her voice. She wanted a break, but was fearful.

"Shelia, c'mon?"

Silence dripped from the sterile cold bricks.

"Alright then," the young man announced. "How about I go get lunch for the both of us and we eat it down here while you work."

"That's sweet," she said, her voice going faint. "But you and I both know that I'd never get any work done if you were down here alone with me."

"Is that right?"

Billy's face twisted into a frown as he heard them kissing.

"Now get out of here," boomed the young woman's voice from the morgue, and Billy dashed behind the door again. The rest of their words were lost in his hurry.

He was no sooner hidden than did the young man pass over the threshold of the stairwell. Billy held his breath. The guy ascended the steps rather nosily. Billy noted that he wore blue scrubs and had blond hair, but he could tell no more than that, and quite frankly he was thankful at not learning anything else about him. To do so would have meant being privy to an awkward and very private display in the wrong place, at the wrong time, or having the young man come upon him in the stairwell. Neither prospect seemed appealing, and he was glad that he did not have to endure one or the other. All that was required of him now was to think up some kind of diversion that would cause the young attendant to leave the morgue so that he could rescue his corpse and get away.

Though now, at having seen where she was located in the building, discerning a bit of its labyrinth, and guessing where his car was on the outside, he didn't have a clue as to how he was going to get Jamie out of here. *Some hero I turned out to be*, breathed Billy into his shoulders, feeling all the more ridiculous as time passed. He sat behind the opened gray door and waited until providence or luck or something brilliant sprang to mind.

XVI.

Shelia Rhodes stayed in the morgue and worked. Billy nodded off a few times, waiting for an idea to form. He was awakened by a squeaky thud. He poked his head around the opened portal and saw Shelia wheeling a corpse to the elevator on an uneven gurney. Its loopy wheel went around wobbly and clanked a steady rhythm. The body on the lopsided top was covered in plastic and a sheet. Shelia depressed the elevator button and waited. Billy pulled behind the opened door and listened for her moving the corpse onto the lift. He didn't have long to wait.

No sooner had the elevator doors shut did he spring into action. But Billy quickly found that his legs weren't quite ready for the sprint. A cramp formed and throbbed in his thigh and he was stiff all over. He'd been sitting on the cold concrete floor for far too long. His rear had become tingly and it hurt to move. When he shot through the morgue doors there was only one body bag left up against the wall. Billy went straight to it. He fumbled for the zipper, eventually finding its small black end he pulled it halfway down. He tossed the flap back and Jamie rested before him, eyes closed. Silent.

She looked like she was sleeping. He didn't know what to say or do. He stood there awhile as a gloom fell over him. The gravity of this moment was heavy. He had expected to find her here. He'd followed the breadcrumbs and spied on her ordeal all morning long. But this moment was singular and defining. Even in death she was beautiful, and that beauty gnawed at Billy's gut with teeth. Slowly, he zipped her back up and walked to the doorway of the morgue. For the first time since it had all begun he actually felt like giving up and going home. She was dead, after all.

He was standing where the dead belonged. For a long time he just stood there, betwixt one place and another, unable to move. Worry fled from his mind as to when the attendant would return. He figured it would be soon, but he was feeling small and insignificant. The monument of the room pressed upon him as doubt crept into his memory. Billy wasn't so sure anymore that he'd actually talked with her that morning, or spent the past few days tracking down her killer. *What if I've been dreaming?*

Nothing was so sure as the coming of the Reaper. He held everyone's time card. Billy felt this in his marrow. Jamie was lying in that awful black plastic bag, not moving, not breathing – still as the grave. *Why isn't she moving and talking now?* Billy didn't know. They'd only started to discover what had happened to her. *Or did we?* His morning felt real, but nothing was so final as death. At least that's what Billy had thought until Jamie Lund proved otherwise.

He turned toward her plastic shell again and opened it back up. He remembered all those blackbirds circling and swarming around her like a tempest. Surely God's hand was at work here, but was it over? *Has he taken it away?* Nothing seemed so vicious a thought than to be teased by life or fate or whatever before learning the truth of her murder. From the start of it there was more at work than what Billy could even begin to imagine. If nothing else, he had that to hold onto to.

"You better wake up, Jamie Lund," he pronounced with conviction. "You better wake up from this or so help me God I'll bury you myself in an unmarked grave. You hear me?" He shook the mantle of his thoughts. "Damn you. You never did know when to quit. Don't start now."

Billy zipped her back up and crossed to the elevator at the far end of the darkened hallway. He looked for the control panel but only found a keyhole. The lift was key activated.

"If it's not one thing, it's another." He sighed.

Moving to the closed utility door he turned the handle. The lights were off inside and he couldn't see as much as an inch from his face. He searched for the switch. He expected to be in a broom closet or small storeroom for sheets and rubber gloves, but when the lights flickered on, fluorescent bulbs spattering and spitting, he found that it was nothing like that at all. The room was tiled with small green and white tiles and led through a bathroom to a short row of lockers, past two shower-stalls, a very large hamper, and a rack laden with towels. Billy closed the door and investigated further.

At first glance there did not appear to be any other exit or entrance into the locker room than through the door in which he had just come, but he soon discovered a small rectangular window at the end of the lockers. There was a bench installed into the wall under the window, so Billy climbed up. He still had to stand on the tips of his toes to reach the bottom of the little, rectangular pane, and he could just make out a parking lot on the other side of the sandblasted glass. He examined the window's frame and turned a latch. The window only opened about six inches for ventilation. It was not enough space, of course, for him or Jamie to fit through.

He looked at the retractable metal rods that folded when the window was closed and figured that if he could loosen them that he may be able to open the window wide enough to squeeze a body through. It would be tight, but not impossible. Billy grabbed one of the rods and wiggled it. It was sturdy, but not so much so that he couldn't knock it out. He looked around for something to hit it with, but found nothing. Climbing down he recalled the tray of tools in the morgue.

Billy quickly crossed to the locker room door. He turned the lights off before he opened it, and even then he only opened it a crack. He didn't want to arouse suspicion if someone were lurking about. He was excited and felt time, once again, pressing on his back. He listened to learn if the attendant had returned. Once he was confident that he was still alone he bolted from the room into the place of the dead. He looked for anything that would aide him in his peril to secure an escape for he and Jamie. Bonesaws. Scalpels and knives. Clamps. He soon discovered an odd looking bone cutter that resembled a regular ole bolt cutter. It disturbed Billy to think about what they used a tool like that for as he picked it up. He shook his head as he fled from the morgue into the locker room, trying not to think about it.

He was half way to the window when it occurred to him that the attendant only had to come into this room to find him vandalizing hospital property. It wasn't like the door had been locked. She most likely had a locker in here. So doubling back, Billy turned off the lights and carefully wound his way through the room. He knocked his shins against a low-lying bench and yowled. He crashed into a locker, once or twice. He cursed at each explosion of painful surprise and was deeply thankful when he turned the corner and saw a little light softly streaming through the sandblasted glass. It gave him a clear path to his destination.

The day was wearing on him heavily. By the time he had mounted the wooden bench, opened the window, and tried to cut the first metal arm anxiety had worn him out. He pulled on the ends of the tool, but it wouldn't budge. The metal was tougher than what he had thought. He tried again, putting his back and legs into it. It was at such an awkward angle to reach. But little by little he clipped away at the rods until a swift smack with the side of the bone cutter dislodged the window from its hinges. He barely caught the falling pane in time, before glass shattered against the wall, making his whereabouts and movements obvious for anyone in earshot to discover. He was just about to place the window back in its frame, jump down, and get Jamie when the lights suddenly cut on, exposing him in his escape.

XVII.

There is a long corridor on the fourth floor of Mercy General that connects two main buildings. Each building was built in different decades by different generations under extremely different management. Throughout construction these new wings were touted to possess all the modern amenities that one could ever want in healthcare. This was the pitch for every consecutive wing that was built in addition to the original hospital. Progress and healthcare, the epitome of patient care was quickly absorbed into the hospital's long history to become both relic and platform for the next age to criticize and condemn for new growth. A hodge-podge of design, Mercy was constantly under renovation.

At the end of the corridor in the old building, from the fourth floor, Shelia Rhodes took a service elevator up to the sixth floor and traveled down a connecting hallway to the building that the university had built. From there she went down three floors to a room in search of the intern that was supposed to have come for the body that she now wheeled through the hospital. Upon learning that no one was in the third floor classroom, the smart woman took the cadaver to the freezer in the basement, where a different intern relieved her of her burden so that she could make the long trip back.

Delivering just one body that was slated for university use was only half of what she needed to do. To say that she was thrilled at having to cart two cadavers up and down three different buildings would be stretching it quite far. She had more than enough work in the morgue to keep her busy past her shift, and though taking care of supplies for medical studies did not, technically, fall within her job description, Shelia always seemed to be the one doing it. She had half a mind to put the bodies back in the large walk-in cooler, shut the door, and wait for the class's instructor to come get them himself. But it was not a choice she could make. As long as Stan was her supervisor she would be crisscrossing, going up and down lifts, and barreling through long stretches of hallways with medical remains. In truth, and she knew it, it would have been easier for her to place the body in her car and drive it around to the other side of the hospital than to walk the great distance on the paths that many different architects had designed. So, when Shelia opened the locker room door and turned on the light her legs felt a little weary.

Billy froze in place. Hearing her enter one of the bathroom stalls, a loud hiss of flowing water soon echoed off the tiles. He gingerly placed the window back into its frame and secured it with the latch. His heart thrummed in his throat. He stepped down from the wooden bench and hid behind the last row of lockers.

He guessed correctly that it was the female attendant when he heard her sigh into the sink, washing her hands and splashing a little water onto her face. He breathed his own sigh of relief when the light suddenly cut off, surrounding him once again in delicious darkness, instead of having the woman make her way through the lockers. Billy assumed that he wouldn't mind her going to her locker if it meant that she was going home, leaving Jamie unattended. He could do with something less adventurous right now and was more than eager to have this whole nasty business behind him.

In darkness he crept from his hiding place to the door. This time he had a better go of it, making his way against the South wall with his hand outstretched before him. He cracked the door open, but still heard the woman fidgeting around in the morgue. He had little choice but to wait.

Billy didn't have to wait long. He heard her pass and board the elevator with his back against the inside bathroom wall and quickly made his way to the tray where he'd procured the bone cutter. He returned it to the exact spot where he had found them, though as he was fleeing over to Jamie's body bag he noticed a short rectangular box.

There was nothing too extraordinary about this box. It was made of cardboard and had a company logo printed on it like many throughout the hospital. It wasn't even the box that drew Billy's attention to it, but rather the contents of the box that made him pause and think. Because sticking out of the box, like tissue, were rubber gloves. It was the gloves that caused Billy to stop and reflect on all the surfaces and instruments that he had touched since sneaking into Mercy.

He still wore Mehal Priyaranjan's ID around his neck, and he guessed that the clipboard was still behind the stairwell door. It wouldn't take a seasoned detective like the one he'd met this morning to figure out that he'd been down here messing about. Billy was sure no police data bank had his fingerprints on file. But he wasn't too sure that they might not soon acquire them once that shifty-looking special investigator began poking his nose into why Jamie was dead in the alley behind his duplex. It was to this association that Billy snatched up a pair of rubber gloves, placed them over his mechanic hands, and began retracing his whereabouts, wiping, he hoped, his fingerprints off everything he had touched.

He used the bottom of his tee shirt to clean the bone cutters and other instruments that he had picked up in his search for a tool. He went back to the bathroom and grabbed a small hand towel from the shelf and began wiping down the window frame, glass, broken hinges, sections of wall, the light switch, doorknobs, and several lockers that he thought he had laid a palm on when stumbling around in the dark. He even wiped down the metal on the swinging service doors, the lock on the elevator, and almost every inch behind the opened stairwell door, including the door itself. Unfortunately however, Billy did not clean up the clipboard, having every intention to take it with him when he left, as well as the ID badge that swung around his neck.

It was to the young mechanic's ingenuity at trying and make everything look as normal and ordinary until the last possible minute. He didn't want to leave any trace of his existence until the discovery of the missing corpse, and so sought to mask his devious theft in every conceivable way. To this effect, Billy kept Mehal's clipboard behind the stairwell door as he went in search of another body to put in place of Jamie in the black plastic bag.

Unfortunately, before he found a cadaver that roughly matched her size and shape he saw more dead bodies than he'd ever wished or cared to see in a lifetime. The back wall of the morgue was full of mortal remains behind square little metal doors. Men – young and old. Women – shriveled and bloated. The corpse of a child shot in three places along its chest and face was most disturbing. Billy felt nauseous. He actually thought he was going to throw-up at the sight of the young boy. As hard as he might try, Billy found it difficult not to look at the huge, gaping death wounds that he had suffered and feel loss at everything the child would never know or experience.

He did not wonder why this young man, ripped from life long before his prime, was not granted the luxury that Jamie had been afforded. He did not consider why death chose that person instead of somebody else. Billy's objective was clear. He needed to get the girl and get the hell out of here. It was all quite simple, but he was appearing to have a difficult go at it. Once he'd found the appropriate duplicate, Billy unzipped Jamie and was lifting her out of the bag, as carefully as he could be, when he heard above him the wide green door opening and closing and the clomp stomp of heavy shoes and the jangle of keys barreling down the steps.

XVIII.

"Gaddammit," Stan muttered into his sleeve when he noticed that Shelia had not gotten the body ready for its autopsy and analysis.

He'd been to two crime scenes this day and the second one was the worst. A double homicide, and suicide, as it turned out. Quite messy. Three bodies with bits of each of them needing to be collected and bagged so that he could figure out the human puzzle. It had fouled his mood. It didn't help any that the first corpse, which had roused him out of bed early this morning, confounded his medical practice and teachings. The least he could have hoped for was to have it prepped and ready to go when he returned with the wagon filled to the hilt with gory remains.

"Where is that girl?" asked Stan of the air as he entered the office, turning on the light, and setting his briefcase and spent coffee cup down.

Billy watched the elder man moving about from a small adjacent room at the back of the morgue, next to the freezer wall. He'd barely had enough time to stuff Jamie back into the bag, avoid zipping up her hair, close the drawer on the body he'd picked out, and hide when Stan Hamerstien came raucously into view. Billy was shaking and breathing heavily, trying to slow his pulse by taking huge slow breaths when he'd rounded the corner of the cubicle and slid out of sight. It had been too close for comfort. He almost had her out.

Billy didn't recognize the newcomer from earlier this morning, but guessed correctly that he was the man the attendant and her boyfriend were talking about earlier. A small hope flickered as he spied Stan leaving the morgue with a bundle of keys held in his hand. This hope was soon dashed when Billy overheard the medical examiner run into his assistant in the hallway coming off the elevator.

"Where have you been?"

"Delivering those bodies to student studies like you asked me to do."

The attitude in the attendant's tone was more apparent when she walked into the room. Her face was squished into a conveyance of annoyance. Stan followed her in.

"Mr. Gunderson done?"

"Yes," she announced, turning to face her boss. "And so is the old lady from yesterday."

"Good," replied Stan, the tone in his voice softening. He reached out to hand Shelia the keys. "Got three in the van that I need you to bring down."

Billy noted how her whole body sighed at the man's request as she accepted the key bundle. He walked over to the freestanding tray where Billy had found the bone cutters.

"There's two small bags of pieces also. It was a nasty one."

"Joy," Shelia sarcastically added as she left the morgue.

By the look and sound of it the two of them did not appear to be going anywhere anytime soon. A headache was forming behind Billy's eyes due to his lack of nourishment. He had no idea how long he was going to have to remain cooped up in this small cubicle of a room before one of them came, turned on the light, and saw him cowering close to the floor.

Everything loomed toward ruin. Billy kept running through his head what he was going to say to his parents when they came to bail him out of jail. He regretted starting this whole horrible affair, and it was times like these that he wished the dead simply had enough respect for the living to stay dead. A volley of *Ifs* plagued his mind: *if only she'd never left. If only she never gotten herself killed. If only she never came to the garage. If only she would have stayed inside. If only…if only…* But it really wasn't Jamie's fault. He was the one who went bounding after her like some knight in medieval times to rescue the fair damsel. He could have stayed home and watched TV for all the lounging he had done in this cold, dank place. But he didn't. He followed after her.

Stan went about preparing the far table for an autopsy. He placed a smock over his dress pants, shirt, and tie and donned those elbow-gripping waders that Billy saw Shelia wearing earlier. Every instance that brought the medical examiner closer to unzipping Jamie Lund and placing her on his table was met with prayers of some strange calamity from Billy that would enable him to abscond with his unnatural haunt. It was ridiculous of course, the buildings of Mercy General were built with the finest grade materials that money could buy, and it was often reported as one of the safest structures to go to in case of a terrorist attack.

Billy felt helpless. Soon the young attendant was loading up the morgue with three new gurneys, each loaded with its own plastic bag nightmare and a smaller black plastic satchel with what Billy assumed housed those fleshy, human pieces he had heard about. He was awarded a small reprieve when Shelia informed Stan that she was going home. From what he gathered from the muffled conversation her shift had ended several hours ago.

Billy had no concept of time while cooped up in the morgue. Everything was laden with that god-awful feeling of dread and suspended timelessness. Minutes felt like years. Seconds ticked by like hours. He was excruciatingly bored. And it did not serve well that he had to remain motionless and soundless, lest he was discovered. Billy passed the time in agony, anticipating Jamie's inevitable display on the examiner's table.

What if she woke up in the middle of her autopsy? Billy imagined the screaming. It was a foul mess indeed. He raised his head to the cubicle's window to keep track of what was happening. Like the bullet-ridden corpse of the little boy, it was hard to look away. Had Stan been paying better attention and wasn't accustomed at being so alone in his work he would have noticed Billy's crown sticking out above the frame of the pane.

Events had grown all too surreal again for Mr. Kimmel as he witnessed the medical examiner placing Jamie on the table. The slow pull of the zipper that released his dead ex-girlfriend into the lasting care of the doctor felt like claws scratching down his spine. It would be weeks before he forgot that horrible sound. Stan depressed a button on the recorder and started talking to himself.

"July ninth, Stan Hamerstien, Coroner for Passiac County, district 8, conducting the autopsy of a Jane Doe found in the alley off East Lexington Street early this morning, of the same day. Was also the attending medical examiner on site. I am removing the victims clothes."

And so he did, describing each artifact he took off Jamie's body. He folded every article of clothing neatly and placed each item into a single evidence bag for later analysis by another department. In due course she was naked, lying on the cold metal table with Stan moving around her slowly reporting into the digital recorder his initial observations. Billy felt as if the man was intruding upon her most private nature. Though, he found the ordeal intriguing once the doctor began talking about the bruising around her neck, attributing it to strangulation.

The man was methodical in his approach to Jamie's corpse, even going so far as to bag the lint he found between her toes. An awkward moment arrived for Billy when the Coroner began examining her pelvic region more closely, raising both her legs into stirrups. Billy received some small reprieve to learn that there weren't any signs of sexual trauma. The analysis of her body and the collecting of evidence progressed smoothly until the doctor announced his intention to begin the autopsy with a single incision.

He closed his eyes. *It's now or never.* Billy didn't want to hurt anyone, but he couldn't let him start slicing up Jamie. Stan was poised over the corpse to make his first cut when his cell phone rang. It bleated annoyingly in the sparse tiled room and Billy jumped. A bramble of nerves, he watched the doctor pause and glare at the phone. But he didn't move. The man seemed set on finishing his examination. Billy braced himself to attack, but after several loud bursts from his ringtone Stan decided to answer it. He shut off the digital recorder, and to Billy's pure resolve, returned the scalpel to the tray from where he had grabbed it.

The medical examiner was pleasant enough at first with whomever he was talking to, but that quickly changed when he couldn't get out of the service he was being asked to perform. Agitated, Stan

removed his smock and hung it up. Then he set the sealed evidence bags aside on the long worktable and disposed of the elbow-gripping waders and rubber gloves. He grabbed his empty coffee cup and hit the light as he left, leaving Jamie spread out on the table for later.

Billy waited for all the noise to cease in the entire underground area before he unpacked himself from the darkened corner of the morgue. He rose, noticing how a safety light softly illuminated her body. He approached her cautiously as the silence and black emptiness of the morgue absorbed around her. He stared into her sealed eyes, naked against all inspection, and truly wondered if she was in fact just like any other corpse now, frozen in its space and time, complete in its bounty of breath, decaying.

Time was a cruel jest, and Billy simply did not know how much of it he had left to finish rescuing his fair dead damsel. Lifting her over a shoulder, he made his way to the locker room again. He placed her just inside the door, using her slumped demeanor as a wedge to keep it open and stream light into the very dark hallway as he went to retrieve the clipboard from behind the stairwell door. Billy was shocked to discover that it had been shut and it was, of course, locked. He huffed and cursed at his misfortune. Now, he could no more reclaim the clipboard with his fingerprints on it than leave this dreadful place, except through the same window that he intended to shove Jamie out of.

Worried and frustrated, he returned to the enclosed room, thinking it best to clothe his dead ex-girlfriend before he stuffed her, unceremoniously, out of the broken window frame. Rummaging through the clothes hamper for something she could wear, Billy came across a pair of blue scrubs. They were stained with blood, but he didn't think Jamie would mind too much in her current condition. He just wanted to get her out of here before anybody else rolled up on him, making his life that much more difficult.

With the scrubs in hand he went to Jamie's inert body and began dressing her. It was harder than he thought. With no aid from her at all her limbs were like floppy anchors. A few times he found himself wanting to hurl curse words at the girl for being dead in the first place. It wouldn't have done any good, of course, just aggravated himself further when he still had to contend with gravity and her languid, lifeless form.

After she was dressed in the blue scrubs, looking very much

like a passed out intern at some medical school frat party, Billy gently lifted her in his arms and carried her to the bench. He didn't remember her being so heavy. *Dead weight.* Once he had laid her in place under the window he went back to the front of the locker room. Passing the bathroom stalls and the showers, rows of lockers, the laundry bin and sinks, he turned off the lights. This time he was thankful for wearing the rubber gloves, though his hands had started to sweat and felt sticky hours ago.

Darkness enveloped him once more. He stood in place waiting for his eyes to adjust to the dim light that drifted across the back of the room from his little escape hatch. It was tranquil, those few moments he waited in the dark. The better part of his day thus far, he was close to the end of it now. When he returned to the dead girl's side and opened the window he recognized his problem. If just putting on a pair of oversized pants and shirt was a pain in the ass then sticking her whole body, limbs and all, through a tiny hole above his head was going to suck.

"Sorry about this," he reported to Jamie's limp, doll-like body as he struggled to get her into position.

With his arms tucked under her armpits he exhaled once for strength and courage and hoisted her toward the rectangle of dim light and fresh air. She was heavy. Dead weight. Her body wanted to fold in on itself in too many places and crumple like a slinky toy down a flight of steps. Billy strained to reposition himself and get a better grip on her torso. It wasn't working. Her chest was pressing uncomfortably upon his face. He was starting to pant and let an arm and leg drop.

Catching his breath, Billy repositioned his hands and pushed with all his might. Her head banged nosily against the little window frame, but he couldn't stop for that. Getting her through wasn't going to be pretty. He was happy that she wasn't conscious to complain. After a few more failed attempts, he brought her down and tried another tact. Grabbing her around the waist, using the flat ramp of the wall, he twisted her as if rotating a dial, manhandling her head, neck, and shoulders through the window. It was a small feat. He stopped and held her there, catching his breath. Jamie resembled a squid drooping out of a box.

Billy squatted down and grabbed her by the thighs and pushed. Clumsily, she moved forward – inch by inch. A few more heave-hos

and she'd be completely through, though he wasn't sure if he'd break her neck in the process. He tried to alleviate the pressure off the delicate parts of her body, but it wasn't easy going. When he'd gotten all but her feet out the window he struggled to move her aside so that he could climb through.

Maneuvering his own body across the tiny rectangle was difficult. Half way out he needed to grab onto Jamie's scrubs and pull with all his might to wiggle his legs through the narrow orifice. Once he was through though, Billy rolled onto his back and panted, staring at the coming night. Dusk was falling all around them and he was quite anxious from the whole ordeal, nervously shaking. Any minute now and somebody, anybody, could easily drive by, or walk past on their way to their car. Except for a small hedge, which was a few feet away from the window, he was completely exposed with the corpse.

"Well, that was a pain in the ass," he barked to the stars, rolling his head to the side.

Jamie resembled a messy lump more than a person. Her eyes were lazily open and stared blankly back at him. It was a sobering expression. He quickly caught his breath, stood, and looking around, dragged Jamie behind the low-lining hedge. It couldn't be helped. He needed to find his car and he'd be able to do it much faster if he wasn't carrying her around. Billy went back over to the tiny ventilation window and pulled it shut, wedging a bit of wood from one of the hedge's trimmed limbs between the pane so that it would remain closed. After that he quickly walked to his car, which was two parking lots over, and drove up to the curb as the sky darkened and the streetlights began to glow more brightly

Behind the bush, he rolled Jamie onto her back. Her hair was knotted. Her face and scrubs were smudged with dirt and green-grass stains. Her fingers were jammed into balls on the lawn. She looked worse for wear. Billy removed several dark amber tresses from her silent, sullen kisser and hoisted her up, carrying her nonchalantly to the car. As he laid her in the back seat and shut the passenger's side door, he thought he vaguely detected the scent of rain on the wind.

Climbing behind the wheel, he pulled from the curb as if nothing was remotely out of the ordinary. It had been a helluva day, but it was done. For better or for worse...it was done. No matter what happened now, whether she woke up or he found a grave for her somewhere far outside the city limits, he was in too deep to turn back. The die had been cast and Billy drove a dead girl back to his apartment. He was tired, hungry, and sore. He never thought that he'd actually make it this far, but he did, he kept telling himself, "I did it."

As he lit from the hospital drive to the main street, the jagged buildings of Mercy General shrinking in his rearview mirror, rain began to fall. Softly at first, with large chunks of water, beading on the windshield. Billy was thankful for the sight. It imbued a refreshing scent wafting up from the street. All day long he'd been eating recycled air. So, he parted his window and let the rain gently wash his face.

XIX.

Billy was woken from the knocking at his door.

It had been an uneasy night. Once he had finally gotten Jamie inside, laid her out on his bed and cleaned her up, he was exhausted. His innards felt like a tangled fray of raw emotions. He was wired. He stood for a time looking at her reposed features, waiting for something to happen. He half expected something to happen. But nothing did. Standing there, he memorized every line and curve of her form, but he soon began to feel more like a stupid fool.

After eating nothing all day, Billy thought to finally vent his bottled energy with food, but even that was asking for too much. Standing in the light of the opened refrigerator, with his shadow cast on the far wall, he searched for something to nibble on. Billy knew he didn't want to cook. Yet he also didn't feel like eating anything from the places that would deliver. So he stood there, blankly staring at the same meager offerings until he eventually shut the door.

He fell into a comfortable chair, took his boots off with groans of relief, eased his sore feet up, and was asleep within minutes. There he stayed until an ungentle rapping woke him from that deep and mighty slumber and he lumbered to the door rubbing the crust from his eyes.

He staggered over his haphazardly laid boots. His hair was a wild chestnut of spikes and as he opened the door the sun bit his eyes. He squinted violently, blinking until he could see that nobody stood beyond his opened door. Confused, he shuffled out, chewing the dry film in his mouth as he looked to his neighbor's side of the porch.

Two middle-aged callers waited as his neighbor opened the door. This wasn't the first time that he'd mistaken the banging on his neighbor's door as his own. They were wearing suits. Except the woman. She donned a fine flower printed dress and wore a smart hat that had a frilly bit that covered the top of her forehead. His neighbor, Greg Meyers, wore a suit and so did the other gentleman. They all looked prim and proper and Billy was about to shuffle softly back indoors when he heard his neighbor speak.

"Morning, Billy." A chipper voice. "Quite the commotion we had there yesterday, huh?"

"Yeah," croaked the frazzled young man.

"Seems some poor girl was found dead in our alley," added Mr. Meyers, more for the benefit of his friends.

"Oh, my Lord," exclaimed the thinly wry woman, placing a hand to her heart.

"It's a shame," announced the neighbor as he locked his door. "To be taken so young. I heard she was barely twenty."

"That is a shame." replied the other finely dressed gentleman with a rich baritone voice.

"We'll have to pray for her," pressed the woman with a concerned and crinkled brow.

Billy watched as they all made sympathetic faces and drew from the front stoop one after the other.

"See you at church later?" Mr. Meyers asked with a smile.

The other two turned and looked up at Billy. He had started attending on a regular basis before the dead girl entered his life. Ironically, it was only after Jamie had broken up with him and moved out did he begin to fill his Sundays with the Bible. He felt the pressure of their eyes.

"Maybe later, Mr. Meyers. It was a late night."

"Well," the old man smiled, "God be with you either way. You take care, Billy." He waved and started off.

"You too, Mr. Meyers."

Billy waved back. The thinly wry woman kept her gaze on him as they all walked to the sidewalk. If he'd known any better, he would have sworn that she knew something was up. It was unnerving, the way she glared at him like a sinner.

Billy nodded, smiled, and watched them shrink away down the block. He shuffled back inside his half of the duplex and closed the door. It clicked into place louder than he'd like and the immediate departure of sounds made his apartment all the more silent and lonely. Billy went to the bedroom. A knot formed above his eyes. Jamie was just as he had left her.

He entered the bathroom, leaving the door open, and relieved himself. The loud stream stunted the cold silence that the corpse lent to the air, to the bed, to the entire room.

"Did you hear that," Billy added as he took a piss. "They're gonna pray for you." He chuckled and shook out the last drops, zipped up, and reentered the bedroom. "They're gonna pray for *you*."

He stared down at her, thinking about how he was the only one that needed prayers if she didn't wake up. *My little zombie girl – dead to the world.* He cracked his neck as a fly buzzed around the room and landed on Jamie's spiritless, stiff cheek. Billy sighed and went back into the bathroom to brush his teeth.

XX.

Out of the shower and Jamie still lay there, a cadaver in his bed. He'd already figured that he was going to burn those sheets and get some new ones. Around game time, he turned on the television for the pre-game report.

Throughout the interviews, speculative plays, grand proclamations, and highlights from both team's previous games played Jamie still remained as motionless as a stone, Billy's own personal Albatross. When the first field goal was kicked Billy's eyes began to wander more to the partially closed door than to his TV set.

When the score was 21 to 15, Jamie was still acting defiant and Billy was starting to get nervous that she'd always remain an oversized paperweight. When night hurried down the skyscrapers and buried its Nubian face in the heat of the concrete and fell on the wanton creatures trolling through desperate streets there was still a cadaver lying in Billy Kimmel's bed.

All day long and nothing had changed. Except for the fact that more flies had found their way into the room, and she was beginning to stink.

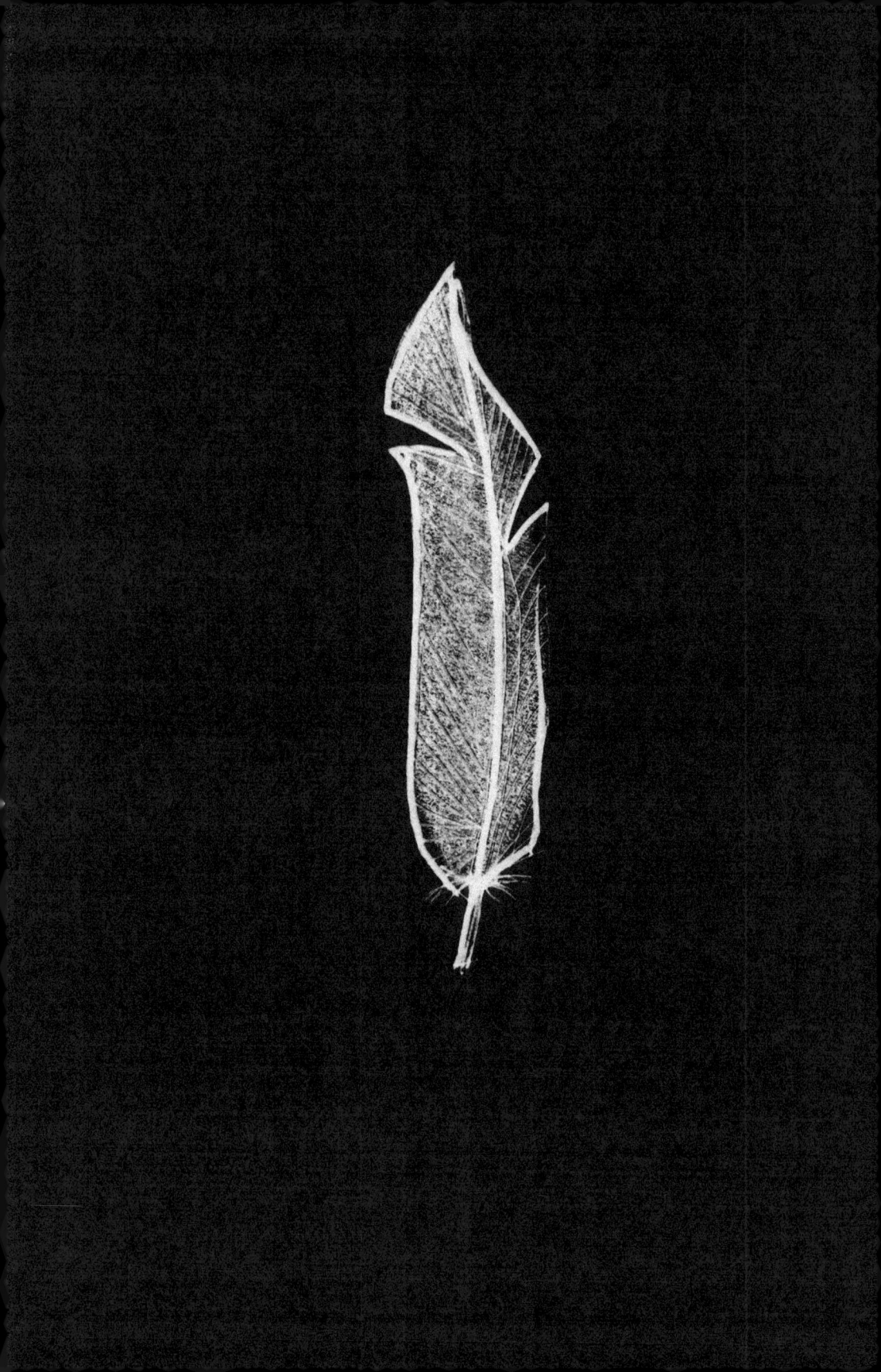

XXI.

By morning the smell emanating out of the bedroom was unpalatable. She reeked. Billy was flabbergasted at what to do. So, he dosed her in perfume from a tiny bottle that he had found a week after Jamie had moved out. He'd always meant to return it to her. Though, he never figured on it being in such an odd manner as this.

He tarried around the dead tethered bed, getting dressed. Flies upon flies had gathered, annoyingly buzzing around her stiff-laden corpse, cutting the air with high-pitched stings. Billy cranked up the air conditioner to lower the temperature in the rooms of the apartment. He'd slept on the couch last night and was awoken by the sounds of a movie coming from the TV set. Night of the Living Dead, in glorious black and white. Billy hadn't seen it since he was a kid.

The film had scared him then, feeling alone in the house as his parents slept and every room between his bed and the television set, dark. The film looked ridiculous to him now. Zombies trying to enter the house, tearing through boarded up windows, in search of live, warm flesh to eat. If only the filmmaker had known what the living dead were really like he would have thought twice about starting such a nonsensical fad. *The dead are boring. The living dead...are more so!* But the film did put a knot in Billy's stomach, so he turned the set off and lay on his couch, the one he and Jamie had moved into the apartment, and thought heavily about the events of the past few days.

Sometime during his analysis of the natural ebb and flow of the universe, which had been working quite nicely since the dawn of time, he compared the only other instance that he knew of the dead rising. By Billy's reckoning it had taken place in Jerusalem over two thousand years ago. He chuckled and shook his head. The thought was ludicrous: *Jamie Lund and Jesus Christ, undead rebels of the apocalypse.* If any similarities existed then he was her apostle. *Ridiculous.* He chided his folly as he fell back asleep. The only thing that was evident now were the bothersome little insects, drawn into his abode by a fine and natural calling.

At work his mind was elsewhere. It was obvious what he needed to do. Matters with Jamie's remains would only get worse. He needed to get rid of the body and start living his life again. Yet in truth, he did not want to bury Jamie in some obscure way. He wanted the miracle. He wanted a life extraordinary. He wanted the dead girl. But it wasn't meant to be; there really wasn't any real proof that she had ever been anything other than what she currently was – a lifeless corpse.

"Hey, Hector," called Billy as his boss walked through the garage. "You remember that girl from the other day?"

"Yeah," he said. "The short one with the black hair?"

"Yeah." Billy nodded. "She seem real to you?"

Hector laughed at his employee. "Eh, a little pale for my taste, but real enough." He turned to leave, but added, "next time you take off work for such a girl, you know, take her to the beach. Both of you, get some sun. Live a little."

He had some small proof. She had been more than what she was, but it didn't alter the situation any, and the situation was grim. Perhaps after he had disposed of her he'd take a couple days off and Hector's advice to go the beach and lounge in the sun. Ease back into his old life.

On the road home with the day behind him, Billy was absolutely convinced that Jamie had to go. For whatever reason faith was belly up and his apartment wasn't going to be host to an extended family of oversized gnats any longer. He'd just have to chalk it up as a fluke and forget about the whole mess and never speak about it to anyone. And if that didn't work, drinking would always help. Billy was already beginning to feel better at finally making a solid decision and was confident in his method of disposing of the girl's remains.

Hector knew a man named Warren who had a salvage yard and stripped old cars for parts and compressed the rest down into scrap metal that was then melted for recycling. Billy had taken a few clunkers over to Warren's place that were junking up the parking lot at the garage. It was as grand an ebb and flow as Billy had ever seen. It would meet his needs nicely. All Billy had to do was sneak into the yard, stuff the dead girl into one of the cars that was slated to be compressed into a huge metal cube, and once it had been melted for recycling her remains would be incinerated into nothingness. It seemed like a perfect plan.

The only trouble was that when Billy returned home, he found two policemen waiting for him at his front door.

XXII.

"Mr. Kimmel," announced the Special Investigator as Billy stepped from his car. "I thought you said you didn't know the girl?"

The accusation was smart and yellow, hitting Billy like a lead pipe. *Colonel Mustard. On the sidewalk.* The police detective wore a curvy, warm smile and dark sunglasses though dusk was close at hand in the sky above. He extended his hand to Billy as he descended the steps, but the man's smile did not comfort him any. On the contrary, it made the hairs on the back of his neck rise with alarm.

"Do you remember me from the other day? We met in the alley."

Billy accepted his outstretched hand and shook is head in the positive. "Yeah."

"Special Investigator James Riley," he turned to the uniformed officer that accompanied him. "This is Officer Langford. I believe the two of you exchanged some information the other day."

"Yeah." His world was tilting.

"I was hoping that we might exchange a bit more information." There was that smile again, oozing across his face.

"Well, I'm just getting off work and it's been a long day; not sure what I can help you with." Billy tried to sound more tired than he was, afraid that he was coming off as sounding annoyed and guilty.

"I understand that, Mr. Kimmel; I do. But unfortunately for people like Officer Langford and myself, who work regular jobs, much like yourself; criminals, on the other hand, work twenty-four-seven. I hate to impose an inconvenience, so we'd greatly appreciate just a few moments of your time."

Billy understood the threat of arrest. "Of course," he said, waiting at attention.

"Inside please, Mr. Kimmel?" asked Special Investigator James Riley with his arm leading to the tomb that was Billy's apartment.

Though phrased as a question, Billy knew it wasn't a request, and he was lost at what to do. Officer Langford's eyes drilled into him like meat hooks. His every word and move was being scrutinized by two trained professionals. Billy exhaled softly as he climbed the steps leading to his doom. The holstered gun on Officer Langford's belt loomed larger than real life. As he slipped the key between the metal legs of the lock, Billy imagined what was to follow: Aroused by the scent and the partially opened door, the two men would stumble upon the room and find Jamie lying prone in his bed, and from then on out he'd be sleeping in a hard prison cell.

It was inevitable.

Billy imagined the shock and horror that his neighbor, Mr. Meyers, would suffer upon hearing the news that the dead body, which was reportedly discovered in the alley was found in a bed so close to him where God-knows-what-had-been going on! He wondered if the old man would tell his church friends about how sick he thought Billy had always been. Would they pray for him then as he sat on death row for a crime that he did not commit?

Even as he opened the door the rank stench of perfume knocked the three of them in the face. The air was frigid and created a barrier over the threshold. Officer Langford and the Special Investigator both wrinkled their noses before entering.

"I accidentally spilled a bottle of perfume this morning. It was my ex-girlfriend's. I'd just found it. I tried to clean it up, but..." Billy looked from each man to the other. "I'll open a window."

He cracked the one in the kitchen, where they had entered, and crossed quickly to the bedroom. Billy closed the door behind him and opened the terrace doors, spying the dead girl as unceremoniously still and inescapable as ever. He tossed the edge of the bed sheet over her and reentered the living room, shutting the door completely, and found both men standing nearby.

"What exceptional blue carpeting you have. Don't see that every day, do you?"

"No, sir," replied Officer Langford.

Billy moved toward the kitchen, hoping to draw the policemen away from his bedroom. "It came with the apartment when I moved in. You said something about me knowing the woman in the alley?" He wore a concerned look across his face.

"Ah, yes," the detective replied. "I have a photo of her here somewhere. High School yearbook picture. I believe you also went to the same school as she did." He fumbled through his pockets and uttered her name. "Jamie Lund." He turned toward the officer, ready to ask if he had the photo.

"What?" Billy felt weak in the knees, despite the fact that he already knew whom it was. There still remained a small hope that with her body gone they would not have been able to ID her. Billy never did put two and two together as to the ink stains on her fingers and so suddenly the room was a Tilt-A-Whirl.

"I'm sorry," the detective announced. "The photo can wait. But you know who I'm speaking of now, don't you Mr. Kimmel."

"Jamie?"

"Yes." He flipped open a small notebook and read her address like a question.

Billy had never known her new address. "She's dead?" His eyes searched the two men, even though he knew better than most. "That was her in the alley?" He acted as if he grappled with the news. "What happened to her? Why was she there?"

"Well," shrugged the Special Investigator, "that is what we are trying to find out."

"Yes," he nodded accordingly. "Of course, what can I do to help?"

Billy felt as if he wanted to sit, but was afraid to invite them further into the apartment and make them feel comfortable. Besides, the only place to sit on his half of the duplex was either in the living room or outside on the front stoop. So he awkwardly stood in the kitchen throughout the interview.

"When was the last time you saw Ms. Lund?"

Just a few seconds ago when I covered her with a sheet. "Uhhh," he appeared to think on it. "A little over a month ago, I suppose. We broke up a few months before that."

"So you dated." Riley wrote in his notebook. "How long?"

"Since high school."

"Sweethearts, then."

Billy felt uncomfortable by Officer Langford's hard stare. "You could say that."

"Can you think of any reason why she would have been in your alley, Mr. Kimmel?"

That question had been driving him crazy for a couple of days now. "How...how did you say she died?"

"She was strangled." The detective was blunt, eyeing him.

"Strangled?" He recalled the Coroner making that same claim.

"Officially," stated Riley, moving toward the fish tank, "we are still waiting on the Medical Examiner's report. But I'm fairly certain." He leaned down and watched Merlin swimming back and forth in his tank. He tapped the glass gently.

So they don't know she's gone yet.

"Was it a mutual break up?" The cop rose and began slowly pacing in the direction of the bedroom.

"Huh?" replied Billy.

"How would you categorize your break up with Ms. Lund, Mr. Kimmel? Was it mutual? Did you dump her or did she break your heart? It must have been serious if you hadn't seen her in such a long time before your last association."

"She came by to return some stuff that had gotten mixed up in one of her boxes."

"So, you lived together?"

The question sounded like an accusation. "Yes. Here actually. This was our first, well…only place."

"Ah," said the detective, raising his head going silent as he stopped near the closed bedroom door looking cautiously around the room. At some length he turned to Billy and drove the point home. "So she broke your heart."

He hadn't even asked and he knew. The man could look at Billy and tell that Jamie had dumped him and it was hard and it was bitter and that it still affected him. What chance did he have at duping the detective that her body was so close at hand? Billy watched him as he crossed the blue shag carpet and began feeding his fish.

"Have you tried speaking with her girlfriend Loni?" Billy asked. "They hung out all the time. She might know a lot more about what Jaime had been up to than I would."

"Is that why you called her, Mr. Kimmel?"

Billy spied Merlin gobbling up the soggy flakes and a log lodged in his throat. He'd forgotten that he placed a call to her phone while they were at the restaurant. He shook his head, trying to pass it off.

"Loni?" I haven't spoken to Loni since–"

The Special Investigator popped up from behind the tank, cutting him off. "I hope you don't mind, I took the liberty of procuring your phone records, on the chance of our meeting, and discovered that you called the deceased Friday night at 9:57pm."

Without hesitation or want of indifference, James Riley stretched his hand out with folded copies of the phone records he was talking about. Billy didn't need to see them, so he waved it away. The detective slowly returned them to his pocket and waited for Billy to make his account.

He sighed. "I dialed it by mistake. I hung up before she answered. I just didn't want to speak to her after…" He ran out of rope for his lie.

"Was that why she was here, Mr. Kimmel? Did she come to see you and the two of you had a fight?"

"What?" Billy scrunched up his face with the question. "No! I told you the last time I saw Jaime was little over a month ago. I didn't even recognize her in an alley and now you're telling me my ex-girlfriend is dead, and you wanna grill me simply because my finger slipped on my cell phone and I chickened out?!"

Special Investigator James Riley stood by the closed bedroom door again. "Are you dating, Mr. Kimmel?"

"Huh?" The question threw him for a loop.

"The perfume?" Riley stated with raised arms.

Billy felt defeated. "It belonged to Jamie."

"How interesting." He smiled again greasing his face as if it were sex wax. Then the smile vanished with a wipe and he paused as if to listen. "Do you have company, Mr. Kimmel?"

Billy didn't understand and quickly fired off a "No. Look, it's been a long day like I already mentioned and I'd like to get some dinner before it gets too late."

His tone was biting and accurate for the turn of the interview and Special Investigator James Riley just stared at the young man as he listened to the sudden pounding of wave after pounding wave of cascading water emanating from a shower's stall as it trickled through the thin plaster and wood of the walls. Billy's facial features must have changed or altered in some way because the detective smirked, a crooked, high-knowing line that caused Billy to shiver.

Or it could have been the sound of the shower that made him quake. It was hard to tell. But what happened next was simple enough. The detective fished a business card from one of his pockets and added, "do keep in touch."

He strode to the door with Officer Langford as Billy's eyes banged on the closed bedroom door. There was such excitement flowing through his veins that Billy's toes, for want of crossing that room and finding out for certain if it was a particular cadaver or not, caused them to tingle.

The Special Investigator stopped cold in his tracks. "Do you mind if I take a clipping of that rug? For the missus, you know? It is such a unique color."

Dreamily, Billy agreed and James Riley bent down by the edge in the kitchen, at the room's divide, and snipped a few strands of velvety blue shag into a tiny evidence bag. He folded them neatly and placed them in a pocket that also contained Billy's phone records. The detective never did find and show Billy that high school yearbook photo of Jamie, and it was the farthest thing from Billy's frame of mind at the moment. He neither wanted to see the picture, nor cared. He just wanted the two men to leave so that he could race to the bathroom and see for himself the wondrous miracle that was abound.

Billy took the business card, but the two policemen exited the apartment way too slowly for his liking, leaving him shaking and standing by the kitchen door. His heart pounded great giant thuds as he crossed the kitchen and the ocean of his living room – it was all really just a few short strides. He opened the bedroom door as if lighting a match to the kindling of the frame. His bed was empty and faded blue hospital scrubs lay haphazardly on the opera of the floor. They told a story that lead to the bathroom. The misery of how Billy had acquired them and how Jamie had worn them was all but an acid memory. The young man was positively electric at seeing them empty and crumpled on the carpeting.

Steam rolled past the opened doorway of the bathroom, rising like smoke from a fire. Billy stared into the mist with his own disbelief. A murky, feminine shape lathered itself beyond the flimsy skeleton-frosted curtain. This was not a time for niceties. Billy urged to know. His heart was drumming in his throat. His breathing was a decomposing engine of raw power and verve. He moved the shade back slowly and the entirety of his world, with all its cages and misperceptions came undone.

The heavens, in its infinite jest, looked up at him through doughy blue eyes, distilled by murder, boundless from the laws of Man. Her soulful keep wept through a tiny river of factory water. It revealed her body as true and real as he could ever have hoped or imagined, and then he collapsed. Billy fell toward the tub's basin. His eyes fluttered skyward and he did not know that instead of landing on a hard painful surface he fell into the sure, quiet, naked arms of death.

XXIII.

Billy woke to a grinning corpse.

"You're all wet, silly."

"Huh?"

"You collapsed."

Water drummed around him. Her smile was a tranquil veil that lifted him to his feet. After so much, he couldn't believe his eyes.

"I did."

"Yeah. You did."

He touched her damp, matted hair and felt her ears poking through the waterlogged locks. He placed his hands on her shoulders and felt her sonorous bone underneath palpable flesh. Her eyes were two pale grains of sand nestled in the dune of her face. She stared at him with compassion, resting her hands on his drenched shirt and chest. His palms cupped the back of her arms. He felt like lifting her up. He pulled her to him and it felt to Jamie as if he intended to kiss her, there in the shower.

"You're getting all wet," she professed with verbrato.

"I don't care," he declared, drinking her up. "You're alive." He laughed and his whole face was beaming like a lighthouse. "You're alive."

Her smile waned and she pulled back. "Go dry off and we'll talk."

But Billy just continued to stare at her naked form as if she were a mirage.

"Ok?" she implored, beginning to feel awkward.

"Yeah," he breathed, shaking his head, but he did not move. "It's really you, isn't it?

Her smile widened to a bright laugh. "Yeah, it's really me." The wonder on his face astonished her like spray painted graffiti. "It's Ok. I'll still be here."

5"You better," he proclaimed and Jamie felt a rustling beneath her breasts.

His smile was a cup pouring into her torpid, lifeless heart. "I'm not going anywhere for awhile."

Turning to leave, Billy stepped from the shower, but cupped her cheeks in his palms and gazed upon her one more time. Her vestige was so unlike recent days, entombed in rotting slumber.

"Go on," she said. "I'll be with you in a minute."

Jaime watched him disappear before she closed the curtain. He couldn't stop staring at her. Inside the little shower shell the water was beginning to grow cold, but Jamie did not feel it. Even the pulsating billow of thousands of droplets of hard-driving liquid on her skin only felt like a barrage behind a heavy insulated cotton wall. It was enough though to ground her to this temperate perch. For just minutes before Jamie had bore wings and soared like an angel through vast and open skies. The tepid stream hollowed her and drove the sensation of feathers away. The languid stares from the boy made her welcome home harder to bear. There were so many things she needed to tell him.

Jamie stared down at how the water pooled and circled around her feet. She wiggled her toes. *Extraordinary. Such delicate things, toes. Nothing like talons.* She smirked. *Seemingly useless, unable to grip branches or wires or pull carrion or dig for worms, yet they are wonderful to posses. Simply a wonder!* Being back in her body felt like entering a grand hall of an old house, familiar yet strangely cold.

Upon closer inspection, Jamie noticed an odd metal band around her right big toe. She couldn't remember ever wearing a toe ring before, so she lifted her foot and found there a soggy piece of yellow paper stuck to her sole. It was of card stock and was connected to a bit of wire that wrapped around the digit that she had seen. Jamie removed it. The ink from the handwriting was blurring from its wetness, but the printed matter was intact. It read: *Mercy General; No. 9652-3.*

"Travelling without me I see," remarked Jamie to her body as she set the card on the sink.

XXIV.

"Do I even want to know what happened to my clothes?" she asked as she exited the bathroom wrapped in a towel, drying her hair with another one.

"They were put into evidence bags," Billy said sitting on his bed.

"Ah," she uttered, continuing to pat her hair with the towel.

Flies buzzed in and out of the opened balcony doors.

"What happened?" Billy asked, his words thick as gravy. "One minute you're sitting on the balcony and the next you're lying dead in the alley surrounded by cops."

"You know that guy with the dark eyes and olive skin that I said I remembered from the party?"

"Yeah."

She sat on the bed beside him. "I saw him standing in the alley and I went out to him." Her eyes searched his face. "He spoke to me inside my head. Not with his mouth; his lips didn't even move. He told me that he felt sorry for me and breathed a tiny piece of himself inside of me. He said he knew what was going to happen. So, it's because of him that I'm here."

"But how did you wind up...dead, I mean, not moving in the alley?"

"He was leaving and I touched him."

Billy's eyebrows launched. "You touched him?"

Jamie shook her head up and down. "Yup. I touched him."

"Well," his face went wide and blank and he rose from the bed, pacing, "that explains everything."

Jaime chuckled, but she could tell Billy was deeply riled. "He was radiating like a sun. I couldn't help myself..."

"So, what you're saying is the guy's a giant bug-zapper and you were a timid moth"

Jaime burst out laughing, a quick snort of mirth.

"I'm serious," he said with fervored steps. "Why not? You're dead. You know a man who glows and I saw you swallowed in a cyclone of birds. It makes sense. Sure."

"It does?" she asked, rising, collecting the towel around her chest because there was nothing about his expression that told Jamie that he understood anything.

"Yeah." Billy had a pitch and a vibrato in his voice that was wildly confident. "You said you were alive because this guy breathed some part of himself into you. So it only stands to reason that when you touched him you gave it back."

"Huh," uttered the dead girl, sitting back down on the edge of the bed. "I didn't think about it like that."

"Makes sense to me," finalized Billy, pacing back and forth across the room. "Do you remember anything after you touched Mr. Magic Man?"

"Everything."

Billy's worried feet came to a halt. He stared down at the delicate creature and waited. But the girl sitting on the edge of his bed merely looked up at him in silence.

"WELL..." he urged through the strength in his hands.

"I'm not sure I can even explain it," shot Jamie to appease the man. "I can scarcely believe it all myself. So I don't expect you to understand."

"Believe me," interrupted Billy. "I stopped trying to make sense of it awhile ago. Continue."

But Jamie drew quiet, looking at his rattled features. "It must have been hard for you."

"What?" He looked at her pale, oval face. "Oh...it was nothing."

Jamie didn't believe him. She grabbed him by the wrist, bade him to sit next to her and tell her everything that had happened since she'd been gone. Billy sighed and began.

"You were dead, sweetheart. The cops came and everything. A full light show; the whole nine yards. I had to steal you from the morgue." Billy smirked and chuckled, thinking about it. "I waited all day, got bitched out by a hooker, nearly got locked up in the process, and I had to stuff you through a window no bigger than a matchbook. So if you notice anything broken or bruised it's not my fault. I did what I had to do."

He rose again and resumed his terse pacing.

"Thank you." Jamie added with a small voice. She moved her limbs and rolled her wrists. "Everything's fine. In full working order."

But Billy just nodded, struggling with a valley of words. "The cops were here today."

"I know. I saw them when I flew back."

"What do you mean 'flew back'?" He turned on his heels.

"I flew," she simply added. "When I touched Horus I—"

Billy threw up his hands. "Horus? Who's Horus?"

Jamie made a catch-up-face. "The guy in the alley. He—"

"Isn't Horus some Egyptian thing or another?

"God," corrected Jamie. "He's an Egyptian God."

Billy's pacing stopped cold. His mouth stammered with

something to say, but the ramifications of what was being discussed had vastly, and too quickly, widened beyond his grasp and scope of the real. Finally, Billy uttered "Ok. Why not?" He looked at the dead girl. "Why not an Egyptian god. He's hanging around, got nothing better to do with all of eternity, probably bored, and it just so happens that you run into him at a party on the shore, and then again in the alley behind my house. So, he gets around." Billy shrugged. "Why not?" He chuckled and tightened his mouth into a firm line, pitching a thumb toward the kitchen. "I'm getting a beer. Do you want one?"

Jamie quietly shook her head no and listened to the thudding of his work boots as he crossed the living room and opened the refrigerator door. He yelled back that they were all out of beer. Jamie felt for him the best she could, but there simply was too much to take in. As for herself, her body did not feel the same after her ordeal. Its pallor of death and slow decay felt more comfortable. She rode her skin with more ease. Having collected the jewel of her soul in a thousand beaks to return it to this singular vessel had been a trial, in and of itself, that hadn't yet completely washed away in the shower. Billy returned, leaning against the doorjamb and asked her to continue.

"When I touched him I was immediately pulled into this great light and then I was a part of the sky. I was everywhere at once and yet...nowhere. I saw myself in the alley but I couldn't move. As hard as I tried I kept being taken away from myself like I was drifting on the wind. And for the longest time I didn't know what was happening. I was scared, but I also knew it was all right. Once I started to calm down I began to notice that I saw more places at once than just regular-like with having a single set of eyes, you know?

"It took me awhile to figure it out. But I was in the body of the birds. Once I understood that, the rest was easy and I began to feel each and every single one of them as myself. You can't imagine how it felt Billy to be alive in a hundred different bodies all connected by a single consciousness and yet acting independent all the same.

"I flew across the city, over fields, and states. I bathed in a stream, ate worms and crickets, and followed a migration North for a spell. I remember swooping down," she danced her tale with her hands. "I cawed with the rise of the sun and slowly I focused my intent on just one of the birds and it was through him that I was able to call all the others back to me." She paused and stared up at Billy.

His features were calm and serene.

"In essence, I captured myself and returned to find my body lying here instead of the alley. Had you not opened the balcony doors I never would have been able to fly in here and drop my soul back into my body. It was like before; I was pulled through this light. One piece at a time, like dropping pebbles from my beak. Eventually I woke up here, but the air was stifling. I couldn't breathe. I had gotten so used to doing it when I was the birds. Suddenly all there was, was this choking perfume, gagging me, and the only thing I could think of was to wash it off."

Billy smirked and made a pitiful face. "You were starting to smell."

"I was?"

Billy nodded. Jamie looked herself over and sniffed her armpits. It wasn't every day that someone tells you that your rotting flesh is stinking up the place. She sniffed a wrist, but couldn't smell anything. So, she rose and crossed to him holding out her hand for him to smell.

"How's it smell now?"

Billy leaned in and sniffed. "Better," he said with a nod.

She circled herself in her arms. The warmth that she had gleaned in the shower had dissipated. Jamie was beginning to feel the gloom of death upon her exposed shoulders once more.

"So, what did the police want with you?"

"They think I killed you."

"Get outta here," she voiced. "They do not."

But Billy didn't budge. "Yes, they do."

He turned and walked into the living room.

"But why? How?" she stammered after him.

"I don't know," he said, squishing his shoulders up to his ears. "But that detective guy gives me the creeps."

Jamie sat on the couch, pulled her knees in tightly, and rested an elbow on one knee and her chin in her palm thoughtfully. "So, I guess this means I can't go back to my place?"

"I guess not."

For a dead girl, Jamie exhaled. The best she could under the circumstances, though it was more of a slumping of her shoulders than an actual exhalation of worried breath. "What am I going to wear?"

The look on her face was priceless and Billy started to laugh. "Shut up. It's not funny."

"Yeah. It is," he joked. "I have a hand towel you could slip into."

She made a mocking face, but eventually joined him in his folly and it was a great tension releaser – the two of them, laughing again. After awhile, Billy had a thought and ran from the apartment to the Chevelle. Outside on the telephone wires and perched on nearby rooftops were the darkened bodies and feathery hosts of Jamie's flight of fancy. Billy was happy to see them again, though he thought there would be more of them by her tell of it.

Quickly, he got what he needed from the trunk and ran back into the house. He set Jamie's shoes down in front of her as she stood. The dead girl looked from them, and their worn out soles, to her jeans clad knight, and said, "Ok. That's a start."

XXV.

Jaime's feet were propped up on the coffee table as she watched reruns of The Simpsons, waiting for Billy to return from a half day at work and the thrift store. She lounged around the apartment in one of Billy's larger tee shirts. It was the only thing they could find for her to wear. The sensations of wearing wings were becoming less prominent with each passing of the clock.

When Billy returned he set several bags on the coffee table in front of her. It felt like Christmas. Giddy and excited at her new wardrobe, Jamie rummaged through each plastic bag making a deliberate mess.

"Wait here," she announced, "I'll try these on."

With that she dashed into the bedroom, taking a couple clothing items in hand. Billy eased his boots and socks off, sighing into his cracked imitation leather chair. He was tired. The events of the past few days had worn him out, and even now that Jamie had come back he found it difficult to truly rest.

He longed for a shower. Grease stained the creases of his hands even though he had washed them. The underside of his fingernails was black. He had felt a little weird about handling the merchandise at the thrift store with so much tar caked under his nails.

"Well, whudya think?" she asked, attacking the room in a pair of tight-fitting jeans that hugged her curves and a hot pink T-shirt with a worn out decal of a teddy bear and the word 'Naughty' in a disco font.

"Nice."

She held up a finger. "Be right back."

And she was. Jaime tried on two more pairs of pants, some shorts – which she didn't like, because they showed too much skin; three more tees, and a hoodie before she tried on the dresses that Billy begged her to wear. She paraded each ensemble before him, cracking jokes, being the runway model. Their laughter made her cheeks flush and full with an illusion of life, and while getting dressed she found that her joints were aching. Her muscle felt dry and stiff, and as the afternoon lengthened to night it only got worse.

Jamie especially liked the socks that he had bought for her with multicolor finger toes and the penguin version where each toe-end oscillated from black to white. The shoes that he'd picked up for her were another matter. Only one pair of sneakers actually fit well enough to wear. With the ones she already owned Jamie didn't feel that they were necessary. With so much lavished on her, she was beginning to feel bad that she'd caused him to spend his hard-earned money.

She wished that she could pay him back. She had the money sitting in her bank account, but they had decided that it would be best for her to cut all ties to her former life now that the police had gotten wind of her death. All in all, the day's haul wasn't that bad. Most of the clothes fit, and they'd had some fun playing with them. Billy made room for her in his closet and a dresser drawer before he crawled into a shower to wash the rest of his work away.

As the hot water met his skin and Billy was pulling the shower curtain back he noticed Jamie's wrinkled toe tag resting on the bathroom sink. It was a concrete reminder that despite all their laughs and acting normal death was hot on their heels. It danced in the halls with them and that somewhere, out there in the city, lurked the man that had killed Jamie Lund. The police were looking for a killer to pin on the body that they had found in the alley behind the duplex, and Billy wasn't too sure that the police were looking for the same man Jamie was.

A bitter coldness tingled over his skin as he closed the shower curtain the rest of the way and completely stepped into the stream of soothing liquid. Despite the circumstances and the whole crazy affair of having to steal her from the morgue, Billy was happy to have her back. It was better than her not being here at all. He'd always felt that he could open up and be himself around her. It was something he missed when she had moved out. Now that she was back, he didn't want her to leave. But Billy knew that thought was foolish. She was dead, and not even some Egyptian god could have changed that.

Long after Billy had cleaned the grease and grim from his person he soaked in the cascading pound of the shower. Motionless, he stood there letting it rain over him. Breathing slowly, Billy was simply glad that she had woken and that he wasn't cleaning the dirt from his hands at having to bury her in some obscure place or have her bones crushed in an automobile vice.

After his shower, Billy settled into some dinner and a spot of TV. He insisted that Jamie take the bed again, as he hadn't yet changed the sheets. But after last night with him sleeping on the couch and her awake all night with his head resting in her lap, and all the wonderful new clothes, Jamie changed the sheets on the bed so that he wouldn't have an excuse. But being so active made her muscles and joints ache even worse. So, Billy walked down to the corner store and picked up several bottles of lotions and cremes.

They talked for the longest time as Billy rubbed nearly all the ointments into her joints and body parts. It seemed to help moisten her flesh and muscles, making her body more pliable. She told him about her many adventures while being a flock of birds. Most of it sounded boring or gross. But Jamie was intrigued by it all, and it was, he had to admit, fascinating to think that her spirit had broken into so many tiny pieces, yet still retained one essence.

They both wondered if that was what real death was like. Jamie's circumstance was not the norm. They couldn't measure her after-life with what truly lay beyond the veil of this mortal coil, but felt they hit upon something with there being a bright light involved.

Eventually, sleep found Billy wanting and he took his tired frame to bed. The dead girl sat out on the terrace and watched him sleep for a bit. The night was warm with a gentle breeze. Her black-winged angels watched her, as she watched them, considering the moods and fluctuations that she had witnessed this evening from Billy's aura. She wished she knew what it had meant, if it had meant anything at all. She was now convinced that it did. Horus's gift was a singular invocation, and so far, from what she had learned there was nothing about it that she should take for granted.

So she made plans to visit the local library in the morning. It was a great excuse to show off her new clothes. *Well…*her nearly new clothes anyway. Billy had a computer, but Jamie thought the thing was still connected to dial up. He rarely used it and he never was one for surfing the net. Jamie couldn't even remember the last time that she saw the thing turned on. And besides, it would feel good to stretch her legs a bit after flying around everywhere she traveled.

This added development of the police fooling around with her corpse while she was out was not a good thing. It hastened what little time she had against her. Jamie could feel the decay of her cells and knew that the aches and stiff joints were only the beginning, though she didn't want to say anything to Billy about it yet. She'd learned a lot on her spiritual walkabout that she wasn't completely sure on, and didn't want to say anything until she was. Her connection to her flighty feathered friends was strong, but she knew she had to get home, back into her own skin, or else vanish forever and never know or find the man that did kill her.

Time, it seemed, was always falling on her head and now time ebbed at her bones with a finality and crueler embrace than she could ever imagine. Death was not a pretty sight and she didn't know how many more days she had to feel pretty, or as near to it as she could muster.

"Pay it with the heart, not the flesh," Jamie recited, recalling Horus's words to her that day in the alley.

It seemed so long ago since she'd dragged herself from the river and made that fateful long walk home. So much had happened since then. And there was still so much left to be done. Jamie stretched out her hand, feeling each bird and their rapid breaths in their small frail bodies. Like the conductor of an orchestra, she moved and they lifted into the air, a great big blanket of wings beating with such music, vanishing on their mission. A few remained to keep the dead girl company. To these feathered friends, Jamie bid good night and reentered the apartment.

She shut the doors and lay down next to Billy on the bed. His breathing was deep. He was dreaming and Jamie hoped they were good dreams. The world and all its dark appetites could slip away. All that harshness of life was beyond the confines of this bed now and further, lay beyond the borders of these windows and doors. The night was a lonely place, so Jamie lifted Billy's arm and curled into the warm space that his body made for her. Without waking he pulled her closer, nestling his jaw over the curve of her head. She lay her ear to his chest as his breath washed over her like fine imported silk. His arm encased Jamie within his shell. He was the warmest thing she knew. So, for the rest of the night she lay entangled with him listening to the thrumming of his heart as he slept.

XXVI.

"Cancer," explained Jaime. "Her husband, Herbert, had cancer for the longest time and last year he died. Ever since then Rose has been living alone with her two cats, Simon and George."

Billy mouthed the names of the cats with morbid fascination at the sheer fact that she knew their names, before he asked, "Why did the Librarian let you take home all these books without a card, because you knew the names of her cats?"

"No, silly," she replied, basking in the sun as it streamed through the windows. "I listened to her, you know. I really sat down and listened to what she had to say. She's a very nice lady. We talked all afternoon. She made tea." She accentuated the elderly woman's kindly act by raising her eyebrows.

"She really misses him, though." She sat back down on the couch. "Like she was his moon moving around his planet in orbit and then poof...one day the light went out and she's just drifting, you know?" Jamie held onto that thought for a moment like there was deeper importance. "That's why she volunteers Tuesdays and Thursdays at the Library. I think I'm gonna go back Thursday."

She flew off the couch again and Billy followed her with his neck.

"I still don't see how cancer has anything to do with checking out library books?"

"I told her I had it."

Oh, now it was beginning to make sense. "That you had it?"

"Yeah." She shook her head enthusiastically as if she'd already explained it sensibly enough the first time. "My library card is in my purse, which is God-knows-where! Probably with the bastard who killed me. So, I don't have a driver's licenses or any credit cards anymore. I mean, how would it look if all of a sudden I started checking out books and making charges when I'm supposed to be..." She shrugged nonchalantly, "you know."

Jamie took a few steps and then turned on her heels. "This whole being dead thing really gets in the way of living."

"Hadn't noticed," quipped Billy, mostly to himself.

Jaime opened the refrigerator as if she was looking for something to eat. "You sure you don't want me to make you something for dinner?"

"I'm fine," he announced for the third time. "I picked up a burger on the way home."

She stood on the threshold between rooms. "You should really eat something more substantial than that."

"I will from now on," he said, barreling through a deep sigh.

Her flip-flopping was getting to him. She had been an electric ball ever since he had come home from work. Fervent. Bouncing from one subject to the next as often as rooms in the tiny apartment, blurring all the lines and independent moments of her day into one, ever changing, elastic tunnel of slip-stream verbiage at a heightened rate.

"I told Rose I had cancer and that I forgot my purse when I was dropped off at the library."

"And, she bought that?"

"Well dah, silly. Obviously." She sat on the couch again. "Don't I look like a cancer patient?"

To this Billy agreed. Her pallor had not changed or improved since she returned. Though the smell was better, it was obvious, even at a first glance, that something was not quite right.

"Anyway, she's a really nice lady, a little bit lonely, and she let me check out the books. Oh!" She exclaimed suddenly with a shout and sprang off the couch again. "You should hear what it says about you."

Around the coffee table, past the chair and Merlin the fish, over the carpeted section of the apartment to the stiff linoleum floor of the kitchen, Billy watched her thumb through the pile of books that were stacked on the kitchen counter. It was an impressive stack for anybody with or without a library card. It was refreshing to see her in such high spirits, but it was also tiring to keep up with her pace.

"I ran into your neighbor today," she threw across the room.

"Meyers?" The thought of it made him nervous. "Did he recognize you?"

"No," she replied, pulling a single book from the stack. "Why would he?"

Billy stammered. "Well...you lived here."

"Oh," mentioned Jamie, stepping into the room, "that's right. I forget that." She shrugged. "He didn't seem to notice. He did tell me about the commotion in the alley, though. Very dramatic from his point of view."

"Dramatic from his point of view," chided Billy a little frayed by his experiences. "I was the one who-"

"Don't be such a queen," warned Jamie as she flopped back down on the couch besides him with her nose in the book. "He wanted me to tell you he's moving out at the end of the month. Said the neighborhood just wasn't what it used to be." She took a brief pause from the pages and looked up. "He's moving in with his sister, or something like that."

Nimbly, her fingers flipped back and forth through the pages as she laid the book in her lap. It rested there like some plush cat as she stroked chapter after chapter for the passage she wanted to share. "Blue is the energy of the spiritual teacher..." she began reading.

"So, I'm blue?" he interrupted with a hard wrinkle deforming his features.

"Well, mostly. It changes and moves around depending on how you feel at any given moment. But everyone has dominating colors. You're mostly blue. There's some green, a little yellow." She paused, peering at him intently as if she was looking straight through him rather than at him. "With purple spikes that get lighter or darker all the time."

"Huh," he voiced. "And, you can see this now?"

"Yup." She shook her head in agreement and continued. "It says blue represents one who is intuitive, sensitive, patient, and kind; compassionate with a peaceful nature, yet one who knows how to focus in order to accomplish goals. Blue is a protective energy and one of contentment. Someone with blue energy often helps, encourages, and nurtures others with equal firmness and affection. Blue also opens the throat chakra and teaches us to own our voice and to speak our truth with quiet integrity. People respond to blue's sensitivity and caring and naturally want to confide or confess. Blue is also an energy that may appear presently in periods of transition and change." Jaime looked up from the book. "Are you going through a period of transition or change?"

"I don't buy it," he grunted. "It contradicts itself."

She quoted again with a nod. "'Teaches us to own our voice and to speak our truth with quiet integrity.'"

"And you believe this stuff?" He went to the kitchen for something to drink.

"It's interesting. A place to start."

Billy wryly smiled as he poured himself a glass of water. "So, does this mean that you're ready to confess?"

"What would I have to confess?"

Billy did not answer, but as he reentered the room Jaime noticed that a color shifted in his auric field. Unsure of what it meant, she flipped through a few pages and read a few lines. They offered only vague generalities. His color shift was specific and she felt that it was confined to the two of them.

She took a stab at it. "You want to know why I broke up with you?"

"I was only joking," he said, easing into his recliner.

"No," she demanded. "You wanted to know. Your color changed; you wanted something from me and I didn't give it."

Billy felt like protesting, even though it was hollow and she was right. But he stuck to his guns. "I was only kidding. Really?"

The air snapped with brutal coldness. Jamie knew he was lying and he had the audacity to hide behind the television set, turning the thing on instead of dealing with the emotional baggage he carried for her. So fragile a thing was a live, beating heart. It was a virtual minefield.

Jamie closed her book, got up, and walked over to Billy. She picked up the remote from the arm of the cracked leather chair and turned the TV off. "I was afraid," she confessed. "I was afraid of becoming too comfortable with you and falling into a mediocre life. It seemed like that was where we were heading. It's always been easy to be with you and once we started to live together I was scared that there was never going to be anything else. So, I ran. It was never from a lack of love."

Silence stretched like taffy between them, but Jamie did not move away. She wiggled her finger across the top of his hand until he reluctantly held hers. Slowly, his dominant blue returned more brightly to his field and she knew that her honesty was the right thing for the moment. He deserved to know. He'd never asked for the train wreck of these past few days, but he remained stalwart and true to his character in the face of deep fear. Jamie knew that she owed him much. After a short spell she returned to the book and the couch as Billy watched TV.

A full quarter of an hour passed before he asked, "Can anyone see auras?"

"Yeah," she replied, pulling her head from the text. "With a little practice."

"Ok," he said, sitting up in the recliner. "How do I do it?"

Jaime quickly read a few passages, closed the book, and told him to join her on the couch.

"Ok. Pick a spot and look at it. Like the third eye or chest chakra with the person in front of a white background." She turned and looked at the pale wall behind her. "This'll do. Now, you're supposed to stare at the spot without moving for about a minute. Then with your peripheral vision you look at the edge of the person and you'll start to see their aura."

"Alright," he said, thinking it sounded easy enough and began focusing on the girl's brow.

But the earnest expression on Billy's face made him look as if he were pushing out an ardent turd. Jaime couldn't keep herself from laughing.

"Stop it. I'm trying to concentrate."

"I know. That's what's so funny."

He broke his line of sight. "Ha, ha," he joined dryly.

After a second or two, Jamie straightened up and Billy resumed his zealous stare. But after a short bit it began to make Jaime uncomfortable.

"What are you staring at?"

"Your collar bone," he informed, keeping his focus.

"It looks like you're staring at my tits."

He sighed exasperatingly and broke his eye line again. "You don't really want me to do this, do you?"

"No, it's not that," reported Jamie. "It just felt like you were staring at my chest."

"Well, I wasn't."

"Ok." She repositioned into an Indian squat and aligned her spine the best she could on the old floppily couch. "Try it now. I promise, I won't move. Or, laugh. But this time look right here." She pointed to the space between her eyebrows, to the area where one's third eye was presumed to reside. "The book says this is the best spot."

Billy glared at her for a second. His shoulders felt like a packet of straw boxed too tightly. So, he shook them out, cracked the tension in his neck, exhaled, and began again. For over a minute he concentrated on Jaime's Ajna Chakra before he allowed his peripheral vision to wander to the borders of her frame. After only a few seconds of this he looked away, deep in thought.

"Was anything there?" she asked doubtfully. "Did you see it?"

"I'm not sure."

What the fuck does that mean? Jamie waited, but he only grew quieter. "C'mon, tell me," she urged after a time. The silence was biting.

"I'm not sure," he restated bitterly, seeing the odd forms clearly in his memory. He hesitated a moment and then did his best to described what he saw. "It was like you were outlined in a thick black crayon, and that that was outlined by a thin golden band. The blackness wasn't moving. Though it appeared to absorb inward around you. But the golden band was moving. It pulsated like a heartbeat. At first I thought it was radiating out from you. But it was apparent that the gold band was radiating into you."

"Oh," she said and that was that.

Jamie picked the book back up, turned around in the seat, and delved quietly into reading again. The silent reply felt awkward at best, but Billy didn't know what else to do or say. He returned to his comfortable recliner, the one he'd bought when he started working at the garage, and watched television. His mind lodged more to the soulful dead girl. After awhile, when dusk had drawn down and the air outside had cooled she closed her book and took up residence on the front stoop.

All afternoon the apartment doors had been opened to catch cool summer breezes. Billy watched her sitting on the front step, just sitting, before he got up, turned off the television and joined her outside. He sat down beside her, not uttering a word. Sometimes there weren't any good sounds, except silence.

Jamie leaned into him, curled her arm under his, and rested her head on his shoulder. And there they both sat that evening, nestled like penguins on a glacier of concrete, listening to the cadence of the city.

XXVII.

When the shutters of the world had closed and the big cold eye in the Cimmerian sky had dipped behind its zenith, she felt it. They called to her from far away.

Many miles.

It was an unmistakable feeling. Her joints and muscles were cramping again and she was all out of cremes. Billy was fast asleep and through the fog in her decaying brain Jamie spied a house. It rose like a dream, built on a cascade of feathers, with mortar and brick. Tacky statues decorated the lawn, appearing etched as if from steam. The pavements and streets nearest the house was still wet from a summer rain – the same rain that had darkened the skies over the duplex this past afternoon.

Shrill caws lit her ears, excited, begging the dead girl to come. The lights in the house twinkled like stars, distant and faint, the hour was late, but someone was awake inside. Jamie closed the balcony doors as she came in the apartment and strode to her slumbering champion. She woke him firmly, but gentle.

Billy's eyes quaked open, staring into her enlivened gaze. Moonshine splayed across her pale extremities ignited through wet planes of glass. Her eyes blazed with a fire that lit a clear path to follow. As he groggily rubbed his eyes, Jamie rose, strode to the bedroom door and simply said, "C'mon. They've found it."

XXVIII.

Billy was in the car and driving long before he ever actually felt awake. The air bristled an unusual quiet as they left the duplex and the dead girl was just as tight-lipped. A light rain spattered the windshield, beading tiny droplets in the Chevelle's wake. Jamie directed him. Billy had stopped asking where they were going awhile ago and settled into the road. He just drove. It was his purpose he came to realize. He owned the steed.

After some time, isolated with the intensity of the quiet girl, Billy began to feel as if the wind racing over the metal hide of his car was his breath, that the gas pumping through the engine was his blood, that the headlights cutting a keen path before them were his eyes. His focus became as intent as hers.

Above them, unseen by the shield of the car and the nighttime sky was the map. Flying above the wet tarmac and the wind-swept trees and all the brilliant dotted streetlights flew *her* army, leading the charge to the house in her vision. Soon they had left the dense, claustrophobic architecture of the city and tunneled down its suburban veins on wider streets. The murder of crows flew overhead, breaking the drizzling rain that fell on them.

When Billy's car had pulled gently onto the street where the birds had brought them, they dispersed on rooks of branches, wires, and rooftops. Suddenly being here again, Jaime remembered the street. She was laughing in the passenger seat of the dark stranger's car. She turned to see who was driving…but only saw Billy. The stench of freshly polished leather was pungent in the air, but not in the Chevelle.

It was on that other night. Wheels churned the tarmac on this road then and she felt good. Giddy. Alive. Sexy.

Jamie didn't feel sexy now. She didn't feel much of anything, except that she was one step closer and that she didn't know what she'd find inside. The house was a mystery. They were big on this side of town – *Expensive!* Finally, someone had taken her someplace nice, to someplace she thought was special, and they had killed her.

Jamie recalled feeling like a "somebody" that night. She felt exceptional sitting next to that man in his expensive car. The engine had a different hum than the Chevelle, though it was just as finely tuned and purring. She wore the short black skirt to show off her legs. She wanted to impress the driver. Jamie reached into the decaying recesses of her death-addled mind to see the man's face, but he was painted in shadow. Billy was bent over the steering wheel looking at her wanting to ask her where they were, but waiting for a sign as to which house it was as the road ended at a beachhead.

"It's the one with the light on," she uttered, shrinking farther into the leather of her seat.

Up ahead he saw it. A beachfront Colonial, three stories by the look of it, and it was decorated with classical statues of nymphs, dogs, and water lilies throughout the front yard. Billy pulled to the side of the short street and killed the engine. He turned off the lights and they sat in darkness. Save for the tiny sprinkling on the roof of the car there was silence.

Jamie just watched the house as Billy waited. Two BMW's were parked off to the side of a semi-circle driveway that was illuminated by Victorian styled lamps. The yard was well taken care of and there was an ivy-covered fence with a small wooden door about a man's height that had a crescent moon carved in the top of it.

In her slow-rising memory the mansion and its immediate street were surrounded by lots of parked cars. The atmosphere of the house was lively and festive, they were celebrating the Fourth of July. Fireworks could be seen on the horizon over the beach. People were walking between the house and the water.

Jamie recalled that there was a pool in the back yard as well as a Koi pond in a Japanese garden. There were three double-sized grills blazing, manned by a catering staff that served the guests all night. Jaime walked through the rooms in her mind, entering a billiard and game room, a marbled kitchen and bath. There was a chandelier in the foyer. She remembered climbing up the mahogany styled staircase so that she could get a better view. That was when she first saw him – the man with the olive tanned skin and deep set eyes. *Horus* – her god of death.

"So," asked Billy after a time. "What's next?"

"I don't know," muttered Jamie. "It's not like I have a plan."

"You knew how to get here well enough."

Jamie leaned forward and pointed up at the blackbirds. Billy understood now. He watched her watching the house for a few seconds, and then sat back and spied on it too. It seemed the order of things. Billy huffed when the automatic sprinklers turned on. Water filtered the already damp lawn and a fine mist gathered around the antique styled lights. It was obscene.

"Kinda late for a visit, don'tchya think?"

"Lights are still on. Someone's up."

"Maybe they're on vacation and left the lights on to make it look like somebody was home." As if on cue to make Billy look the fool, the square little blast of yellow light in the upstairs window on the far left went out. "Well, that blows my theory."

"I'm going in."

"Definitely not," he said turning.

She looked at him firmly with her eyebrows raised. "I'm going in."

"Are you mad? That's breaking and entering."

"No," she stated flatly with a resolute jaw. "Dead."

Billy sighed uncomfortably and heard the lock on the car door unlatch as she pulled on the handle opening the door with a soft clank.

"Why the hell do you want to go in there?"

Jamie stopped and turned, looking squarely at him. "You see that house?"

Billy noticed the trimmed hedges and overly saturated lawn again for wanton effect.

"Yeah," he uttered, missing the point.

"Well, that's it." Jamie told him reverently. "That's the house where I died."

XXIX.

Against his better judgement, he watched her disappear into the rear of the house through the wooden, crescent moon gate. His stomach churned uneasy. He would've liked a moment or two to prepare for breaking the law again, but she had told him to wait. He was in enough trouble with the police as it was and she didn't want him to get into any more.

"If you're going in, I'm going," he assured.

"This is something I have to do. You don't. Just wait for me here."

"I can't let you go in alone–"

"What's the worse that can happen?" she interjected. "I'm already dead."

Before he could argue again, she leaned down and kissed him and told him to wait. It was a small smooch. A 'lil peck. A friendly 'I'll be right back'. It stalled Billy's intentions long enough for her to reach the front yard. Breaking the law was becoming a habit with Jamie around. *We were never so adventurous when we were dating!*

The backyard was mostly how the girl remembered it, though there was less people and decorative lighting. Chlorine from the lagoon shaped swimming pool filled the air as tiny drops of rain danced circles in the water. The filter drain gurgled with a slow, perfect rhythm. Brass statues of cranes, partially hidden in the gardens watched her ascend the path from the shadowed gate to the sliding glass doors. Behind the

Moroccan tiled porch the rooms inside were darkened.

She tested the locks until she found one that hissed quietly open. Someone had forgotten to close up shop. Moon-glow washed the hard marble floor and Persian throw rugs. It fell across a box of genuine white leather couches and loveseats nestled around a large, blackened flat screen TV. She recalled people seated in them talking.

A Windsor pearl mantel framed a cold fireplace. The scent of ash faintly clung to the air. A few pictures adorned the shelf. Portraits of children growing and grown. A sport pic from a weekend of scraped knees and sweaty jerseys. There was an accomplished graduation smile, cuddled anniversary poses, and an elated wedding three-fold that sat squarely in the center. It was quaint. Average. Normal. And Jamie wasn't exactly sure why she was here or what she hoped to find.

A digital chime pulled her attention to the opposite side of the room. A trendy city centre floor clock clanged twice more. 3 a.m. It sounded exactly like a traditional grandfather clock, but it wasn't, and Jamie couldn't tell the difference. She moved from the living room through a large dining room and study to the foyer. In each room the air was still - antiseptic. The lack of lived-in scents told Jamie that a cleaning crew had been busy recently, or that the house was vaguely absent of the family that decorated the mantel. *Perhaps the people are away, like Billy had thought, and the light was on a timer. But would they leave one of the back doors unlocked?*

She stared up at that chandelier. Darkened now, but in her memory it was magnificently lit. A 1778 Monticello replica, two tier, that hung at a point over the huge hall. She climbed each timid step half-expecting a creak from a loose board to give her position away like marking an 'X' on a map as she gazed upon the unlit splendor of the hanging glass array. A plush red velvet carpet fell like a waterfall down the mahogany staircase, winding in an arc to the third floor. Jamie felt as if she were floating.

Clinking wine glasses, steady murmurs of disembodied conversations hallucinated in her ears. A deluge of people dressed better than she was passed her on the crowded staircase. From this vantage point she could oversee the party, reveling in the breath-taking splendor. Guests cloistered into small pockets. Dance music pumped from strategically placed Bose throughout the house and garden patio. This was where she saw her dark-eyed stranger descending the red waterfall toward her. He whispered a greeting in a strange language that she did not understand. All night long Jamie kept feeling as if she was waiting to exhale. It was the first time in her life, and unfortunately the last, that she felt elevated to the social status that she had dreamed of.

The man whom she later knew to be Horus ran his hand across her face. She remembered feeling flush and warm in his stolen embrace. Encapsulated in his propinquity the crowded launch of the party disappeared and all that remained was the crowning specter of the stranger's gorgeous eyes. They bore through her as he spoke again. It was still in a language that, for a time, she wouldn't understand. Jamie had to cross that threshold of death and have her spirit broken into a thousand shards before she could even begin to know what he had said to her on that cascading stairwell.

It felt as if it had been years since the party, but the dead girl knew better than that. The summer month was still upon them. Faded glitter and cheap-made popper wrappers with their burnt edges could still be seen lining gutters and filling empty doorways and stoops within the city. It was what the evening's rain was washing away. The mansion may have had several cleaning crews visit since then, but time had not lost any of its savage irony.

"I will lift you on wings and what will be bitter will be no more," recited the dead girl from memory.

It was what the Egyptian had whispered to her on the winding staircase. Then he did something completely unexpected and forward. The strange man leaned down and kissed her. He pressed his savory lips against hers. She felt his tongue penetrate the gate of her teeth and dance with her muscle. She did nothing to stop him. How could she, wrapped in his powerful charisma? Their breaths mingled as their saliva twisted in an ardent embrace.

Even after the sudden passion of the kiss she felt his body pressed against hers, though he was already descending the stairs away from her. Her loins were two wet oysters aching for more than what he had casually given. He smiled wryly at her and she watched him go, as mysteriously as he had come. All that evening Jamie was waiting to exhale. The hue of the Monticello Chandelier cast its golden ray upon her and it felt good to be alive.

Jamie eyed the darkened hallways of the upper level now and

did what she assumed she must have done on that evening of her death – climbed back down the red velvet waterfall. She crossed the foyer in a daze and entered the room on its opposite side just as an iron hand clasped her arm in a hardening grip. It was all too familiar and sent her mind reeling.

"What was that?" she recalled the angry voice berating, "Did you think I wouldn't notice?"

"Let go," she demanded. "You're hurting me."

"And in front of everybody. I told you how important this was." He held her tighter, jerking her shoulder up as he pulled her closer to him.

"I didn't even know the guy," she confessed, staring into a handsome face twisted by jealousy. He crowded her, flaring his nostrils as he spoke. *This isn't like him*, she thought. His cheeks were ruddy. His hair neatly trimmed. He kept his voice low and terse, for just the two of them; his clear blue eyes stabbed her womanly features like daggers. "Honest. I don't know why he kissed me."

"Yeah?" her escort spat, releasing her. "Didn't look like you did anything to stop him either."

That should've been a sign right then and there, but he looked so hurt. "I'm sorry," she uttered, but the young man's face disappeared.

"Who the hell are you?" the angry voice barked in place of the man from her vision. "And what the hell are you doing in my house?"

The man's hair was messy, graying, and thin. His cheeks were scruffy. He hadn't shaved in a day or so. He twisted the hold he had on her arm in the same way that the man from her memory had done. Though this guy was portly, older, he was dressed in a bathrobe, opened around a hairy chest, pair of boxer shorts, and slippers. Jamie quickly recalled him from several photographs that trimmed the mantel.

"I'm sorry," she repeated again, still lumbering from her recollections.

"Wait a minute," he breathed, scrutinizing his burglar, and dragged her over to the desk. He fumbled around and turned on a nearby tabletop lamp. "Don't I know you from someplace?"

Her eyes grew as big as his as she squeaked an unsaid answer. In the dim light, each recognized the other. They had only met once and then only talked for a brief time at the party.

"I know you," the man hissed in a throaty baritone voice.

"No, you don't," Jamie informed.

"Yes, I do," the man exclaimed with growing disgust. "You're supposed to be dead."

"Happy to disappoint!"

As she spoke, Jamie pressed her free hand against the man's sweaty chest and pushed him off her. His mind was stuck on the details of her face, collecting the facts of what he thought he knew from this unexpected discovery. He fell away and bumped into the desk, jostling the lamp. It tipped over, breaking the bulb. Jaime didn't hesitate. As darkness enveloped them, she ran from the room.

"Hey?" he called after her. "You're supposed to be dead. You're supposed to be dead."

Jamie didn't look back as she fled through the house. Fear weld to her ribs as she made for the sliding glass door where she came in. The bright sudden flash and mineral boom that sounded like a firecracker made her think of the party on the Fourth of July and the man that had taken her to it. But it didn't effect her as drastically as it did Billy.

He was sitting in the car when he saw the desk lamp turn on through a downstairs window and wondered what Jamie was up to. It made him glad when it finally went out, but something about the way that it did wasn't quite sitting right with him. He never had the chance to figure out what it was, because when the gunshot lit fragments of the house through windows of half-closed curtains he knew something had gone horribly wrong. He was already across the yard, heading toward the gate when Jamie broke from it and yelled at him to "Go!"

Both of them barreled to the Chevelle as front lights ignited tacky statues and the wet lawn. Locks on the front door where turning against their gears as Billy was backing out of the short street to the two-lane road that had led to this section of beachfront property. Jamie hadn't even closed her door properly when his wheels had peeled out, squealing down the street. The dead girl's avis merchants swarmed behind the black machine, obscuring the angry man's line of sight.

But it wasn't the fury of birds clamoring in the air outside his house that upset him most. He wasn't even bothered by the fact that lights were beginning to flicker on from the few neighbors he had. What bothered Aaron Scopelliti so much was that he'd told Tony to get rid of that nosy bitch and he'd lied. But then again, he helped carry her strangled body to Aaron's car. He was proud of him then. It gave him points in the organization. The broad looked dead enough when they tossed her in the trunk. *Didn't groan or nothin'!* But Tony must have lied and botched the job if she was snooping around his place past the middle of the night. The girl was supposed to be dead. Who knew what she overheard while hanging at the doorway for Tony like that.

Wouldn't have happened back in the day, thought Aaron, *we trained our broads right. Best they listen, or bam, one in the kisser!*

XXX.

Billy couldn't get it out of her fast enough. What had happened inside the house, why all of a sudden lights were flicking off and on, there was a gunshot, and she was yelling at him to go. He had her explain it to him twice. By the time they had returned to the duplex he was feeling good that no one was following them and there was little chance of them being traced back to his place. For all sensible reasons, as far as Billy was concerned, the whole nasty business was over and done with. That was until they got home, turned on the lights, and Jamie took off her hoodie, throwing it on the back of the chair.

"Jesus Christ, Jay," he exclaimed, "look at your back."

She turned. "What are you talking about?"

"Take your shirt off," he asked, crossing the room in a few short strides.

Oblivious, she obeyed. "Thanks, I could use a rub down, my joints have been really stiffening up."

"It's not your joints I'm worried about," he said as he squat down in front of her. "It's the hole in your gut." Billy stared straight through a bullet hole to the other side of the room. It was the size of a nickel. "Didn't you feel it?"

"Feel what?" Jamie twisted and looked down. "Jesus Christ!" Anger flashed through her eyes. "That fucker shot me!"

"I know."

"Gaddammit," she exclaimed as she looked at the shirt she was holding. "I liked this one too." She paced away from him and cursed. After a minute of frantic stomping she stopped, looked at Billy, and asked, "how bad is it?"

"I can see all the way through and the edges are burnt a bit."

"Really?"

"Really."

Jamie exited to the bathroom. Its light spilled on the carpet through the opened bedroom door. Billy just listened to her as she went off, gazing at it in the mirror. It wasn't lost on him that if she weren't already dead they'd still be at that house. If she were alive she would have bled out. Even if he could have gotten her to the car they'd be at Mercy General right now and he'd be worried whether or not she was going to make it. Instead, the biggest dilemma that Jamie had to face at the moment was whether or not she should keep the tee shirt with the hole in it or throw it away.

Billy crossed to the toolbox in the kitchen and pulled out a roll of duct tape. When she came out of the bathroom he knelt beside her, tore off two short strands of the sticky-back tape and covered the holes in her right flank. It was the sort of bodywork the auto-mechanic could handle.

"That should keep you," he said as he rose.

"Really?" Jamie asked with an expression that told him it wasn't necessary.

"Really," responded Billy as he replaced the tape back in the box. "Now, let's see about those joints."

Jamie exhaled at the thought of it and cracked a stiff patch between her shoulder blades. The pops and snaps of drying cartilage and bone along her spine was so loud it caused both of them to pause and reflect. Though neither said anything about it. It didn't sound good…and it was creepy.

Billy joined her on the couch and started rubbing a coconut scented lotion along her back, shoulders, and neck. Jamie moved her

hair to one side and held it. Her profile looked dainty beyond the
curve of her rotator cuff and arm. Her eyes darted to him and as he
worked his way down, Jamie slipped out of her bra.

She always felt more alive when he touched her. Things
felt closer and yielding, instead of miles away. His hands were
unmistakable charms. Massaging the pains of death away, she trembled
a little every time his fingertips brushed the sides of her ribs. She went
limp, melting into the slow, steady rhythm of his palms. His hands on
her neck were an aphrodisiac and Jamie felt a longing she didn't know
she could feel. Leaning into him with her eyes closed she pulled his
hands across her breasts. Her chin titled skyward as his thumbs grazed
her nipples and her lower lip quivered for his taste.

The young man didn't keep her wanting for long. He pressed
his warm lips to her cold receptacles and squeezed, pulling her closer.
The shape of her form against his chest and legs again was heartening.
Jamie let go of his hands, twisted around, and grabbed his face as they
kissed. He cupped a breast with one hand as the other traveled to her
neck and gripped her firmly at the base of the skull.

Then just as suddenly and surprisingly as the embrace had
started Jamie withdrew. She pressed her forehead against his face,
clasped his neck with quaking hands, and bit her eyes shut. Billy panted
with ire breath. She had no such engine pounding for all her fire.
Quickly, Jamie grabbed her ruined shirt and ran from the room, from
the apartment, into the slow-moving light of dawn.

Billy let her go. The kitchen door swung wide in her absence
as he climbed down from the height of his desire. There was definitely
something wrong about the kiss, yet so damn right. Billy mostly
thought about its flavor. Jamie didn't taste the same, and as odd as it
sounds he wasn't sure if he should go brush his teeth or run after her
into the doe-eyed morning. He had never put his tongue in the mouth
of a corpse before, so he was a little lost as to what to do next.

XXXI.

The rain had started again as dawn broke over the soggy city. Her black feathered entourage flew above her like a mood. Jamie crisscrossed blocks, wound through alleys that she never would have gone down before and returned to the apartment when she began to feel crowded by too many people, radiating too many colors on the streets – *going to work, going to bed, going to play, to eat, and shop.* She wanted to find Billy there in the tranquil den that had become her haven, but only found remnants of his ghost and the wafting scents of the breakfast, which he had cooked and ate. Jamie assumed he went to work.

The day was gloomy and shit. *I never should have kissed him.* But Jamie couldn't shake the feeling of how bad she wanted him either. Falling into him like that was so natural it hurt. But she had her chance and let him go. She walked out and left him wondering what he'd done wrong. If she could only go back she'd marry him. She was sure of it. He was a good man. But the vanity of her desires had gotten her killed.

Every lofty hope or wish to be something other than what she had been was now made mute by the irreversible fact of her death. She stood on that staircase, with her fate sealed, dreaming of being somebody that she never was and was never going to be, and it was painfully obvious. *I never should have left him. He was the one for me.* What consummate viciousness it was to bear witness, so plainly and clear, to the path that one should have taken? Jamie ached with a pure knowing. She wanted a do-over. She wanted to go back in time and yell at herself about how all she thought was wrong. Billy *was* right and true and good. He was honest and would've loved her through all the wrinkles and pills, trips to the hospital, that old age brings. They could've had children and he would have been a great father. *Why didn't I see that then?*

Jamie caught her reflection in a bit of glass in the patio doors. Her skin looked jaundiced and pasty. Her hair hung like a dead rat. She spied her pets, sullen in the rain-swept morning, with their wings folded back, their necks tucked in, heads down, so that the water rolled off their beaks. Every now and then a random caw broke the eerie silence of her thoughts as one of the blackbirds shook the weather from its feathers. Then, it rolled its head back into itself again, tucking its face under the edge of a wing, feeling the hate and confusion that the dead girl felt.

Jamie had waited to exhale. Caught up in the whirlwind of her life. Being at that party was like holding her breath and that bastard had choked it out, leaving that breath lodged in her neck, never to escape. Always and forever, Jamie Lund will be waiting to exhale. *Damn it! Where are you?* She wanted Billy so badly. She wanted the comfort of his shape, the ease and peace of mind that she could, at any time, reach out and touch him. Jamie knew it was selfish, rude even, considering how she'd dumped him for the asshole that had killed her. *Was it really because of his car that I went out with him? Was I really that shallow?*

Jamie knew the answer and despised who she used to be. *So what? The man had money. He flashed it around. That didn't change the fact that he was a dick.* Jamie stomped through the apartment, pacing and enraged. *The heart wants what the heart wants*, she remembered telling herself at the time, making plans to move out. Now, here again, climbing the same four walls reciting the same ridiculous little line as if it ever meant anything real. Billy was real and her heart didn't want him then. Now it's a decaying relic and it had no right, no voice; hell, it didn't even keep time anymore! Jamie's desires were just passing shadows, and because of that she hated herself and craved a worthy distraction.

So when the rain thinned and the clouds broke, letting thin streaks of sunshine poke through, Jamie decided to return to the library. Perhaps there she could live vicariously through Rose the life she'd never have with Billy. Rose's marriage to her husband had been a good one and the Librarian always had funny tales and tidbits of vitality that soothed her spirit and passed the hours of each unending day in a cup of tea. Even though the dead girl didn't have the stomach for it, she felt that this dreary summer morn would simply vanish with a friendly host and a warm cup of brown liquid.

When she'd climbed the steps to the library, spending time with Rose was all she could think about. She'd convinced herself that it was exactly what she needed, a little girl time, and that the lurid kiss and lingering feeling about Billy Kimmel were just that... *lingering feelings* – phantom emotions from a past life that meant nothing. Though, when she stuffed the books on auras through the little slot return she didn't see Rose at her usual place. So she went traipsing down an aisle that she'd deliberately walked past the last time she was there: *World History*.

Back and forth she paced, pulling out books as she kept an eye on the front desk looking for the kindly Librarian. Soon a small stack weighed her down and she sat in the middle of the carpeted aisle, reading snippets about ancient Egypt and Egyptian Gods. It occurred to her suddenly that when she was alive she never went to the library. Even during high school she preferred to look things up online at home or in the computer lab. The library was a mythical place for nerds and geeks that weren't as hip and cool as she was. Though when she thought about it, she remembered how Billy used to use the school library for book reports and she'd always ride his ass about getting the synopsis online, instead of reading the book. He said he liked the quiet of the library and that his computer hummed too loudly.

Jamie sat up and looked around. Rose still wasn't at her desk. She listened to the still vibrancy of the hallowed halls until a small chuckle of laughter broke the otherwise tomb-like grip on the city's book repository. All roads led back to him. No matter how far she traveled or what she did or where she went she couldn't get away from thinking about Billy. Even death wasn't an obstacle or a resistance; Billy Kimmel was the centering stone of Jamie Lund.

The dead girl didn't like this thought, regardless of how true it was. It caused her to revisit the morning's bad ideas in triplicate. She knew with a desperate lucidity that she should have stayed with Billy and that if she had she'd be alive right now, and instead of hiding behind the near-vacant walls of the library she could've been out there making a home with the man that loved her or getting a suntan on the beach. She was never one to let summer slip away behind the churn of air conditioning.

Frustrated and on the verge of rebooting her ill mood, Jamie snatched a few books on ancient Egyptian religions and waded through a short line to speak to the African American woman that was hogging up Rose's station. Jamie couldn't help but notice how the woman's aura was bounding pinks and greens from behind the desk, but once her eyes fell on her it altered by rippling spikes of black and white. *I should have worn my sunglasses. It's always in the eyes. Stupid.*

"This is all for you today?" asked the Librarian pleasantly enough.

Jamie peeled her eyes off the woman's field. "Is Rose around?"

The black energy of her aura seeped into the vibrancy of her greens and pinks, mutating them. "Oh, I'm sorry. Rose no longer works here. She passed away yesterday. Did you know her?"

Jamie just stared at the woman, dumbstruck.

"Was she a friend of yours?" the Librarian asked

"What?"

"Did you know her?"

Jamie couldn't speak. She just wagged her head from side to side, telling the Librarian, no.

"Oh," the woman mused, shifting her glasses more snuggly into the crook of her nose and started scanning the serial numbers from the books that Jamie had brought to the counter. "May I have your library card?"

"I, ah…" Jamie stepped back.

The Librarian looked up from the stack of books with disconcerting eyes and asked the young girl again for her card. Jamie didn't answer. She felt as if the vast expanse of the library was closing in on her shoulders. She felt cramped, squeezed like an ancient accordion whose billows had cracked. Her lips trembled as if to speak, but she only backed away and ran from the building, throwing open its huge double doors that had lions embossed on the metal.

She ran away from the Library's stone edifice with no concern as to where she was going. It was all a blur. The people and their auras blended into the shock and grief that Rose was gone, the architecture and traffic melded into a sold permanence that spurred Jamie to dip down alleys, block after block, and pound pavement until she felt purposefully lost. She did not pant or run out of breath. She could have traversed the whole distance of the state had her will held out.

But she stopped when the sun was high enough in the sky and all around her were unfamiliar faces. Her body shook with a great deluge, though she couldn't cry. She barely knew the woman, she was old, and now she was gone. Jamie didn't understand any of it. She just wanted to cry like a normal girl. She wanted to fold her face in her hands and have it all out. Have the drama in the sea and the sky drive through her frail system and wash away all her rancid regrets. She couldn't love the man anymore. She was dead. She had her chance and blew it. She didn't have a shot at what Rose had with her husband and now the woman wasn't even here for Jamie to yell at, or ask what the flavor of tea was that they had shared.

The only thing the dead girl had was a Technicolor-world seen through bleached eyes and felt through a drab shell. Death wasted everything and kept no quarter. *He didn't have to come for Rose like he did. He could've waited a day at least. He didn't have to come for me!* Jamie started walking and after awhile found with ease that she'd wound her way home. Not back to Billy's place as she had intended, but to her apartment, her quaint, quiet (*barely lived in*) apartment.

Jamie stared up at the door like it was diseased. This place didn't belong to her anymore. Just like Billy, it was a shadow of the past that held nothing for her now. But Jamie couldn't help wondering if the window was still busted out in the alley. She had to look. Around back someone had covered the gaping hole with a piece of plastic and it was swathed by yellow crime scene tape on the outside. The bright line and indecent lettering made her curious. As she neared the broken pane she heard voices coming from inside her old place.

"Look, it's nearly the end of the month I can't leave it like this," spoke a baroque accented voice that she recognized as her Ukrainian landlord. "I've got renters. Renters who can pay rent and who want to move in; you understand."

"Yeah, well..." spoke a voice that she didn't know. "As touched and all as I am by your problem, your apartment is still considered a crime scene in an ongoing investigation and I don't want you or anybody else in here until I say so. You got that?"

"Yes, but–"

"No, yeah but," the other man quickly spat. "You remember the girl that lived here. The one that paid rent for the month…"

"Yeah, I remember her," the Ukrainian defended. "Nice girl; cute face."

"Well, that nice girl is dead–"

"I know, you already tell me–" the landlord tried to interject, but he was cut off again.

"Well, I'm telling you again. Stay out of here."

"I'm not in here I tell you."

"Don't lie to me. Don't lie. I saw you poking around, going through her stuff."

Jaime stood on the tips of her toes, peering through the bottom edge of the filmy plastic to get a look at the man her landlord was talking to, but all she could see were their blurred figures standing in the hall.

"I'm sorry her murder was an inconvenience for you," the figure of the cop shouted. "But it's not an opportunity for you to go riffling through her stuff. In my line of work we call that stealing." The cop held up his finger in mid-air to silence the landlord as he moved again to worm out of it. "I don't want to hear it. You stay out until I say otherwise. You got that?"

The blurry figure of the cop placed his hands on his hips.

"Yes," she heard her old landlord squeak and she wanted to laugh. He was such a prick.

"Are you sure?" The cop asked. But when her old landlord started to answer, he interrupted on purpose. "If you aren't, don't tell me you are. Because, if I catch you in here again I'm going to arrest you for obstruction of justice, or shoot you. Though, I haven't made up my mind which."

Jamie crouched below the window's edge and clamped a hand over her mouth, stifling a torrid laugh at her landlord's expense. *This must've been the guy who was at Billy's when I returned.* She crept up and stuck her finger through the plastic sheeting to make a hole and then peered through.

Only the cop was standing in her apartment now. *He must've scared Mekal off.* She looked him over the best she could through the little spy hole she'd made and decided immediately that she liked him. He wasn't at all the type that Billy had made him out to be. He was even kind of cute, and he'd stopped Mekal and his greasy fingers from snooping around her place. That had to count for something. But when Special Investigator James Riley saw an unwelcome eyeball poking through the plastic that he'd put up, he stomped across the room to give yet another asshole another thumping.

Jamie didn't stick around long enough to hear what the cop might've said if he'd caught her at the window. His fine demeanor quickly vanished to an unpleasant look, and instantly she knew what Billy meant when he said that he gave him the creeps. Riley had a menacing glare and it never crossed her mind that the cop wouldn't hesitate to pull his gun and shoot her if he felt so inclined. It was such a small hole in the plastic that she was perplexed that he'd even seen her at all. So she ran. She ran from the alley on feet of enduring nature and this time didn't stop until she was sure, absolutely sure, that she was good and lost. There was just something about this day that she couldn't quite get away from. But she was damn sure gonna try!

XXXII.

Thunderheads rolled across the heavens on late afternoon winds. By dusk it was raining again. Neon beat the wet pavement like crystal. Tires sliced the air with song. The dead girl was walking. Her birds huddled in the rain, roosting a few blocks at a time, moving when they only felt the invisible tether of their leash stretched too thin for comfort. They had not eaten as much today as they would have liked. She stopped on occasion to let them forage, but Jamie was always too cagey to hang around in one place long enough.

When the city had darkened, by night and by clouds, Jamie realized that her dead dry skin was beginning to absorb the sky-water more than it was beading off of her. She wanted to be home and out of the rain, but her wanderings had taken her far and she still had a long way back to the duplex. One of the things she noticed that she hadn't read about in any book was that the auras she saw reflected off the wet sidewalks, shops, and streets. Jamie found this intriguing. Energy shadows, passing unseen by normal eyes, were a carnival of cotton-candy distraction that kept her busy for awhile. Though, eventually she stopped and leaned against the brick of a building under a metal yawning.

It wasn't long after that that Jamie spied a car in the road that had stopped. Its headlights were in her face so she couldn't see the make or model. She tried to keep her head low, out of sight, but when the streetlight changed and the vehicle stayed put longer than what was expected Jamie began to get a little nervous. Much to the dismay of her waterlogged pets she was on the move again. But the car kept pace. Jamie ran and the sky above her lit with a hundred dark tiny shapes following after.

The car revved its engine and picked up speed, chasing Jamie down an alley. The dead girl was trying to put some distance between her and the stranger that was stalking her. Headlights cut a crisp path in front of her, casting her shadow long up the sides of the buildings. She could feel its heavy metal presence barreling down. It would soon be on top of her. But the bright stream of oncoming headlights and hurtling steel was overcome by a swarm of crows and the vehicle was forced to stop. The driver opened his car door to a discord of sable feathers and fervent wings. He shouted.

"Jamie, stop! Jamie, wait! It's me. Stop, its Billy."

Through a thick fog of beating wings and the thudding pulse of her sneakers on the alleyway, Jamie heard Billy's harried cries. She stopped. She became still, but the wall of screeching beaks and menacing talons did not disappear. They flapped before the young man, blocking his way. Slowly, Jamie walked through the dense air of her army and found Billy standing by the opened door of the Chevelle waiting for her.

"What the fuck, Jay?" Billy snorted as she neared the car. "I've been looking for you all day."

Jamie gently lifted her hands and the crows rose into the air with an impressive rush. Billy felt fear for the dead girl then. Small, but real, though it was there. She was becoming something otherworldly and it didn't sit right with him. She didn't answer his question or move away. She just stood there like a lump in the pouring rain looking at him like a sad sack. Billy stood there too. It was hard to feel anything other than pity for the girl in this moment, but he was getting wet.

"C'mon," he said. "Get in the car. You're soaked."

He climbed back in as she walked around to the passenger side, opened the door, and entered. The thud of her closing door encapsulated them both in the dry, humming womb. Rain clanged on the roof in hard staccato beats. Water dripped off Jamie's upper lip. Her hair was matted to her head. She looked worse for wear, but she

was here. Billy had her once again.

"You alright?" he asked.

"Yeah."

"You wanna talk about it?"

Jamie shimmied her head from side to side. "No."

"Ok."

Warm air blasted from the heater. It was good and toasty. As Billy put the Chevelle in reverse Jamie attacked him. The vehicle lurched in the small alleyway and Billy threw it in park as Jamie stuck her tongue down his throat. Her lips were cold, yet soft. He accepted them and embraced her passionately. Her hands moved from his face to his chest, around his neck, and to his crotch. He pulled the dead girl closer. She climbed onto his lap. Dripping wet, she ground into the stiffness of the live seat. Billy pulled his head back, gasping for air as Jamie suckled the heat from his lower lip.

He pressed the tips of his fingers tightly into the nape of her neck. Her hair was mushy and clung to the creases of his fingers. Jaime caressed his face with her lifeless hands. The fire of his flesh bled into her palms like a sponge. Billy had thought about just this sort of thing earlier today, assuring himself that what had happened during the meassage was never going to happen again. She delicately planted kisses on his panting lips falling to the oak of his neck. He trembled and it passed through her, a tarnished ache within her loins. His head swooned as her tongue flicked the apple of his throat, his chin. She found his mouth wanting.

The kiss was ravenous. Their hands hungrily ate at each other's clothing. Groping and pulling. Billy's hands followed the undeniable curve of her ribcage to the arch of her back as his nimble fingers flitted under her damp shirt, unclasped her bra, and pressed into her decaying flesh. She began to writhe against him like a dancer. He cupped her breasts and they felt good – alive and eager. Her hands trailed from the bend in his neck, down his heaving, broad chest to the joy she felt in his pants. Hurriedly, she unbuckled his belt. Loud clanks disappeared with a hand dipping under his shorts that grasped his engorged member. Her touch excited him further and he kissed her neck, hungrily. The scent was less than intoxicating. Jamie smelled old – *stale*. The days in his apartment after rescuing her from the morgue plagued his mind. It was sobering.

Jamie's hips swiveled and ground into him with the ache of her dead flower as her hand massaged him up and down. She wanted him. Now, in the car, in the alley, Jamie needed him inside of her. More than anything else, she craved Billy with everything she had. Billy pulled back, tracing her outline against the headlights beyond the bubble of the car. She was beautiful. *Still beautiful.* But she wasn't alive. He moved his hands to her shoulder to say something, but Jamie fervently kissed him and grabbed both hands and placed them over her quivering breasts. She squeezed his hands so that he would squeeze her and began to remove her wet hoodie and shirt.

"Jamie?" he breathed between her lips.

"I want you too," she croaked from the back of the throat. "So, bad..."

Her mouth was all over him. She grabbed a chunk of his chestnut hair and pulled as she pressed her dank jeans into the opened area of his pants.

"Wait..." he panted in short breaths. "I don't think we should–"

"It's alright," she said, tugging at the top of his jeans to remove them from his hips. "It's alright."

"No, wait."

Reluctantly, Jamie stopped. She stared at him, her hair dangling in front of her face. "What?"

"I don't think we should..."

She kissed him hard. He returned the lip-lock for a moment or two and then pushed her back.

"I'm sorry. No." He shook his head and avoided her eyes. "It ain't right."

Jamie, pissed, climbed off him, moving toward the door.

"Wait," he sighed.

But she didn't want to be around him. Her passion turned to hate. She pulled down on the handle and the door opened and the rain fell in.

"Jamie, wait!" he yelled, grabbing her arm.

"Get the fuck off me!"

She struggled, but he held firm. If she couldn't have him, then she didn't want to be anywhere near him right now. She yelled at Billy to let her go and he yelled at her to listen, "just listen!"

She went still, wanting to cry. The rain beat against her legs and the opened door, but she didn't care.

"I love you," he said, like it would make a difference.

But those three simple words broke the girl into a thousand pieces. Her shoulders sobbed and quaked, whereas her eyes could not. She turned and fell into him and he held her tenderly. Jamie knew that he loved her. She'd never doubted it in all the time she'd known him. It wasn't his love that she craved. It was his body, his manhood. She needed to feel like a woman again, like a whole, live, woman again. But all his love couldn't give her that. It couldn't make Jamie Lund feel like something she wasn't.

For the longest time he didn't know what to say. He held her quietly until her shoulders stopped heaving and a little while after as she curled against his chest in the front seat. Rain pounded against the upholstery and he eyed it disdainfully not wanting to disturb her any further. When she righted herself in the seat next to him and shut the door, asking to go, he pulled from his pocket a piece of folded paper.

"What's this?"

"I went to the DMV today," he explained as he finally geared the car in reverse and backed out of the alley, onto the street. "I spoke with my Mom's friend, gave her what we had, and she came up with this."

Jamie unfolded it and looked at a single sheet of paper with names, license plate numbers, and addresses. There were about five or six listings.

"You got this today?"

"Yeah."

Jamie scrolled through the names, but none of them jumped off the page like she expected.

"Well, shit," she exclaimed, "why didn't you say so?" Billy looked at her oddly as he passed under a green light. She smirked and continued. "Here you are trying to get into my pants when we got leads to track." She knocked him in the arm. "So like a guy."

Billy chuckled and let her have it, cruising down the street. He couldn't give her anything else. As badly as he wanted her, he couldn't. He needed to be stronger than his basic temptations. He needed to fall into the love he had for her that went beyond physical display, or else he felt they were both doomed. The dead girl had a purpose. That simple piece of paper she held proved it

An ancient Egyptian god had breathed life into her murdered body so that she could avenge her own death. Billy had tasted Horus's breath on her lips and imbibed her decaying flesh. Nothing could change what already was, regardless of how either one of them felt about it. Slowly, he wound his fingers between hers, and for the rest of the drive, held her hand.

XXXIII.

That night they stopped at one of the places on the list before they went back to Billy's. But it wasn't the right car. She sat staring at the blank TV screen as Billy slept in the other room. She held the list lightly in her hands, going over it again. She set it down and picked it up a dozen times over the course of the night, listening to the rain until it stopped, sometime before dawn.

Billy had asked her to lie down with him as he fell asleep, but she declined. The crush and feel of him was too much. He didn't argue. Jamie yearned to go outside for a walk as he slept, but the rain kept her bound indoors. She paced the small flat. Once, Billy was woken by her tight, terse stomps. He lay there listening to her strutting back and forth until he fell asleep again, wishing that there were something he could do. He knew she was climbing the walls, but they simply had to deal with it. Time, he reminded himself, would take care of it.

The hours wore on like an eternity and she stared at the blank face of the TV. At her own reflection. Living through these long quiet nights was the worst and Jamie felt like a freak. A *real* monster. A candidate for Ringling Brothers and Barnum & Bailey's Circus. For the longest time she sat there and considered applying for a spot in their sideshow. She even thought up a stage name – *Sheri Underwood, The Incredible Walking Talking Corpse!* She imagined the circus flyer and life under the big top, but always returned to the list and to the names printed there waiting for one of them to speak.

But none of them did. *Maybe I never saw his name written down,* she considered. *Maybe that part of my brain has decayed*, she thought. But the list remained the same and so did her reaction to it. She wished Billy would wake up and that they would get started and find this guy and get it all over with. She wanted it behind her, though she didn't really know what she was going to do once she had found him. The list demanded that she think on it.

I could kill him. It would be right and just and make the world a better place. Truly, a piece of Jamie felt that that was what she was meant to do. But something small inside bade her to think. Killing him outright, as he had done to her, didn't quite sit so squarely upon her shoulders as she once believed, and Jamie wasn't sure why.

Morning found her, not on the balcony where she once promised to reside through each sunrise, but down in the yard walking around in her bare feet. The grass was cool and damp. The dew soothed her sore ankle joints and toes. She'd decided that before they reached the next location, down on the list, that she needed to stop at Wal-Mart or CVS and pick up some make up. Her blackened gaze through the turned off television screen told her that there was some up-keep that must be done. Her eyes and cheeks looked sunken and sallow. Her lips were thin and pasty. *No wonder Billy didn't want me. I'm a freak.*

"No," she said aloud. "You're a cancer patient."

And thought of Rose.

XXXIV.

Billy woke, more by Jamie being louder than usual than his natural alarm clock going off. His premature stirring could not sway his sights. They were fixed like a compass, pointing North to track down the rest of the addresses that he'd gotten yesterday at the DMV. Jamie didn't share his bustling enthusiasm as he showered and shaved. She was simply pleased not to be alone in the apartment anymore and was looking forward to getting out of the house.

By dawn, Jamie had memorized every crack and nuance that could be had in his half of the duplex. There wasn't much left for her to curb the crushing boredom and she wished that she had at least kept one of the books on auras to keep her company during the long nights. Sleep, she realized, made the dull slow drip of existence bearable. Without it time was just an enormous piece of cold taffy, constantly stretching, that never broke. It plodded on and on and on and on. Sleep broke the rhythm. Sleep renewed one's vigor, giving them a false sense of time and purpose. Sleep chopped the taffy up into small, manageable, life-sized bites that the mind could handle.

Since the morning of her death Jamie had not slept. Her only brief repast was suffering rigor mortis in bed. She heard the taffy pulling, felt it being stretched, counted the seconds; watched, with eyes burning, every minute change of light. Sleep, as it turned, was just another thing she envied Billy and everyone else that took it for granted. It was agony to endure every infinitesimal tick of every single night and day. Somewhere in all the madness of her afterlife she prayed for an off switch.

In the time it took Billy to shower and shave, Jamie could have knitted a complete bedspread and matching throw rug. In the time it took him to get dressed, Jamie thought her head was going to explode.

"What?" He yelled from the other room, asking her to repeat what she had said. But she merely informed him that she hadn't said anything, grinding her nails into her palms, as he finished buttoning up his blue jeans.

She spied on him as he dressed. Both of the doors to the bathroom and to the bedroom were left ajar. Just enough so she could revel in his nakedness and eye the piece of him that he had denied her. She gruffly snorted before he had asked what she had said, and when the peepshow was over she crossed to the fish tank, using it as a mirror, to apply makeup. Sometime in the wee hours of the morning, when Billy still snored comfortably in bed, Jamie had run down to the corner store and bought a few things. The two Koreans that owned the place were kindly enough, but she could tell that she made them uneasy. Her knocking about when she returned was what woke Billy.

Behind her reflection Merlin swam. She did her best to look alive, but it was becoming useless. Even though Billy hadn't said anything, she knew he could tell. Death always made an obvious impression upon the living. Jamie also knew that at some point she was going to have to deal with her slow decay, but not today. Today was the day that they were going to track down the man that had killed her. They should have circled it on the calendar, entered it in their day-planners. Today was the day, and Jamie wanted to look her dead best. The color of the lipstick she applied had been chosen specifically for *him*.

Merlin dangled in front of her wanting the thing behind the invisible wall to open the sky and deliver food. But the thing just held there playing with itself. He crossed his domain many times, but the thing did not open the sky and bring him any food. He wished it would go away. He didn't like the look of this one. The other one was ok, though it didn't bring food as often as the fish liked. When Jamie had fixed her face, she spied the fish staring at her and thought of Oscar. This was the replacement fish, the one that had come after she had left. She liked Oscar. She missed him. There were a great many things that Jamie Lund often missed. Sleep and Oscar were only a few that she counted. So Jamie flicked the glass with a hard fingernail a couple of times, because the fish in the tank wasn't Oscar and she felt a deep-seated hatred for everything that was gone.

Finally! They were on their way, moving toward the door. Jaime affixed a pair of sunglasses to her freshly painted face, pulled her hood up, and entered the sun. She flew down the steps, but was forced to pause as Billy locked up. *Everything is taking forever!* Agitated, her leg shook and she swore that it had taken Billy longer to get out of the house than a Junior Miss Prom Queen. She sighed and bounced her hands, nodding her head to the dreary beat of time. It was unbelievably unbearable. Though, when he bound down the steps and joined the fidgeting corpse there were only a few short paces to his car at the curb. As he leaned down to unlock the passenger side door a familiar voice broke his stride.

"Mr. Kimmel. May I have a word with you?"

Jamie knew that voice and stiffened. She'd heard it yesterday in her old apartment. Billy stiffened too from the polite swagger in the man's tone and turned around.

"Hello Detective. What can I do for you today?"

"Please," smiled the cop, pulling his attention from Billy to the girl that stood behind him. "It's Special Investigator. I work with the Crime Lab. Detective makes me sound like a character from a Mickey Spillane novel."

He peered at the girl, but she lowered her head and turned it aside. Billy stood there waiting nicely and noticed that he hadn't brought the other officer with him this time. He considered it a good sign.

"We were just on our way out," informed Billy, trying to distract the cop from Jamie. His heart thrummed in his throat.

"Good," the Special Investigator chimed. "Then you won't mind making an extra stop."

"Where to?" Billy asked apprehensively.

To this, Riley merely smiled broadly. It made both Billy and Jamie very uncomfortable. "To the police station, of course. There are a few things we'd like to discuss with you."

"Can it wait 'til–"

"I'm afraid not, Mr. Kimmel," the Special Investigator cut in. "I'd prefer that you came of your own recognizance, though I am prepared for the alternative." Riley put his hand on his hip, close to his gun, cocked a devilish grin, and turned sharply to Jamie. "Excuse me, but do I know you from some place?"

Jamie shook her head from side to side, looking at the ground. "No."

"You look awfully familiar," he said as he took a step forward.

Billy's heart sank and his hands began to tremble.

"Are you sure we haven't met?" Riley asked again.

"Positive," stated Jamie and added, "I just got into town."

"Huh," the investigator breathed, thinking for a moment before he asked the girl for her name and to see her identification.

Billy thought it was all over now. Game up. That all his rancid fears, which he'd felt while hiding out in the morgue, were about to come true. *It can only get worse from here*, he assumed, but Jamie surprised him with a quick answer at no hesitation or thought.

"Sheri Underwood," she said. "My purse was stolen and with it all my IDs."

Fueled by Jamie's great lie, born partially by truth, Billy perked up. "We were just on our way to file a report."

"Then it appears we're both heading in the same direction," stated Riley with a slow turn of his head to his suspect. "How fortuitous."

"Yeah," Billy nervously laughed. "Imagine that." He started to move toward the driver's side of the car. "So, we'll see you there."

"I don't think so, Sport," the Investigator barked, breaking Billy's stride. "We'll take my car." He indicated Jamie with a short wave of the hand. "You're girlfriend here can follow us if she wants. What is that?" He asked, doing the same motion in front of his face. "Some kind of Goth thing?"

"Yeah," said Jamie wryly. "I like the dead."

"Huh," breathed Riley again. "I like country music, though I work with the dead."

"How droll," replied Jamie flatly, wishing that the cop would simply leave them in peace.

"Not so," added the detective. "The dead have a way of surprising you."

No shit, thought Billy, dreading every moment of Jamie's resurrection about now.

"Just the other day," continued the cop with ease, "we had a corpse disappear on us." He snapped. "Just like that. Must've got up and walked away."

He said that last part glaring at Billy and the poor boy felt the ground slipping away, cracking under his feet to the fiery depths of hell.

"Well," piped Jamie, much to Billy's chagrin, "the dead have a way of doing that sometimes."

"Yes, they do," oozed Riley from lips that were shaped too pleasantly. "Yes, they do."

"We should get going," stated Billy urgently as he crossed to Jamie and handed her his car keys. "So, ah, I'll see you there? You'll follow us down, right?"

"Sure," replied Jamie, giving Billy's hand a firm squeeze for reassurance as all her bottled energy drained into the street.

"Ok, let's ride," said the overly excited suspect to the Special Investigator, acting chipper and nonchalant. "Not a huge fan of country music myself, but I won't mind if you play it on the way to the station."

Riley let the fool pass him as he watched the girl in the hood and sunglasses. There was something about her that ate at his gut. Riley didn't like it when things gnawed at him in an annoying way. Ever since he'd stepped foot in that alley this case had gnawed at his gut in a peculiar kind of grate. It made him uneasy and hard to please. Now, his biggest body of evidence had gone missing and he was grasping at straws to even bring this guy in for questioning. But straws and a blue strand of carpet hair were the only things he had at the moment. Straws…and his gut.

Jamie moved to the driver's side of the car and unlocked the door, watching the cop and Billy as they climbed into an unmarked vehicle. Jamie didn't like the man. He was getting in the way. His aura was pulsating reds and purples that were cut with swathing shards of orange and green. It didn't bode well, his field, too much strength and intuition for her liking.

As she climbed behind the wheel, fired up the Chevelle, and pulled behind them, following them down the street Jamie felt a desperate urgency to resolve this nasty business of her death before Billy was fingered for it. Time, it seemed, was once again not on her side. She felt its hands crushing her neck, squeezing the air from her lungs, and pushing her over a concrete bridge. *There has to be a way to get Billy out of this. There just has to be!* The only consolation that Jamie felt now was that at least he hadn't been arrested…*yet.*

XXXV.

Jamie waited for him in the parking lot of the police station. It was even more boring than being at his apartment. She considered taking up smoking to give her hands something to do in these long hours of constant tedium, but wasn't sure if she'd be able to even inhale and exhale any of the smoke. She considered taking up many other bad habits now that it wouldn't matter all that much how it affected her. If she wanted, she could eat mountains of sweets and cakes, drink like a seasoned alcoholic, never exercise, and she'd retain her trim girlish figure. In fact, she reasoned, *I would lose weight with the more junk food I ate and the more alcohol I drank.* It seemed like the perfect plan, and by the time Billy emerged from the darkened doorways of the city's crime lab, several hours later, she'd even devised a marketing scheme for her new deathly diet and an infomercial.

Jamie noticed the black ink smears along his fingers as he walked up. He tried to clean them inside, but they still left a stain. The permanence of her undead existence in his life had also become a stain. Jamie felt it, and felt his frazzled energy as he asked her to get in the car. His dominant blue was suffering and all the poor dead girl could do was feel sorry for him and hope that the universe had something better in store than Billy going to jail for a murder he didn't commit. But the universe was never kind or known to be all that compassionate. A vacuum inhabited by gas, rocks, and fire, it never shared its plans with anyone. Fair was a carnival show, a pony ride, not the actual turn of events.

"Well," he said as the Chevelle took the street, "they know you're gone and I'm their prime suspect. They kept asking me the same questions over and over about you and when we were dating. How long we lived together, and all that junk."

"What did you tell 'em?"

"I told him the truth." He turned toward her with a frayed brow. "Well, all that I could. But that guy…" Billy shook an angry finger. "He knows something, Jay, I'm telling you. He knows something that he ain't saying, and it ain't good. He's biding his time."

She rested her hand on his arm. "Sorry."

"Don't," he said, squeezing her hand. "Don't be. It's not your fault. It's that bastard that killed you and we're going to find him and bring him to justice for what he did. So help me."

As he spoke, Jamie noticed Billy's blue rising through his field. It made her feel good and happy to see his color again. She liked his fire, his drive. And he was right, they needed to find the guy that had killed her. They really didn't have much choice in the matter. If there was any chance of ever getting rid of Special Investigator Nosey then they needed to find Jamie's killer, wherever he was, and bring him in. Jamie pulled out the list. She set it on the seat between them, asking which place they should go to first.

After some small discussion they set a course and headed for it, but it wasn't what they were looking for. Jamie had seen enough of the man and his car through her tattered memories to know what the vehicle looked liked, and that he was classy. That he had money and showed it. The first place they went was on the outskirts of the city in a low rent neighborhood. Definitely not the right place. So, they backtracked to a deeper locale in the city, but that wasn't it either.

The address was a row house that didn't look familiar to Jamie, but they couldn't rely on that. She might have never visited her killer's residence. They had no way of knowing for sure, so they searched up and down the street for the vehicle with the corresponding license plate, but couldn't find it. So they waited. Searched side streets and waited some more.

"They collected DNA from me," Billy told her as they posted

guard in the car. "Some lab geek in a white coat swabbed the inside of my cheek with a long Q-tip."

"Then I guess it's a good thing you weren't slobbering all over me until after the police found me in the alley." But her dry attempt at humor didn't come off as well as she would have liked. "Don't worry. They don't have anything on you. You didn't do it."

"I know." But his expression wasn't convincing.

Jamie rolled her head against the back of the car seat to look at him. "What is it?"

"A clipboard," he confessed shyly. "I had this clipboard with me in the hospital that I was carrying around to make me look official. I meant to take it with me when I left, but it got locked behind a door."

"You think they have it?"

"I don't know," he said, falling silent for a long minute. "But if they do they'll know I was there."

Jamie took his hand and held it for awhile, thinking, tracing the ridges of his fingertips. Eventually, a redhead woman in her early thirties came home from work and shuffled two kids into the thin brick face. The vehicle she drove was a Buick. It was not the one that Jamie saw in her vision on the bridge. Hours had passed and another address was crossed from the list. Dusk now toyed in the sky and evening traffic slowed their pace to the next listing.

It was a high-rise condominium downtown that presented a unique problem. The address they had on the printout didn't specify a room or floor number, and the parking garage that the condo was attached to had a gate. Billy suggested going in and talking with someone who worked at the front desk as to where Anthony Sorbini lived. But Jamie thought that if Anthony was their guy they might tip their hand to him by asking a lot of questions. So, they did what only seemed obvious. They parked the Chevelle, fed a meter, and walked into the parking garage for a general, line by line, inspection.

Neither one of them wanted to do it. It seemed like a daunting task, but they couldn't think of any other way. Waiting for hours staked out in front of the parking garage just didn't seem like an option after the last place. It had eaten up their whole day and gotten them nowhere. Even if they did stake it out this guy could enter the building through another route, park in a different location, and they would never know it. So, Billy and Jamie decided that it would be best to just huff it, and tread the umpteen levels inspecting each car one at a time.

They made a sharp plan, each taking one side of the garage, walking down a row of cars. Beginning on the level where they entered they went down and would take the elevator back up if they hadn't found it below and start searching above. Though, at this time of day the garage was filling up. Vehicles moved around them – heading up, heading down. Stale exhaust smells and concrete were rife. Neither one of them found anything by the time they hit the bottom of the garage. With new cars arriving every minute or so as they descended they resolved to walk back up instead of taking the lift.

"Pointless," Jamie sang. "This is pointless."

They had reached the second level above the one where they had started.

"More foreign cars than American; you notice that?" he asked. Jamie just lobbed her head to the side and stared at him like she cared. "Just saying."

She heard it before she saw it and turned in its direction. She stopped as Billy kept walking. There was something about the car's pitch and tone as it climbed the winding lanes that resonated within her. It felt like the hand of doom reaching across the crowded city toward her sublime throat. Billy noticed her and was going to ask why she'd stopped when a sporty BMW pulled into a fresh space below them. They could see perfectly through the cut in the concrete, over the tops of the parked cars. It was the exact make and model as the one from her memories.

He moved to find a better angle so as to read the license plate number. But by the way Jamie just held in place, standing there like a rook, he felt it in his marrow that it was the man they were looking for. What he didn't expect to see was a familiar face climbing out of the passenger seat. By the long expression on Jamie's face she didn't expect to see her either. *Loni – Jamie's best friend.* They had met on a job that the dead girl held right after high school. Billy knew he had to act fast if he wanted to keep their cover. One look from the blond bombshell and it was over. Then Anthony Sorbini stepped from the car and Billy saw Jamie's hands flinch and tighten. He didn't hesitate any longer.

Scrambling across the ramp, he pulled Jamie aside before she could run over and claw his eyes out. They fell against an SUV in relative quiet. He told her to wait and they watched as her best friend walked to the elevator with her killer. The young man was handsome. Had dark hair, brown eyes, strutted with a confident swagger, and wore a tailored suit. Billy had seen plenty of guys like that dropping off their imported cars for the grease monkeys to fix. They never got their hands dirty. Billy tried not to think about how Jamie had left him for this asshole, but it was hard not to compare.

The dead girl on the other hand, couldn't take her eyes off them as they strolled – with Loni tossing her head back with a laugh and he, placing a hand to the small of her back. Her head swooned with a rush of memories. Everything that she had ever done with Loni had been blocked out by Horus's tender kiss. Years came spooling back to her at once and she knew that her best friend had eyes for the new guy she was dating. She caught her flirting with him at a dinner one night and they fell into an awful row about it. Jamie had avoided her calls ever since. Suddenly, she remembered introducing the two of them at a club, shortly after she and Billy had broken up when she moved into her new place. Every rancid feeling she ever had about Billy from that time in her life also came flooding back like a storm. It caused her to pity her poor pathetic self more than she had. Shame burned in her gut. The veil on her consummate blindness had finally been lifted.

She felt Tony's hands on her, while he was choking her and making love to her. She felt him inside of her and how he made her feel when they were on the dance floor or riding in his car or going out for dinner; such fine restaurants. It was all jumbled up in one great sensation. She recalled the last moments of her life at that house on the beach, ebbing away through his thick fingers as he pushed her against a metal shelving rack in the garage.

She had overhead Tony talking to that fat greasy fellow from the other night. The big man was laying out a drop schedule to the slick Italian for some police on the payroll. Names were mentioned and a shipment at a dock that she'd never heard of before was also tossed around before they noticed her. Anthony had been vague about what he did for a living, but Jamie had found out. Her timing had been unfortunate. But the ironic thing was that she didn't even care about what they were talking about. In her hard moment of clarity, Jamie knew that she would have been okay with him working for the mob. She wanted the fast cars, the fancy restaurants, and the fine clothes. The honest eye of death showed her just how cheap and shallow she was, and that if Tony would have let her live she would've kept her mouth shut and enjoyed the spoils.

She remembered crying and pleading with him that she would never tell. But he slapped her around anyway. He didn't believe her, and told her that he had orders. The sting of his backhand hurt worse now as she witnessed Loni entering the elevator in a low-cut dress, form-fitting, looking elegant. She knew where they were going. Jamie relived every ding to where the elevator doors would open and come to a stop, and they'd walk out. She knew how many rooms they would pass on their way to his suite. Jamie knew the scent of his place and how the silk sheets on his bed felt, and by the look in her eyes, so did Loni.

Billy did not have to ask the obvious question. He knew, so he uttered, "Well," to break the tension after the couple had disappeared. "She looks good."

Jamie turned on him like a snake with hard eyes and said, "Can't you say anything nice?"

XXXVI.

Jamie wanted to stay and see where her killer and former best-friend went when they came out of the condo, but Billy was hungry. He also felt that it wouldn't help them any if they just rolled up on them in some vague place and made a scene. They needed a plan. Billy wasn't going to make any plans until his stomach stopped gurgling and the cotton in his head went away. Reluctantly, Jamie retreated and was silent as the grave as they drove from the high-rise to get something to eat.

She's dating the man that murdered me. It was larger than what she could process. They used to be so close. Jamie kept looking at the printout that had Tony's address and name, wondering why it didn't stand out earlier. Wondering why she'd forgotten Loni. Wondering how she could have let somebody like Anthony Sorbini get so close that he could so easily steal her life. *Is Loni doing the same thing that I did? Will Horus kiss her goodnight when the time comes?*

Jamie refused to go inside the Applebee's and Billy was too stubborn to let her sit in the car alone. So, he ordered his dinner as takeout and ate in the car. The back of the Applebee's parking lot had suddenly become a home to several hundred blackbirds that had descended to roost. Billy didn't even have to ask who the sharp dressed man was as he struggled to balance the Styrofoam tray on his knees to cut his steak. The unanticipated rush of all her faculties bade the dead girl to speak; memories were like popping corn tumbling from her mouth. Talking about it seemed to make everything just a bit easier and besides, she knew Billy deserved to know.

"I met him about a month after I moved out. Loni and I were hitting the clubs pretty hard, and fairly regularly. I wasn't looking to start dating again. Not after us. I was just having a good time, you know. He seemed nice enough…at first. We'd run into him at Angel's Share, the Ballroom, or Table 50. He bought the drinks, we'd hang out; we played the room. Loni seemed interested in him, so I kinda stepped back, but he was interested in me, so she told me to go for it. He knew of a couple cool after-hour places and it started to become a regular thing. We'd run into him, party, and hit some new place that had some thing or another. He asked me out. I said yes.

"Loni acted as if she…you know, she didn't care that we were dating. But I noticed how she started to flirt with him more and more. I'd catch her rubbin' all up against him on the dance floor or moving in the second my back was turned." She paused, shaking her head in thought. "Honestly, I don't think things would have moved as quickly as they did with him if I hadn't felt that Loni was trying to steal him away. He became a competition. Loni and I had a fight and we stopped talking.

"Things with Tony kind of slowed down a bit after that because work picked up. I was vying for a promotion so I was putting in more hours. But we continued dating, going out. It was nice, really, having somebody spending that kind of money on me, going to the chic places." Her eyes flicked cautiously at her quiet host. "I don't think I ever loved him, but it was nice. Different."

"You mean different than me?"

She shook her answer loose. "Yeah. You and me, we'd known each other for so long and we became so used to one another that I think we forgot how to have a good time, just simply have a good time, you know? It was all about the bills and work, planning for the future, and if we were going to have a family or not." Jamie saw the look on his face and reached out, grabbing his hand. He was stiff and cold. "I loved you. I did. But I wasn't ready for kids or the kind of life you were asking me to have."

"I know."

Billy's eyes were tearing up. He recoiled, slowly pulling his hand back and boxed up the rest of his uneaten dinner plate and plastic paraphernalia. Jamie watched him, but he deserved to know the truth regardless of how much it hurt. After all this time she finally had all the marbles in her pocket and she couldn't let it lie. The damned will out. Jamie had to come clean.

"He wasn't anything other than a fling," urged Jamie. "I would have seen that. Given the time, I would've seen that."

Billy stared at her. Without Jamie's words or her hard confession he knew the score. He couldn't judge her. As bad as her leaving had been, he'd reconciled it, and figured that they'd meet again at some point, in some way. They shared too much history together for them not to. He never faulted her for leaving, so there was no use starting now. Life had ruled its verdict on her actions, and it was by Billy's estimation, unkind. Everything else was superficial. The past was only a collection of irreverent details on the anatomy of a life. What they were dealing with now, what was truly on the table, was simply the bitter aftermath.

"So, what are we going to do about it?" he asked after a time.

Jamie leaned against the inside of the door. "I don't know."

"Maybe I should call Loni and tell her—"

"No," Jamie added quickly. "Leave her out of this."

"She might know something or be able to find out something that would help us to nab this guy."

"Or get her killed." Jamie sat up. "He's done enough damage as it is. I won't aid him in doing it again. Once was enough for me."

"Yeah," said Billy thoughtfully, tossing an eye to the birds that were perched on the roof of the Applebee's and other nearby shops, on cars, and standing around in painted lots. He'd become so accustomed to them now that he hardly gave them any notice, but it slowly dawned on him that it probably looked a bit weird to other folk. So, he turned around in his seat and fired up the Chevelle. "Let's get outta here."

The road became the thing – the sound that existed between them. They drove and were thinking, isolated in their own pockets of air. Neither had any answers for what they needed to do. They'd put so much energy into simply finding the guy that now they felt a little lost. Billy hadn't picked a direction when he pulled out of the Applebee's parking lot and he didn't want to go home just yet. So he drove around, filled the tank with gas, and climbed the steep road to Willowmyer's Peak.

"You know," informed Jamie. "I tried to find this place after we broke up."

"Yeah?" he asked with a smug grin.

"No luck. Got lost. Drove around for hours."

"Told ya. This is *our* spot."

Jamie curled up in the seat, looking at him, as the Chevelle moved slowly into a makeshift parking space. The nose of the car overlooked a little patch of the city. Night was falling quickly and the lights below were already dotting the landscape. Billy turned the engine off, pulled the parking brake, and eased his seat back, turning to look at the dead girl.

"I haven't been up here since the last time, with you."

"Have you dated anyone since…" she let the question trail off.

"No. Just haven't felt like it. Went out with a couple people from the shop a few times, but mostly I hung around the apartment."

"I'm–"

"Don't," he cut in. "It doesn't matter." He rolled over in the seat and looked at the sky and the city below.

It hurt that he didn't want her apology. But it had already been said. Jamie turned over as well and they both lay there, with the seats eased back, staring at the city as the stars lit the dark blue heaven. Her crows flitted in the wild, foraging for food; Jamie felt their delight. Out of the hard earth and dust-barren realms of the city, the birds were more content.

"We need to find some way," he said "to point the cops to Mister Anthony Sorbini."

"You could make an anonymous phone call."

"Naw. It needs to be something more than that."

Jamie chuckled.

"What?" he asked.

She sat up. "They need hard evidence, right?"

"Yeah," he replied, looking at her queerly. "But where we gonna get it? That's what we need to figure out."

Jamie just smiled at him until it made him uncomfortable and he sat up too.

"What's going on in that brain of yours?"

"Evidence," she claimed, with a devilish smirk. "Hard evidence." She displayed her hands across her own form.

"Oh, no," he said not liking where this was going.

"Yes," she said, nodding up and down.

"No," he refused flatly. "I can't let you."

"I don't see any other way. And besides," she barked, turning in her seat. "It's not up to you. I'm not going to let you get arrested for taking me from the morgue or as my killer when we can easily set the man up who's responsible."

Billy's stomach was a lurch, sinking. He hated to admit it, but she was right. The police were already looking for her dead body and it wouldn't be all that difficult to send Special Investigator James Riley after her real killer if Jamie was willing to play possum through a staged ordeal. It wasn't the best plan, Billy felt, but it was all they had at the moment, and that, at least, was better than nothing.

"Ok," he said finally. "What do you want me to do?"

XXXVII.

Billy's cell phone rang. He'd just rolled out of bed and was getting dressed. The sleepy eye of dawn was nipping at the cool shoulders of buildings and Jamie was on the back porch.

"Hey, Hector," Billy answered, holding the phone between his cheek and his shoulder as he buttoned his pants.

"I need you in today," squeaked his boss's voice through the tiny machine.

"I can't. I'm finishing up that thing we talked about."

"Yeah, well…I think I've been lenient enough. I got triple the cars and less staff."

"I know. I know." He noticed Jamie watching him and moved into the other room. "And I appreciate it. I'm not trying to mess up your business and stuff."

"Billy, we go way back, but I gotta get these cars done, bro."

"Listen, could I come in tonight? And bang it out? I just gotta finish this thing, you know. And once it's done, it's done. I'll be there like regular."

There was a long silence. Billy paced, slowly, eyeing the dead girl through the half-opened doors, thinking about their plan, praying for miracles.

"You better," added Hector finally.

"I will," Billy said. "Promise."

He hung up feeling the gods on his side and the wind at his back.

"I'm going to the little store for supplies," he said as he crossed the blue shag to Jamie. "You want anything?"

Her face went placid and she just stared at him.

He got her meaning. "Ok, I'll be back in a minute." Though, as he was leaving he threw across the room, "Be ready to go when I get back."

Like she'd been anything but, for hours now. Her shoulders drooped and she rattled her head, looking out across the barren yard. Some people were moving through the alley – heads down, looking grim. It had been a cloudy sunrise behind the smog of the city, but it was clearing up. And getting hotter. It was going to be a scorcher today. She could feel it already. The moisture in the air was wreaking havoc on her bones. She ached. Her muscles were sore and the rising humidity wasn't helping.

Billy went to apply lotion on her decaying epidermis last night, but stopped, asking if he thought it would mess with her DNA. She considered it and thought it best if they just left it alone so that her skin and hair follicles would be particular to her natural condition. Though, he did replace the duct tape over the bullet holes. As night drew on, waning into the dawn, she'd become more and more achy and stiff. It had put her in a foul mood and she wasn't looking forward to playing "full dead" in the trunk of Tony's car with the god-awful heat and humidity.

Billy grabbed two snack cakes, a muffin, three sodas, and a breakfast sausage. He was anticipating the stakeout and didn't want to leave Jamie for a minute if he didn't really have to. He even set aside a couple empty bottles just in case he needed to go the bathroom. They had talked about it all night, until he fell asleep on the couch and then went to bed. For inspiration they watched reruns of CSI and CSI: Miami, hoping for ideas, but mostly just enjoyed the shows. They were confident their plan was going to work, but neither one liked the risk involved. Though, they didn't see any other choice in the matter.

He was walking back to the duplex when he saw the police cruisers and officers at his door. They were talking to Jamie. Hands on guns. Pointing, he overheard one of the cops tell her to "stand over here." His stance and demeanor was forceful, as two officers moved inside. Billy held back, and slipped behind a space between two buildings. He watched them. The cop was asking Jamie for her identification and she was spinning the same lie that they had told Special Investigator James Riley the other day. Billy looked for him, but didn't see the detective anywhere.

"Shit," he muttered. "Shit."

Everything was going to hell in a hand basket faster than he could handle. If they took Jamie in it was over. They'd find out who and what she was and they'd catch him eventually, probably in some seedy motel off the Interstate, and then it was off to the little white rooms with the rubber pads and straightjackets.

"Shit."

He needed to get out of here, but feared for the dead girl. Billy backtracked his steps to the corner store as the officers came out of his apartment and gathered around. He spied on them from the end of the street, blending into the other onlookers. He was mortally grateful when the police climbed back into their cars and drove away without her.

He stood there with an earmark of confusion as to whether he should run back to the apartment, get Jamie, and go. But he figured the police had somebody watching his place, so he hung back as the gawkers dispersed, going back inside the corner store to wait.

It could not have been more screwed up than if Billy had been her actual killer. The police had left and she was flipping out. Pacing through the joint, Merlin watched her, but she didn't stay indoors for long. She grabbed his keys, leaving the empty bottles by the kitchen door that Billy had set out, and left, slamming the door as the fish crapped a long, thin black turd. Sprinting down the steps, Jamie glanced casually for a tail or Billy coming back from the store. Seeing neither, she slid into the driver's seat of the Chevelle, fired it up, and headed up the street.

Turning the corner, she slowed and looked for Billy, but didn't see him. Frustrated, Jamie hit the steering wheel and decided to loop around. On her second pass, Billy saw the crows above the street, and then saw his car. He ran from the store. She was looking on both sides of the street, moving slowly, and caught a quick glimpse of him in the side-view mirror as he ran after. She pulled over, getting as close to the curb as she could – a car's length – reached across the seat and opened the door. Billy jumped in.

"What happened?"

Jamie stepped on the gas, cut off an oncoming car, and dipped under the yellow light at the next intersection. She looked in the rearview mirror as Billy turned around in the seat. Neither one of them saw anybody following them - except the usual mass of tiny black shapes flying through the air.

"I heard a knock on the door. Thought it was you."

"Me?"

"Yeah," she yelled. They were both talking loud and excited. "I thought you'd locked yourself out, so I answered and it was the police."

"I saw them."

"You did?"

"Yeah."

"Fuck, Billy. They came to arrest you."

"Ahhh," he eased through his throat uncomfortably, sliding down the passenger seat. "Shit." He turned to the driver, who was huddled over the wheel. "What did you tell them?"

"I told them you were at work."

"No. You didn't."

"What else was I supposed to say?" She looked hard at him. "Invite them in, wait for you to get back?"

"I've got to call Hector," he said, reaching for his cell phone. "I can't let them show up at his place like that."

"Are you crazy?" hollered Jamie.

Billy stared at her. He was thinking about it.

"Lemme see your phone?"

"What for?" he inquired, handing it to her.

Jamie rolled down the window and threw it out.

"What the fuck, Jay!" he screamed, watching his phone shatter into several pieces on the street.

"Didn't you learn anything from watching those shows last night. They can track you using your cell."

"But you didn't have to throw it out the window. You could have just taken the battery out."

Jamie turned and looked at him. He was breathing heavily. His eyes were huge. Everything was intense. Suddenly, she busted out laughing and he soon followed.

"Ah, shit," he said after they'd calmed down some. "What are we going to do now?"

"Same thing we were going to do."

Billy nodded, conceding the point. "It better work."

"It will."

And they drove on, into the posh region of Anthony Sorbini's luxury high-rise suite.

XXXVIII.

They went through the entire parking garage twice, floor by floor, and didn't see Tony's sports car anywhere. Things were not going as planned. It had seemed simple enough last night. To stow Jamie away in the killer's car and have Billy phone it in, and basically, follow the same routine that she'd already undergone one time before. All they needed to do was lead the police to find her body in Anthony's possession and then Billy would be off the hook. Or, so they thought.

But they didn't think it through. Now, as they walked level by level, slowly realizing that the day was turning sour grapes, they came to the conclusion, in bitter words, how their idea wouldn't have worked in the first place. How were they going to stash her corpse in his car if it was locked? Billy never did understand that one. As his feet ached and his blood sugar thinned and he felt dogged by uniformed personnel, his voice became strained and he called the whole idea stupid. Because if they had to break into his car for her to hide then it would be obvious to the police, and the whole case against Mr. Sorbini would never stick.

"Fine," she uttered with a curt voice and started walking to the front entrance.

"Where are you going?"

"Inside."

"What for?" he whined and started to follow slowly. "Jamie?" he called when she wouldn't answer. "Jamie!"

"What!" She stopped and turned. "Do you wanna go to jail or do you want the bastard that killed me to go to jail?"

"You mind keeping your voice down?" he said, picking up this pace, looking both ways through the garage. He didn't see anybody about. "What I want," he stressed through gnashed teeth, "is to figure out what we're going to do next, instead of reacting to the situation. I want a plan."

"You," she spoke slowly and in his face, "go wait in the car. I'm going inside and into *his* condo." She lowered her voice to a hush, "I'll leave evidence and collect evidence, and when I'm done I'll meet you and we'll find some place to dump me and you can call it in." She glared at him with opened eyes and added another point as he was considering what she'd said. "If his car's gone than that obviously means he's not home."

"But how are you going to get in to his suite?"

Jamie smirked. "Leave that to me."

She turned and started on her course again, but he reached out and grabbed her arm. She turned around angrily. "What is it now?"

Her tone threw him off, so he hesitated and stumbled, but eventually said, "Good luck."

Jamie softened, leaned in, and kissed him. He was reticent at first and just when he was starting to return the smooch she broke it off and headed toward the door. "You know," she said, turning to look at him as she went. "One day I won't have any lips. You'll miss my kisses then."

Billy didn't know how to respond to that and headed back to the car. They'd parked a couple blocks away when they arrived, on a hill that overlooked the parking garage gate and guest parking area that led to the front entrance of the building. He spied her crossing the lot as he climbed the hill, feeling uneasy about the whole thing. It'd been one thing after another since she'd shown up at his work and both their nerves were frayed pretty thin. He felt as if he wasn't able to catch his breath and as Jamie entered the building he needed to pee. But he wasn't going to leave her now. Not like this.

"Great," he muttered as he climbed the grass to his car, looking for a bush and seeing none nearby. "What's next?"

The dead girl put on her best smile when she entered. Seeing the back of the man's head as he talked with an employee she put on airs, walking with a purpose, and headed straight for the elevators.

"Excuse me?" a mature male voice rang out behind her. "Can I help you with something?

Jamie stopped and turned, looking down her sunglasses. "Charles?"

The graying gentleman did a double take, not recognizing the woman in her shabby attire. "Ms. Lund?"

"Good to see you to. Been awhile." She smiled her greeting, turned, and resumed her course.

He stammered like she knew he would. "Can you hold on a minute? Ms. Lund, can, can you please wait?"

Tony liked to flash the chicks he brought home to the staff. He had done it several times with Jamie when she first started visiting the condo. He introduced her to the manager, an intelligent man in his late fifties, who had charm and grace beyond his station. Tony told her that if ever she needed anything to go to Charles. He knew everything that went on in the building. He made it seem like a big deal at the time, stroking the manager's prominence, as well as his own ego and inflated self-importance. In the last month of her life, Jamie had gotten to know more about Charles than Tony ever had. She took the time to speak with him when she passed through the lobby.

Jamie preyed upon the manager's reputation, knowing that he would have seen Tony with other women in her absence, and in his duties as concierge to his residents she hoped to exploit the situation. "Yes," she inquired with a hint of annoyance laced with concern.

"I'll need to contact Mr. Sorbini's suite to see if he's expecting you."

It was a very nice way of saying I have to inform the bastard you're dating that you're on your way up so that he can get rid of the tramp he's been sleeping with. Jamie smiled wide and assuring, placing a hand over his as he picked up the house phone. "That wont be necessary. I spoke with Anthony last night before my flight."

"I'm sorry," Charles relayed with raised eyebrows. "Company policy." He began to dial.

Jamie removed her hand, acting nonchalant. "Now how's my homecoming, on our anniversary, going to be a surprise if you call up and ruin it?"

He stopped at the last number and pulled the phone away. "A surprise?" He back-peddled. "Excuse me, Ms. Lund, it's just that I haven't seen you for some time and I–"

She didn't let him finish by pleasantly adding, "There was a death in my family and I was called away. I hurried as quickly as I could so as to make the date. But with the estate and all, I barely had enough time to fly in this morning, drop off my suitcase, hit the gym, and purchase my present." She smiled coyly and winked. "So, if you don't mind I'd like to slip in, unannounced, and well…" She blushed. It took all her will and focus to bring rose to her cheeks.

"I see," said the man, hanging up. "If he is already expecting you."

"Oh," she said, pushing the envelope and playing it up. "He won't be expecting this."

She threw her head back and laughed out loud. The sexual innuendo made Charles nervous. She knew he was too dignified to respond, so she capitalized on it, telling him how good it was to be back in the city and how nice it was to see him again, playing to the man's infatuation. Jamie headed toward the elevators once more, but stopped with a flustered look.

"Drat!" she blurted out. "I seem to have left my key at home." She turned, wearing a frantic face, and walked the few steps that she'd taken away from the desk and said, "Charles, would you be a doll?"

He hesitated, wavering on protocol, so she stretched a fine "please," looking pitiful and sad. "I feel like I haven't even landed yet. I would be eternally grateful."

He softened and smiled. "Nice to have you back, Ms. Lund," and grabbed his keys, telling the Attendant in the office that he was going for a walk.

During the elevator ride up Jamie wove an elaborate lie, partially based on truth from her parents' funerals, about a fictitious Aunt who recently passed away. Charles commented how it was good to have her back, but he hoped she would get some sun, enliven the color in her cheeks with the rest of the summer. She thanked him and said she would, mentioning how Michigan had made her pale. Though she kept her sunglasses on the whole time, feeling that if he saw the pallor of her eyes he'd change his mind. Even she disliked staring into them through a mirror.

The elevator doors opened on the tenth floor, just as she recalled, and they walked the short distance to his door. It was right where she remembered. Jamie asked Charles to be quiet, knowing that Tony wasn't home, but fulfilling the ruse. He smiled and told her again how nice it was to see her. Jamie felt that he genuinely meant it and a bit of guilt rode her icy cold veins. She'd never overtly used anybody in the manner she just had. Charles left the door opened a crack and moved back to the elevator with a whisper.

Jamie held the door handle, smiled once more at the manager, and slipped inside. She immediately closed the door behind herself, and it shut with a soft click. She leaned against it. Ambient light, streaming from half-closed blinds and partially opened curtains created a soft shade to his place. It was exactly how she remembered. Though, there was a new scent in the air. A lingering perfumed aroma. *Loni.*

She listened and looked up ahead. The place was quiet and empty. She crossed the hall into the living room. The paintings he had of women and cars hung up on the wall in a faux 80's styled glam just looked tacky and cheap now. They weren't elegant or rich as she had once thought. The bastard stroked his ego with cheese. The white tiger skin rug under the glass coffee table didn't look expensive and masculine as she had thought. It was nouveau riche, tacky, and heartless. Jamie despised the memory of having sex with him on it in front of the fireplace. At the time it seemed romantic with the flames glowing, incense imbuing the air, candles lit, and an opened bottle of Pinot Noir.

He talked of his family in Jersey and growing up as a teen in the city and she told him about her Mom and Dad and living without them. She thought they connected then, bare-naked on the floor, entwined and talking. She bit the inside of her lower lip in adjunct frustration and moved to take care of business.

Jamie planned on leaving a few strands of hair on and under that ridiculous bleached rug and scraping her arm along the edge of the glass tabletop to dust off a few necrotic skin cells for the city's crime lab to discover. She started touching things at random, mostly anything with glass, to leave very identifiable fingerprints. She noticed the ashtray on the mantle and stuck a few cigarette butts in her pocket. *Nothing like finding these at the crime scene, eh?*

She was turning to move into his bathroom to leave more hair, skin, and fingerprints, as well as, snag some of his hair from a brush when she got a disturbing sight. Tony, it appeared, wasn't away from the condo, cruising around in his fifty thousand-dollar car. Someone else was driving it, so they both startled each other unexpectedly. He was coming out of the bedroom, wearing a pair of slacks and his bathrobe with no slippers or shirt. She was crossing the living room with her sunglasses moved to the top of her head.

He recognized her immediately, though he didn't quite believe it. Even though his boss, Aaron Scopelliti, had chewed him a new asshole about the chick showing up at his place, Tony didn't buy it. He'd watched the light leave her eyes when he strangled her to death. She never made a sound as they loaded her up into the trunk of the Beamer, or when he pulled her out and carried her to the side of the bridge and set her on the broken concrete rail. She didn't even gasp or squeal as he tossed her dead ass into the water. So Tony didn't really think that Aaron was altogether right in busting his balls over lousing the kill. Ordering him to murder his girlfriend had been hard enough, but saying that the bitch had showed up at his place on the beach, and broken in, and that Tony was a "fucked up ingrate" just hurt his pride. It wasn't kosher. But seeing her here now, when he never thought to see her again, Tony began to understand Aaron's hostile approach.

"Didn't I kill you already?"

"You tried."

"Well," he uttered with a long pause. "Guess I'm going to have to try harder."

He advanced on her position, but she fainted right. He dodged to cover her, but she moved back and he grabbed her arm. Tony backhanded her across the mouth. In the memory of that same sort

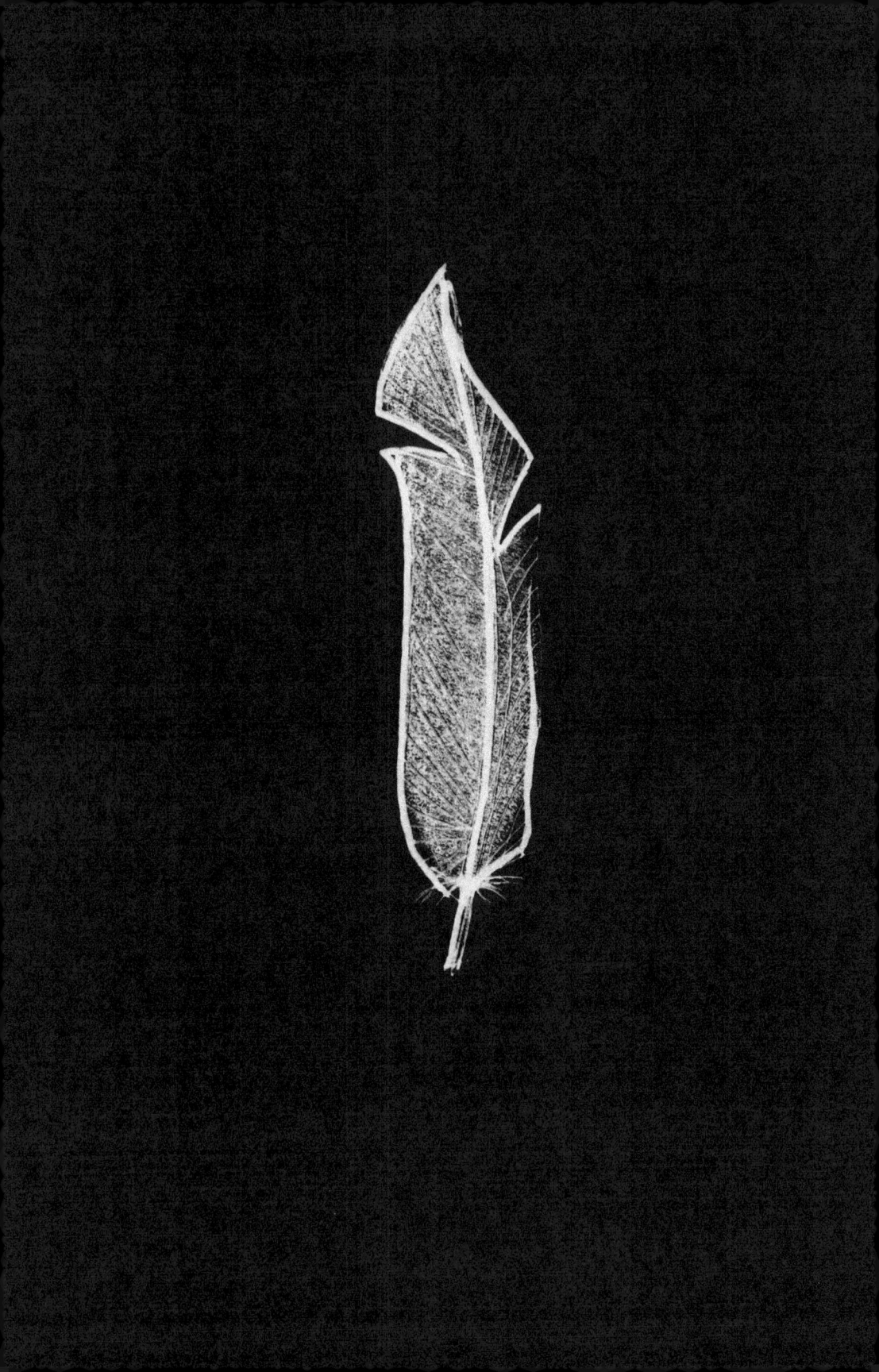

of hit, a little over a week ago, it stung. But Jamie hardly felt it now. Falling across the loveseat she said, "Is that all you got? Big man like—"

He hit her again and shut her up. Jamie stumbled against the wall. "You hit like a sissy," she teased.

Tony pulled back and punched. Jamie ducked under it and he put a hole through the plaster. As she scrambled to get away he reared his arm backwards knocking her in the head with his elbow. It sent her crashing through the glass top of the coffee table.

Jamie covered her face as she went down, but her arms and sleeves got cut. She rolled onto her back as he descended upon her and kicked out, nailing him between the legs. Tony buckled with a hard groan and fell to his knees, cutting his chin on a piece of glass. Jamie scooted back and stood, laughing at how weak the man appeared.

"Why ain't you dead?" asked Tony through spittle and clenched teeth, mixing with the blood on his chin, feeling a sharp pain in his gut and frustration boiling his veins.

"You don't get it, do you?" She moved her hair out of her face; never realizing how a few black strands fell from between her fingers onto the carpet near the fireplace. "You already killed me once. You can't do it again."

He rose to his feet, legs a bit shaken, as she spoke, not buying her bullshit. She was trying to mess with his head. He couldn't let her do that. He couldn't let any broad do that to him or he'd become a liability. Aaron had made that clear the other day. Jamie saw his aura crackling with hard reds and rich oranges, broken and suffering under midnight blue hairline fissures. He was outlined in white, like a chalk diagram. She didn't see it before, but she could see it now. He was broken and unbalanced. He swung at her and she ducked. His momentum sent him spinning, so she laughed.

"You're really pathetic."

He swung again and missed. Jamie took a couple steps back, finding him nothing but a cruel joke. He moved to hit her again, but she fired off a punch. Unfortunately, he caught it and spun her around, trapping her behind her own arms. He pulled them against her chest tightly.

"Dead, huh?" he whispered in her ear and then threw her face down on the edge of the couch. "We can fix that."

He whipped the cloth belt off his bathrobe and jammed his knee into her back before she could get up. He wrestled for her arms, eventually capturing them, and tied her wrists as hard and tight as he could behind her back. Then he flipped her over and lazily moved her oblong against the width of the cushions.

He stared at her, breathing heavy with an ache in his balls. "You think you're dead now, you just wait."

Jamie kept her lips locked. He wiped the blood off his chin and rattled a forefinger at her, telling her in his macho-bully way not to move as he stepped into the kitchen. Jamie surveyed the damage that they'd caused and grinned. It couldn't have been better for her and Billy than if she had planned it. The entire room was a swathing mess of convincing evidence. Though, the only drawback she saw at the moment was that she had to get back to Billy for the rest of the plan to unfold. She felt confident that she would be able to figure something out until she saw Tony marching toward her with the knife.

He didn't hesitate. He stabbed her just below the sternum, all the way to the hilt. Jamie didn't flinch, cry out, or bleed. He looked into her eyes as he did when he strangled her, when all she could think of was *why*. Now, it was her turn to witness confusion and fear wash over his facial features, as he didn't see any reaction from the girl. He was even more dismayed when he pulled out the knife and it was bone dry and she didn't start oozing red. He took a step back and looked down at the knife. Jamie stared at the slice in her shirt. *More evidence.* She would have sighed if breath fueled her lungs, but it didn't, so she looked up at the man who just tried to murder her twice.

He cocked his head to the side at her, wrinkling his brow, and before she could say anything he stabbed her again. He had a strange look on his face, like a kid with a science kit. He pulled the knife out, looked at it, and then looked at her, and then stabbed her again. He chuckled and grinned, gloating.

"So, I guess I got it right the first time."

"Almost," Jamie corrected him as he stood back, a few feet away from her.

"Yeah," he agreed, nodding, and tossed the knife to the floor.

Pulling his cell phone from a bathrobe pocket, he flipped it open, and dialed. He leered at the dead girl, catching his breath and chuckling as mad wisps of violet rippled through his field.

"Hey," he said with a gruff voice into the phone's speaker, swathing his cut chin with his palm, glaring hard at Jamie. "Get a couple of the boys and meet me at my place." He paused with a sick, boasting laugh. "Do I have something to show you."

Jamie didn't like the look in his eye or in his aura. It was changing more violently with the calmer he got. He was teetering on madness, and for the life of her, she didn't understand why she never noticed it before.

"I don't know what you are," he said as he hung up and returned his phone to his pocket. "Or where you came from, or what you hoped to achieve today by breaking in here. But I promise you," he nestled in close to Jamie's face as she tried to move as far away from him as she could. "I'm gonna make sure you stay dead this time."

XXXIX.

"Winner of two Grammy's for best parodied song and the best air guitarist alive, Billy Kimmel!"

Boredom had made him a little silly. It started with the radio – just listening. Then it progressed to singing along to songs he knew the lyrics to and then singing along to songs that he didn't know the lyrics to until he began making up his own words, belting them out as loud as he could. Now he was fantasizing the Grammies, thanking the audience when he noticed the two guys crossing the lot to the front entrance of the condominium.

Even from way up here the guys looked big. Not muscular, or fat, tall with wide shoulders and dressed nice. Billy thought they looked animated as they headed toward the front doors, talking. He was feeling fluxed that Jamie hadn't come back yet. She should have been out of Tony's suite awhile ago. But Billy still held the fort, doing his best to give her time and space to do what she needed to do.

He thought about going in and poking around – to see what he could find. But if someone saw him then they'd be able to give his description to the police and then the men in blue would be able to place him at the scene and connect him to Tony, which would not aid him at all in clearing his name. So, he waited. He sang out of tune, and waited. Billy felt useless. A grand-prized-winning-air-guitar-fool, there simply was little he could do. All his hope was riding on the dead girl. He'd promised Hector that he was going to come in tonight and work on the cars, but the cops had probably been there already. So that was ruined. He couldn't check up on Jamie and there was no way of reaching her if something had gone wrong. *Useless. Utterly useless; just sitting around.*

After about fifteen or twenty minutes one of the beefy guys that had gone in earlier was walking fast out of the building to his car. He was tossing glances to both sides. There was something about him that caught Billy's eye, and it didn't make him feel too comfortable. He turned off the radio and watched the guy climb into his car and pull around to the curb just left of the front entrance, close to a sidewalk passage to the parking garage. The other guy was already standing outside, looking around when he pulled up. He crossed to the back door of their black sedan. Opening it, he cased the lot with a suspicious glance and waved somebody over.

Billy's jaw dropped when he saw a thin, dark-haired man leading Jamie by the arm out of a side door to the opened door of the sedan. The man threw her in and climbed in himself as the other guy got in the passenger seat. The sedan took off. As Billy fired up the Chevelle he saw the crows take to the air, a massive flock, shaking the branches, wires, and buildings where they had been rooted. *What is it about this day?* Things had gone south again. Billy cursed as he backed up, spewing dirt and gravel, wondering what had happened inside the building that had led to this.

He was shaken and nervous as he raced to the street to catch them. By the time he wound down the hill on the little two lane road and was about three car lengths behind them, he wasn't sure if he should ram them off the road or hang tight and see where they were going. When the blackbirds screamed past his windows in a flurry of feathers and thickness he knew that Jamie was making a move. He smiled and breathed a sigh of relief, watching her winged minions attack the black vehicle.

The car lurched, bobbing and weaving, but it soon righted and the air cleared as the crows flew away. Seeing them hurl their little bodies against the machine had been awesome to behold. Other drivers on the street had slowed and Billy thought the birds were going to cause the sedan to crash. But they didn't. Almost as quickly as the assault began, it was over, and Billy didn't understand why. *They should have torn the roof off!* Seeing them flee was disheartening. So, he decided to hang back and find out where they were taking her. Because whatever had made the birds disperse might be tougher for Billy to handle than he thought.

He did not have long to wait. The sedan only traveled about a mile and a half from the high-rise to a construction site where an overpass was being built. Billy watched as they pulled into the area as he continued on. He surveyed the site, and looped back around a quarter of a mile up the road. When he passed the construction zone on his second pass he noticed that they were all getting out of the vehicle and a bridge that would give him a vantage point to see what was going on.

He drove to the bridge and parked on the side of the road just before it, watching in horror as the two big guys picked up Jamie and threw her over a section of plywood into what looked like, to Billy, the makings of a block or truss-base that would one day bear the weight of the overpass. Billy looked around for anything he could do or use to stop this catastrophe. But he didn't see anything. He wished he had his phone. At least he would have been able to call the cops and have them rescue her. But Jamie had thrown it out the window.

Billy was breathing harder and was beginning to panic. As the truck backed up to the walled block he knew they were going to encase her in concrete and there was nothing he could do, except sit in the car and watch. His whole world was blackening in terror. Even the air he breathed seemed to suffocate.

Billy spied Jamie's feathery pets and wondered why they just sat around, letting these assholes bury her undead like that. He didn't understand. They practically tore his head off when he'd found her on the street the other night, but now they were quiet little monsters and Billy didn't get why they just sat there like bumps on a log. He screamed at them from the confines of his car, but it did no good. Thick gray sludge poured into the large boarded up structure from the back of the truck. Rods of rebar jutted straight out of the center of the grotesque box clawing a vacant sky. Billy felt useless. Completely and utterly, useless.

XL.

Tony wouldn't talk to her when they were alone. She was unnatural. He didn't like killing her that first time around, but decided when he was sticking the knife in and out of her like a voodoo doll that he was going to enjoy it this time around. She should have stayed dead. But Jamie never listened. That was her problem. If she would have listened to him and stayed put, like he ask her to do at the party, then he wouldn't have had to waste her. But the girl was too headstrong and thick willed. Tony chuckled when he thought about what he was going to do to her. If she didn't understand that dead was dead the first time, then she was, at least, going to have plenty of time now to learn her lesson properly.

Jamie tried to talk to him, but he ignored her. After he finished getting dressed he paced in front of her, holding the knife, eyeing her as he tried to figure out what she was. He had questions. Sure, who wouldn't in a time like this, questions were only natural. But Tony figured that it wouldn't make a difference if he asked them or not. It all boiled down to the simple commandment, "Thou Shall Not Kill." He heard it at church enough times and had eaten the wafer enough times, but Anthony Sorbini already knew killing wasn't right. He didn't need his victim telling him that, or trying to make him feel guilty about it. He'd killed lots of things in his short life from puppy dogs to people who crossed Big Aaron. This was the first time, though, that one of them had come back to visit.

In an odd way, Tony looked at it like an honor – a badge of distinction. Killing was a necessary part of the business. For Tony, it had become all about business and this little cutie had singled him out. He was feeling special. Being part of Aaron's organization was what he wanted. The money was good, the life was good, so fuck church and commandments and towing the line like all those dumb struggling sheep out there in the world, and fuck this undead girl – *she never knew well enough to listen!*

In Tony's short career, he had already made more dough than his old man in his entire working-class life. Cracking a few heads had gotten him to where he was. It wasn't pretty, but it was the bottom line. Tony wasn't going to let anyone – living or dead – get in the way of what he wanted. Life was too short to compromise.

When the brute arrived with Milo, Tony showed them both his little knife trick with the Lund Piñata. They were taken aback and Milo had to stick her himself just to make sure that it wasn't some kind of trick. It was unbelievable and Tony swore them to secrecy as he asked Milo if his cousin was still working at the site on the overpass. The sick bastard told them what he had in store for the girl and they laughed. They all laughed at Jamie and she didn't like the sound of it.

She called her birds when the boys ran off to get their car and Tony had taken her outside through the garage. They showed up later than she had hoped, attacking the car while they were on the road. She knew Billy was up the hill and hoped that he'd seen her leaving the building with the men. But it had happened so quickly that she wasn't sure if he would have seen them or not. If he had looked away, for only a moment, he could have missed them.

As the birds descended on the sedan, making it difficult for the driver to see, Tony got wise quick and leaned down at Jamie and told her to "make 'em stop or so help me I'll kill her. I'll slit her throat from ear to ear and watch her bleed out through a red smile."

She knew exactly whom he was talking about. *Loni.* The look in his eyes, the calmness in his voice, and the wicked energy of his aura weren't necessary to convince her that he meant every word of it. The bastard was incapable of love. He'd kill her for sport. He'd kill her for vile pleasure. He had murdered Jamie for less. So she called off the attack, dreading the harrowing circumstances that she had not only gotten herself into, but that Billy was now suffering through as well. Her ex-boyfriend didn't do anything except love her and try to help her and she'd continuously screwed up his life. She wanted to look behind them and see if he was following them up the road, but she also didn't want to give it away that she was with somebody else. Loni's life was in danger simply because she dated the creep. Putting more people in harm's way wasn't going to help the situation any, and she knew it.

When they pulled into the construction yard and he told her to get out, Jamie scoured the surrounding landscape, trying to avoid being noticed and causing suspicion. But she didn't see any sign of Billy anywhere. All she could do was hope. He had been there so far. Tony sent Milo to go get his cousin and a concrete truck to get this thing moving along. He kept saying how he had a date later on. Jamie knew he was toying with her, delighting in the fact that he was screwing her former best friend.

She hated him. Now, after all this time and deadly array of events, Jamie hated the sound of his voice and the look of his face. She wished she had never met him. But it was too late. Everything was too late, and it looked like she was going to be buried after all. Not the funeral she had imagined, or teased Billy about, but a funeral nonetheless. Her eyes kept hitting the scenery, but she saw no hide or hair of him. *C'mon, Billy, c'mon.*

"Well," Tony chimed with enthusiasm "here's where you and I part." He bent down to look at her squarely in the eyes and grabbed her jowls, squeezing her face to make her lips twitch. "Have any last words?" He waited a short bit. "No? Good, 'cause I hate long goodbyes and this one was definitely longer than it needed to be."

He signaled for his men to throw her over the planks and laughed when he heard how hard she hit the ground. He banged on the plywood and shouted, "You take care now. It's been real. I'll tell Loni that you said hi."

Tony told the big man and Milo to stand guard and make sure that she didn't get out of it. He wanted her gone this time and it was up to the two of them to make sure that she didn't escape. He informed the two men that he was taking their car to meet Aaron and deliver an update and that he would send someone back for them later tonight after the concrete had hardened. The guys didn't like it, but he was higher up the food chain than either of them, so really what could they do about it? Tony was leaving the site in the black sedan when concrete began to pour from the top of the wood.

Jamie stood up. She could feel the crows nearby, watching. She knew the men were still there, standing outside of her cell. She just hoped and prayed that Billy had caught on and was close by. She thought about what was going to happen to her before it did. Tony had been a little wild with the kitchen knife at his condo and had sliced her abdomen up pretty good. She thought that if she stood in such a way so as to keep the cuts closed that she might be able to weather the hardening liquid until it got a bit mushy, before she could move around without fear of one of her wounds opening up enough for concrete to seep in. The thought of being stuck to this spot for an eternity terrified her, but she needed to be strong now. There wasn't a whole lot she could do, except pray.

When the thick, ugly goo began sloshing around her feet with wet clomp-slushy sounds she was thankful that the spout wasn't immediately over her head. She remained as motionless and as close to the boards as possible while the liquid composite slowly climbed up her body, pressing snugly against her. She stood in a rectangle cavity of dug earth and mounted metal bars shooting straight up. Compressed by four wooden walls, Jamie felt the concrete's awful weight and was deeply afraid. She didn't know how long Horus's gift was gonna last or if she was eventually going to revert to how Billy had found her in the alley. The cold goo wouldn't stop convalescing around her feet. *Is this my real death? Is this the end of the journey?*

The idea of being encased in a pillar of roadway was not appealing at all. Jamie still felt that there were things that she needed to do, things that she wanted to accomplish. But previous experience had taught her that life didn't care what plans were made or what dreams remained unfulfilled. Death was an unexpected trapdoor that opened whenever and wherever of its own choosing. Inch by inch, the forming mortar slurred around her legs. It pushed her a few inches inward, away from the plywood walls. Jamie didn't dare struggle against it for fear of opening her cuts. She wanted to be closer to the edge for when the boards were removed. It was marching up her belly. There was nothing she could do. She felt useless in this, her most dire need. If she cracked open and the soft liquid slipped inside and hardened she was never going to be able to leave this place in one piece. She would remain forever apart of the concrete block.

It was difficult for Jamie not to move. Her hate for Anthony Sorbini increased with every layer of the gray sludge. When one truck had been exhausted of its bounty another one was sent for. Jamie could already feel it hardening around her feet and ankles. It was a slow creep. Milo banged on the side of the plywood.

"How you doin' in there? Comfy?" He laughed, a sick, vicious tease.

Jamie clenched her jaw tightly, keeping a rebuttal to herself. The molding liquid was thick against her neck. It was all she could do to remain still. She never did like tight places. Wasn't claustrophobic, but the thought of being buried alive...or as alive as she was gonna get, was terrifying. An eternity of darkness, caged within your own dying flesh, locked in place, unable to move or scream! She stared at the plank that he had whacked with intense rancor, focusing her will.

By the time the second truck had unloaded its full cargo, Jamie was forced to close her eyes and mouth, seeing nothing but that god awful eternal black. She had no idea how far over her head they were going to pour and felt a bit of the ugly mush seep into her right ear. Entombed in the gray sludge, the dead girl seethed with a raging spleen and pitied them all if she were to ever escape!

XLI.

Billy was horrified as he watched the trucks fill the base container with Jamie in it. He was so upset he had to leave the confines of his car, pacing heatedly. He wished the two goons would leave so he could race down there and do something. But they just stood around talking. Billy was having a hard time with it all. As dusk fell with night clinging to its heels he was exhausted and drained, sitting outside on the grass leaning against the grill of the Chevelle.

Just after dark, and after all the workmen had left, a car pulled into the lot. Billy watched it intently. It crackled over well-worn earth, pulling slowly alongside the two men. Another big fellow got out of the car. Though this man was heavy by fat more than by muscle. He walked with a bit of a limp and obviously knew the other guys. Billy bade them to get in the car, but the new guy just pulled out a couple paper bags, delivering dinner. Billy sighed as he watched them eat, and though hungry, he felt he'd throw up if he let anything pass his lips. Despite his strain to stay awake and keep watch he fell asleep.

Car tires buzzed behind him, singing street lullabies. He woke a few hours later with unremembered dreams and surveyed the construction site. A smile and a bit of energy fueled his steps as he got to his feet, not seeing anyone below. Rounding his vehicle to the driver's side, a set of headlights caught him in the eye as a car pulled off the road behind him. He shielded his eyes and face. Though when the car's engine stopped, high beams still lit him up like a stage. Then the red and blue lights began to turn. Billy's whole heart sank. The driver's door on the police cruiser opened and out stepped an uniformed officer.

"Evening," the shadowed voice said.

"Hello," replied Billy, shaking quietly where he stood.

"Everything all right?" asked the cop as he walked into the light.

"Yeah," answered Billy. "I was just about to leave."

The cop looked in the windows of the Chevelle as he strolled up. "I rolled passed here about an hour ago and saw you on the side of the road. Thought you might require assistance when I noticed you were still here." The man's eyes stared directly into Billy's lit, uncomfortable face.

He felt the policeman's gaze and smiled. "Yeah, I was tired and pulled off the road. Fell asleep, Officer. Sorry to be a bother; just thought it'd be safer to grab a nap than to be on the road."

"Can't you do that at home?"

"Bug Bomb," Billy added quickly, thinking about the last time that he fumigated his place.

The cop just stood there. For a long minute he looked around, weighing the value of filling out paperwork vs. going home. "You leaving now?" he asked after deciding he liked the idea of a home-cooked meal with his wife better than citing this guy or digging deeper to find something that would keep him from being where he wanted to be.

"Yeah; just about to head out," Billy told him and the Officer issued him a good night.

Sitting in the Chevelle, he waited for the cop to pass and the high beams to move out of his eyes and mirrors. Though, as Billy was about to pull onto the road he tossed a glance down to the yard below and saw the three goons poking their heads out from behind the large block. They must have been wondering what the light show was all about and crawled out from the other side of the wood panels to gaze up the hill. Now Billy noticed the black Lincoln Town Car that had arrived earlier a few yards away from the men. He guessed correctly that he must have been a little groggy not to have noticed it when he woke up excited, guessing wrong that they were gone.

He took to the road. Driving usually calmed him if he had a worry, but tonight it did not. He pulled into a Burger King and ordered a sandwich, fries, and coke. He ate half the burger, all the french fries, and drained the coke to the barren ice. He used the restaurant's bathroom to take a piss, wash his hands, and splash his face with water. He glared at his reflection in the mirror – *A Wanted Man*. It amazed him to no end how he could be so close to the cop earlier, with a warrant out for his arrest, for either body-snatching or murder or both, and come away unscathed. It was something, alright.

He thought about everything that he'd been through with Jamie since she had arrived. There had been many close calls and strange occurrences that tested his faith. But despite them all, God's will won out. He stared hard into his reflection, both hands gripping the sink, truthfully aware of how close he was to dumping her body after she hadn't woke once he had stolen her from the morgue. But before he could grab the tarp from the trunk, the one that he specifically placed in there to wrap her body up, she came alive again and rescued him from Johnny Law. Billy stood up. He ran a wet hand through his hair and inhaled deeply. *This is just the new thing. Have faith.*

He drove back to the site with more confidence in resolving the situation than when he had left. The goons were still there, but by midnight they packed it in and drove off. Once the coasts were clear, Billy pulled into the construction yard and parked behind the large concrete base, so as to be less conspicuous to passing cars. He moved to the trunk and pulled out a crow bar. He closed the trunk's lid with a hard thunk, eyeing that unused tarp.

He moved quickly to the block and shouted for Jamie at the nearest corner. He had no idea where she was or where he should begin, so he circled the rectangle calling out her name unaware of the dense acoustic properties of cement and that his feeble shouts fell unheard to the dry ground. When he banged a corner board loose on the backside of the block with the tire iron, Jamie heard it. The hits reverberated through the thickening composite like a dull wave and she knew somebody was out there.

She couldn't move. Jamie thought that once the slump began to harden she might be able to wiggle back to the corner boards without opening her abdomen too much, but when she tried she found pockets of softer liquid contained and surrounded by harder patches.

The block was drying unevenly and those parts that fell first had started to mold around her quicker than the top layers. So, as the concrete hardened she started rotating her body in tiny, miniscule movements, working against the edge of the cement to push it back from her body as it formed so that she was surrounded by a thin pocket of air, instead of being flush to the construction material.

On most parts of her body she was successful at creating a bit of space between her and her prison. It took a lot of patience and will to isolate sections of herself like that. Her head was an altogether different matter. The liquid wound down to her scalp, weaving between her once luscious hair and saturated the hood of her jacket. Her clothing wasn't a great barrier. It soaked up the water from the mixture, but it did aid her in creating her tiny unbreathable space.

When the first clanks reached her location from Billy whacking a section of block, Jamie knew that he had found her. She struggled at what to do. It would take him a week to chip away at the block, piece by piece, searching in vain for her as it continued to harden to stone. So she concentrated, reaching out to her birds. They stood by her, being an odd spectacle throughout the strange day. Workers noticed the birds hanging around, as well as the two Italians in suits. They didn't like it much, but it didn't matter. They knew who ran the site and knew enough to keep their heads down, noses clean, and not ask questions.

Jamie housed within the birds, connecting her spirit to theirs. She saw Billy through their eyes working hard on a distant corner. It was dark and what remained of the moon was high in the sky. The blackbirds took flight without Billy noticing, but soon he was forced to stop what he was doing when the crows began circling the concrete block in a wide, maddening arc. Then they gathered around the northeastern tip of the cube.

He stepped away from the mass, peering queerly at the birds. They looked back at him too. Billy's hands were sore from the blow back by the few hits that he'd made with the metal bar. He breathed heavy, but steadily, and smirked when one of the crows began pecking at a particular spot. He moved to where they had shown him and he put his mouth against the wood for amplification, and yelled that he was coming.

He pried the 2x4 frame off this section of boards and pried the plywood planks away on both sides of the corner to give him maneuvering room, and begin smacking the edge. The concrete was hardening, but not hard. Each hit tore up his bare hands. His forearms ached and it still took more power and exertion to chip away the corner than what he could stand.

"I'll be back," he yelled at the block and went searching around the yard.

He needed something better than the crow bar. It just wasn't cutting it. Billy couldn't handle absorbing each hit like that forever. He feared it would shake his bones loose. But near a stack of rebar he found a sledgehammer. Billy tossed the tire iron by his car, picked up the heavy mallet, and walked back to the block of stone with the full intention of tearing the whole thing down.

Jamie felt his first hit with the hammer in her back. She smiled as far as she could in the tiny space between her chin and an impression of her mouth. Her hero had come. It only took a few solid blows with the blunt end of the sledge and Billy was looking at the bottom of her jacket. She wasn't at all far in, only a few inches. It gave him hope and once an area had been opened the rest around her legs and hips broke away pretty easily.

He laid a hand on her side and told her not to worry as he chipped the block away. Jamie wasn't worried. He'd come. Despite all the odds, Billy was there, and she hadn't suffered any irreparable damage. But that was before he got to her head. Freeing her arms and the side of her face had been difficult enough, but getting her head out of the muck was proving challenging. Her hair was a matted tomb encased within the mold. Billy tried working at it slowly once he freed the area around her eyes and nose, pulling out an uncomfortable looking nostril impression.

He asked her if she was all right once he'd cleared her talk box, but all she said was "get me outta here." Working diligently around her head was proving more tedious than what patience Jamie had left. Gritting her teeth she pulled. Billy yelled at her to stop as strands by trapped strands of her once long black hair ripped from the scalp. The dead girl screamed into the violent night as the birds took to the air, beating their wings. Their mad fluttering flap pulsed through Billy's blood like a surge.

The hood on Jamie's jacket caught her from leaving after a small tube in her ear broke. Hastily, she tore off the thin garment and

poked two fingers down her ear canal. She pulled and wretched a tiny barrel of concrete out of her right ear. It had flesh attached to it and she tossed it to the ground.

The poor girl was a mess. Chunks of block held firm to bits of clothing and she was covered in dust, looking torn and frayed, sunken and sallow. Billy asked her to get in the car, but she wouldn't have it. Angry, she simply said, "This ends tonight," and started walking.

"Jamie," he called, but she kept plodding on. "Jamie, lets talk about this."

"I'm done talking, Billy. I'm going to do what I should have done in the first place."

"What's that?" he asked, becoming afraid. "Are you going to kill him? Is that what you're going to do?" She wouldn't answer. "C'mon," he threw at her back, a flurry of winged vengeance flying above her. "You're better than that. Jamie, you're better than that!"

But she knew she wasn't, and she'd been thinking about it for hours. Perhaps even longer than that, though most recently she'd been fantasizing about killing Tony as the drying pavement oozed around her, shutting her in. She wasn't going to let anything stop her now. The man had killed her. He threatened to kill her best friend. He'd stabbed her as if she was a pincushion, and he'd buried her with hopes of never seeing her again. *How unromantic can one man be?!* Nothing else fueled Jamie's obsessive afterlife than feeling Anthony Sorbini succumb to her hands and seeing the light in his eyes fade and dim – just as he had done to her. *Fairs fair,* the dead girl chimed, *fair's fair.*

Concrete dust spooled off her as she marched with violent, cold steps to the waiting tower and Tony's doom. To Billy's horror Jamie didn't stop to cross the highway. She just barreled into traffic, nearly causing a dozen car crashes. Tires screeched and front ends dipped as drivers slammed on brakes and cut other people off in different lanes. Jamie's blackbirds swooped down and surrounded her, a thin barrier of feathers. Before Billy climbed back into the Chevelle and revved it up she'd crossed the dual lane street and climbed over the hill, disappearing as one black mass.

Billy was agitated and nervous, afraid of what she was going to do, and he almost forgot the crow bar when he left. But he'd learned his lesson with the clipboard, throwing both the sledgehammer and the bar into the trunk on top of the unused tarp. This way the birds were the only witnesses to him freeing the corpse and he was sure they weren't going to squeal on him. He raced back to the high-rise as quickly as he could without fear of getting stopped for a ticket. It would really mess things up to get arrested now when he had to stop her from making a big mistake.

He pulled into the guest parking area as the dead girl was crossing the road that ran in front of the building. She was heading up the neatly trimmed and manicured lawn when he pulled to the backside of the lot and got out of his car. More crows had joined her as she made her way to the building. It was a fearful sight.

"Jamie," he called to her over the noise of wings and caws. "Don't do this. Let's stick to the plan. We can still make it work. C'mon, Jamie. Jamie?"

But the dead girl just stared at him with hard eyes and told him to go home. Billy's heart was a lead weight as he watched her enter the building and her army of feather-companions drive as a single, thick line around the condominium. They circled the building in crazy arches, a wide black wedge against the night, illuminated by half a moon. Billy leaned against his car terrified of what she was going to do, unable to leave the spot.

She walked through the front doors of the high-rise on a death march. Spirals of concrete dust wafted off her as she made a beeline to the elevators. To the receptionist on duty, the stranger looked scary as hell. Most of her hair was missing or braided in shucks of rock. She was thin and gaunt. Bits of stone and dust and concrete fell off her as she walked through the lobby ignoring the young woman's customary calls and pleas. When Jamie disappeared in the lift, the frightened receptionist called the police.

Jamie stared at her mortified reflection in the polished metal of the elevator doors. She looked every inch the zombie that she was. *Real horror show now!* And that made her want to kill Tony even more painfully than she had imagined this afternoon while encased in the platform base of an overpass pillar. Nothing could soothe her ache now or stop the inevitable. Her hollowed out impression on a bit of block down the lane was the headstone that Tony had carved for himself. His actions had wrought his own end.

The elevators opened and the soft ding chimed. Jamie marched to his door, number1033, and kicked it down with one solid blow. The door splintered like balsa wood around the pinched lock and crippled frame. It tore from its hinges and clattered down the small hallway, knocking down tacky prints and busting glass. It made an awful sound, loud enough to wake the dead!

The dead girl moved inside and quickly crossed the expensive cubicle and swung open the French styled doors that lead onto the balcony. Jamie turned around just as Mr. Fabulous broke from his room in a pair of boxing shorts holding a gun.

"You?" he exclaimed with real surprise as he raised the weapon.

"No," Jamie informed, "I brought some friends."

She pushed her arms forward, the master conductor, the focal point of her winged orchestra, and signaled the crescendo. Her army of birds flew powerfully through both opened tiers of the doorway into the room, filling the space with angry black. They circled Anthony Sorbini in an ominous rush, clawing at his pathetic pink flesh. He fired wildly trying to get them away until an unkind beak plucked the tiny firearm out of his hand. He screamed and hollered in pain as her birds worked him over. He thrust about. He tried to run, but it did no good. Tiny scratches and needle-like beaks poked and tore into him, unmercifully.

Jamie watched with a sick smile twisting her face until a womanly scream broke through the room with vicious terror! Her concentration fell short and a few birds thinned. Through bodies, beaks, and wings Jamie saw Loni, naked, save for a bed sheet, standing in the thrown light of the bedroom. She was repulsed and screaming. The young blond woman caught sight of the dead girl and yelled at her to make it stop, to make the wild birds go away, but then something clicked in her eyes and she calmed down a bit. Peering through the dense air of flapping bodies and Tony balled up on the floor crying, she called the dead girl by her earthly name, saying, "Jamie?"

Enraged and empowered, the dead girl just stared at Loni for several immeasurable beats of the live girl's heart. Seeing her now, so close and vulnerable, Jamie lost bits of hate. Nothing but sorrow crashed within her for the girl she once ran with. "Get dressed," the zombie ordered, "and get the fuck out."

It might have been the mean look in Jamie's eyes, or the room packed with violent descending crows, or her boyfriend whimpering on the floor, scratched up and bloodied, that made Loni run from the room in nothing but a sheet. Whatever it was, Jamie was glad that she was gone, because she didn't want her to see what was going to happen next. Her pets dispersed. Took roosts on the furniture or flew back out the opened doors. They'd made a mess of his place. It pleased Jamie to no end, the shambles and destruction she had caused. It was all payback for the life he had destroyed.

Jamie had not willed the birds to kill him. To hurt and to maim, yes. But to kill him, no, that was her charge - her pleasure and act. She stood over her killer, watching him cry and beg to make it stop and felt no remorse or pity for the man. She walked over to his lacerated and bloodied body and picked him up by the throat. She stared into his cold, dead eyes with her cold, dead eyes. He muttered and whined. He simpered and bled. His aura was even shaken and bruised. Jamie gritted her teeth and reared her hand back, forming her fingers into talons, poised to strike her deathblow when Horus's words reverberated around her decaying gray matter.

"Pay it with the heart. Not the flesh."

Tony waited for it. He was too weak to fight against it. Every inch of him ached and was sore. He shook painfully and wondered why the ghost paused. He thought Jamie teased him cruelly, so he egged her on, calling her names, begging the vengeful spirit to end his fierce misery.

Upon reflection, Jamie would never know why she did what she did or how the idea sprang to life in the folds of her dead mind, but it was clear. With her arm stretched back ready to strike, she pushed her hard-fingered hand, with fingernails sharp and eager, into Tony's aura. It felt like plunging her digits into a warm stream. It thrummed and moved around her hand as if alive. She felt the center of his being. She felt the cracks in his soul. In an intimate way she was guided by some deep knowing. Jamie began to realign his fissures and broken essence. She righted the wrong in him, and he wept.

Such a great torrent of tears poured from his eyes, the likes of

which had never been. An agony worse than any pain inflicted upon his searing flesh ripped through the gutter and valley of his emotions. It burned his soul. Jamie bent and moved his karmic stream, twisted and fixed lifetimes of ill acts of godlessness. Tony felt every tug and pull. He crumbled at the invisible yanks and plucks of his spiritual baggage, becoming buried by the knowledge, weight, and depths of his sins. By fixing his aura, Jamie had broken the man.

XLII.

Billy was thunderstruck when the mammoth murder of crows had disappeared into the side of the building. He couldn't believe what was happening. He shook his head and paced, but he didn't leave his car. When three police units cruised up to the front door of the high-rise, Billy held his ground. Right or wrong, he felt he had to wait for her. He couldn't abandon her now and leave her to a fate that he was hoping to avoid. He was on edge and biting his nails as the birds began to flitter out the side of the building. He felt that whatever had happened inside must be over even though he didn't see Jamie outside anywhere.

Through blinking lights, glass doors, and the distance of the lot Billy noticed Loni talking with a policeman. She looked haggard as she hung by the front entrance wearing nothing but a bed sheet. Other residents were moving about too. Jamie had shook the whole building awake. The front of it pulsed blue and red. A fire truck joined the fray and Billy was sure that they had found her, that the authorities had confiscated the dead girl. He watched her little blackbirds for any sign as to what might be going on, any clues as to where she might be now. But they only appeared to be waiting as he was doing. A good portion of the crows had flown away and Billy wondered if this core group that remained had been with her since it had begun. There was no way of knowing, of course, but he wished he could know.

Their coal black eyes and jet-black wings were frightful and unapproachable. They seemed to stare through him rather than at him and Billy wasn't sure if he glinted flakes of blood on their talons or not.

After a good deal of time had passed and things seemed to take some regular course with legal utilities, Billy spied Jamie walking around the small parking lot, coming out of the parking garage. Her movements were casual, so as to not arouse suspicion. He was immensely glad to see her again.

Jamie had exited the same way that she had entered Tony's suite. But instead of taking the elevator back down to the lobby she had taken the stairs, and wound her way through the building to the parking garage. She left Tony crying into his own slobber, a bloody mess on the ruined floor, but he was alive. She had not killed him. By far, she'd done something much worse. A couple cops were coming up the stairwell as she was going down. She heard them below and got off on the sixth floor. She dipped around the corner of the hall just in case they heard her exit, and waited until she thought they had passed before she continued her jaunt to the parking level entrance. From there it was pretty easy. Everyone was focused on the front of the building, and much to her surprise, she saw Billy waiting for her. It made her smile, but she didn't want him to know how happy she was that he had stayed, so she hung back in the garage between some cars until she could wipe the smirk off her face.

Jamie sat on the cool concrete of the garage floor and leaned against somebody's sports car and was pleased when she didn't set off any alarms. She knew who her killer was now and why he had murdered her, and she'd confronted him about it. Quietly, Jamie prayed that her mission and time on this earth would end. She hoped Horus would descend from where ever he was, or pop out from somebody's gas guzzling automobile and take her away from all the cop lights... and even Billy. Jamie felt tired to her core, as if her soul was dragging. Messing with Tony's aura had made her weary.

She wanted to go home. To that place beyond the veil of stars and tears where poets danced with muses and flowers were adorned. Jamie wanted her death. It had come, but she'd heard only half its song. Her eternal slumber was less than restful. Jamie spied Billy through a sea of cars and garish light. He'd been so much to her in life, and in death. She felt blessed to have known him. He made her a better person. She knew that now.

But the man with the deep-set eyes, alluring tan olive skin, and magnetic charisma was no where to be found. Jamie was left alone in her deathly haunt, with no gods descending to take her away. She watched her brave, young man fuss over the happenings in the building and began to feel a little cruel at keeping him waiting when he'd been through so much and sacrificed so much already. So Jamie left the confines of her hiding place and walked over to where he waited with the car. She could tell he wanted to ask her a million things. His eyes were bent to the heavens and creased with worry, but she simply said, "Let's go home."

Billy didn't argue with her. It sounded like the best plan he'd heard all day, and moved into the driver's seat. Inside the Chevelle, he didn't grill her about it. He knew she'd tell him what happened sooner or later. He could wait a little longer to hear it. The only thing that mattered now was simply getting home. It felt like years and miles away. He drove past the screaming lights and line of public work vehicles as slowly as he could while the dead girl ducked below the window frame in the front seat. As he pulled onto the road Billy gave his lovely machine a little gas, eased it into gear, and turned on the radio.

XLIII.

"You know, I heard hair grows for about a year after you die."

"Really?"

"Yeah," Billy replied. "Heard it on one of those Nat Geo shows. Secrets of the Grave kind of thing. So, don't worry. It'll grow back."

Jamie pulled her knees in tighter to her chest. The murky water swished and gurgled around her legs. Billy sat behind her in the bath clipping chunks of concrete out of the last remnants of her hair.

"I must look pretty frightening."

"Oh," mused Billy. "I've seen worse."

Jamie turned and looked at him. "Better not." She rolled her shoulder and held out her arm. Her elbow was a gnarled point. "I can see my bones sticking out. It's gross."

Billy had already noticed her thin condition, but looked at her sunken skin to appease the girl. "Yeah," he added to throw her off the path to a bad mood. "You remember that time after Mickey Donovan's party, senior year?"

"Sort of. I was kinda drunk."

"Yes you were," he said as he dunked the cloth and wiped her head and neck. "But you should have seen yourself the following morning."

"Aww," Jamie chuckled, "that ain't nice."

"I'm not kidding," he encouraged. "You looked like ass. Like unwashed, greasy, rancid ass."

He laughed at his joke and the dead girl turned around, flicking him with bath water. "You think you're funny."

"I am funny."

He turned her back around and snipped off the last uneven end. A pebble of block fell into the water. It was attached to a frayed, cut clump of hair. Billy fished it out and set it on the toilet seat with the scissors.

"Do I smell any better?" she regretfully asked.

"A little funky, but nothing we can't handle."

Jamie pressed her chin to her knees as Billy ran the wash cloth over her back slowly. He was careful not to get any liquid in her bullet wound or those knife cuts that Tony had decorated her body with. He was stunned to learn of the stab wounds. A few of them went all the way through. The knife had left thin lines that parted open when Jamie moved this way or that. The edges of the through-and-through gunshot were now hard. He was not at all unsympathetic now as to wanting the bastard dead, though he was still glad she didn't do it.

He had already cleaned her up pretty well earlier and they drained most of the soiled water after. So, they were only sitting in a shallow bowl clipping the remains of her tattered head. Billy had set aside his old Ace bandage from an old football injury. He thought Jamie could wrap her stomach with it to help keep her together. He asked her to turn the water back on, to fill the tub up, and she did. It blasted hot liquid, pounding the front end of the tub with a soothing sound.

"What do you think is going to happen next?" he asked as he grabbed the plastic wrap, because it had been on his mind since they'd gotten home.

Jamie sat quiet longer than he liked, thinking about everything that went through her head as she exited the high-rise. She had thought she would disappear and fly away as she had before. But that didn't happen. Billy still had a warrant out for his arrest and she wasn't sure if what she did to Tony would do anything to clear his name or not. Though she had to admit, she'd gathered and left quite a lot of physical evidence during their fray. The cops that had showed up to rescue Tony were going to have a field day of forensics. But at this point in the game she still felt that it was a gamble, so she answered, "I don't know."

Billy had her sit erect as he dried her off and wound the roll of plastic wrap around her abdomen so as to seal her non-healing injuries. He tore the clear kitchen sheet off with his teeth, set the roll on the toilet next to the scissors, and finished the makeshift corset with plumber's tape and plastic before he stood up. Water dripped off him. He instructed Jamie to lie down fully in the tub and soak up some fresh liquid because the concrete had also dried her out as it hardened. The dead girl didn't complain. She gratefully slipped under the contained waves as Billy stepped out of the bath.

He watched her as he dried off. She didn't come up for air and it was eerie the way she just lay under the water, motionless and still. He thought about what it must have been like for her in the composite soup. Submerged in the gray liquid, drowning, unable to die, already dead, being buried alive. It was horrifying to think about, and it occurred to Billy how Jamie had awakened in a river. *The waters of life.* That day they had driven around, trying to find where she had crawled from the riverbank seemed like ages ago. Billy smiled thinking about it and Jamie saw him from underwater. She smiled back and waved. But her face never broke the surface.

The next morning they took a drive to the police station. They both thought that it would be better if Billy turned himself in, instead of begin caught unaware and arrested. The plan had changed. Jamie was no longer going to play possum. The construction site had enough evidence and witnesses and ties to Tony that they thought it would be safer for her to remain out of the picture. All morning long they cleaned the apartment with bleach, removing anything and everything that might be linked to her. Though ironically, she was the one that vacuumed the blue shag carpet. Once they'd finished inside, they moved to the Chevelle and gave it a thorough cleaning. The machine smelled new as it pulled into the station's parking lot.

Jamie wished him luck as he went in. She was supposed to grab the bus and hang out at a motel that they had chosen until everything had blown over, but something inside told her to wait. She didn't have long to find out why she was called to stay put, because in less than an hour Billy was making a beeline for the Chevelle.

He was surprised to see her and a little giddy at being released. Jamie had to ask him twice before he'd spill the beans. She figured it was payback for making him wait last night on what had happened between her and Tony.

"They kicked the warrant down due to an arrest," he told her.

As it turned out, when the police came to the aid and assistance of room 1033, Anthony Sorbini confessed to everything. He confessed to killing Jamie Lund and produced her purse and cell phone as evidence of the act. He laid out all the details that only her killer would know. He also told the cops about how her spirit had come back from the dead and how he had tried to bury her at a construction site. From what Billy had gathered in his short stay with the police, the boys in blue had been up all night, at several different locations, combing through grounds, collecting tons of hard evidence.

Jamie couldn't believe it, but it made sense when she considered what she had done. She'd fixed him. She made Tony a decent person in her final moments with him and he'd simply done what any honest man would do. He confessed. He told the truth when asked and took responsibility. Jamie chuckled when she thought about it and her chuckle turned to laughter. The tension that had held them both so tightly together for so long, gripped in constant fear, snapped. They both felt free and easy again. All of sudden Billy was hungry, so he told the dead girl that breakfast was on him, even though it was already noon and he knew she wasn't going to eat.

XLIV.

It was on a Saturday morning when Special Investigator James Riley stopped by. Billy was in the living room doing bills with cartoons yacking away in the background. He only had a few free hours because Hector needed him at the shop. Billy was still playing catch up with all the work that had piled up during his absence.

The mechanic wasn't even sure if he was going to be able to get his old job back after he'd broken his promise to the boss and the cops had come to the garage looking for him. But Billy found his boss a kinder person than what he'd given him credit. So, when Hector had asked his rogue employee what was going on the young man didn't hold back. He told Hector the truth. He laid it on the table, unburdening his shoulders, but the old man didn't believe him. He just laughed and told Billy that it was okay, he didn't have to tell him if he didn't want to. Though, he encouraged Billy to write it down because it was pretty imaginative, more entertaining than what he thought his mechanic was capable of creating, and then he put him back to work. There were cars that needed tuning, driveshafts that had to be replaced, valves sealed, heaters fixed, computer systems rebooted and wired, a transmission refurbished, and brakes wanting adjustments. Billy was the best mechanic he had, so Hector wasn't bound to let him go due to a little trouble with the law. Hell, he was young once, he understood.

"Better to put it out there than to keep it locked away," she told Billy when he mentioned what he'd said to Hector. But she cautioned him on telling too many people. She didn't want him being hauled off in a crazy cart because of her. Truth had a way of being its own shield at times. It was a fine line, but she knew Billy could handle it.

A cup of coffee fueled the young man's brain as he ran the figures from his checking and savings account. A faint knock stirred him to the door and Billy found the detective's smug grin less disturbing than before. It still made him ill at ease to see the cop again. Politely, Riley asked to be invited in. Jamie was on the back porch soaking up some sun, so Billy didn't think it would be a problem. She'd been looking more and more like a corpse lately and had been staying indoors. The lotions and baths weren't having as much effect as they had previously. Too much time was passing and wearing on her skin.

"Been some developments in the case," informed the Special Investigator as he moved into the living room. He eyed the dead girl on the balcony through the opened doors, but he turned and looked at Billy. "Thought I'd come by and tell you myself."

"I appreciate that," lied Billy.

Riley motioned toward a chair and Billy invited him sit as he told the detective that he'd heard something about it from the news and at the station when he went down to turn himself in.

"Yeah," the cop said, rubbing his jaw. "We're all pretty happy with this one. A lot of bad people are going down. It seems Mr. Sorbini, who confessed to the murder of Ms. Lund, has been very forthcoming about his former associates and we've been able to close the books on a couple cold cases. The FBI has moved in, as it appears Mr. Sorbini is being quite cooperative with a few ongoing cases that they've logged. Yeah," he stroked through an unsure brow as he leaned forward, tossing a look at the faraway girl again. "A really neat bow; but we still haven't been able to locate the body of Ms. Lund."

"That's a shame," Billy added.

"Yeah, it is," mused Riley. "I have my thoughts on the matter. The department, at the moment, doesn't seem too interested in producing the body, even though it would make the case against Mr. Sorbini tighter. He was…" Riley leaned back, relaxing his posture, "talking about some crazy shit when they brought him in." He chuckled softly, looking at Billy in that uncomfortable way. "Makes one wonder, you know? But," he added with his hands, "like I said before, we're all pretty stoked at putting a lid on this one. Seems we bagged bigger fish than what we could have hoped for. Just wish it wasn't at the expense of the young woman we found in the ally." He locked eyes with Billy. "You know what I mean?"

"Yes," the ex-suspect answered quietly.

Riley smiled that greasy sideways grin. "I thought you might." He paused and said, "Well," suddenly catching the girl on the back porch watching him as he added, "I don't think we're going to be able to find Ms. Lund's body, Mr. Kimmel. I guess that's all I really wanted to say. So, if you or any of her friends and secondary family are planning a funeral or some service, I regret to inform that you may want to proceed without any further delay."

Riley turned and looked directly at the dead girl. Jamie casually and slowly turned aside, glaring up at the sun. She pulled the shawl that she wore tighter across her shoulders as the cop stood up.

"These things have a way of working themselves out, Mr Kimmel. But I wouldn't worry too much."

Billy stood up too and the Special Investigator reached out his hand. Billy took it. "Thank you for your time, Mr. Kimmel, and sorry for your loss."

"Oh, uh," rattled off Billy, "Thank you for stopping by. As busy as I'm sure you are with this case and others I appreciate you taking the time."

"Gladly," the detective added with a grin, and then looking down, he said, "That sure is one unique carpet. You know that?"

"Yeah, I guess it is."

The cop pulled at his lower lip with his teeth before he added, "I pulled a fiber off the deceased back in the alley. Imagine my surprise when I found a matching carpet so neatly preserved."

"Huh," cited Billy. "Must've traveled with her when she moved out. She did live here for over two years."

"Of course," nodded Riley. "That must've been it."

Billy nodded too. "Must have."

"Well," added the detective, "it looks like you're busy."

"Yes," said Billy walking toward the door. "Again, thanks for stopping by."

Riley crossed to the opened door, stood on the threshold, and turned. "How do you think she got out of the morgue, surrounded by all those hospital personnel?"

Bill stammered. "I am sure I don't know."

Riley's grin was wide. "I'm sure you don't." He moved to leave, but stopped again. Billy felt that awful sinking feeling return whenever this guy was around. He just wanted him to leave. "The perpetrator must have dressed up like a member of the hospital staff to gain access in and out, don'tchya think?"

"I suppose so," he said to appease the cop. "It makes sense."

"Yeah, it does," stoked Riley. "I imagine them, possibly wearing scrubs or a doctor's coat, stethoscope around the neck, name badge, and a clipboard to tie it all up."

The man just glared at Billy knowingly and the mechanic was simply stunned, not knowing what to say or do next. So he did nothing for a spell. But when Riley hadn't left Billy shirked his shoulders, made a goofy smile, and added "sounds like it to me."

Suddenly, Riley slapped him hard on the shoulder and wished him a good day. He turned to leave but stopped once more and told Billy to take care of that friend of his. Then the Special Investigator skipped down the steps, moving away from the duplex to his car. Billy was dumbstruck. He lingered at the door until his neighbor poked his head out to see what was going on, and said, "Hello."

Billy returned the favor and went back inside. He was slightly shaking and felt that the cop knew more than he was letting on. Why else would he taunt him about the clipboard? *And the way he kept looking at Jamie through the room.* It had made him uneasy, and yet, he was oddly comforted by the cop's visit. The way he told him how satisfied the department was by Tony's grand confessions, him leaking information like the Titanic; Billy was confused.

As he joined her on the back porch, Jamie told him to relax and not worry about it as she took his hand and held it. Her fingers were dry and coarse, taught against the bone. Her skin was looking green and wrinkly. Billy replayed his and Riley's conversations over and again in his head until he was content enough to sit by Jamie's side for awhile before going off to work. The bills and account balances could wait. Deep down Billy knew he could handle what he was thinking about. He didn't have to run the numbers, but his father had taught him that it was always best to be sure. A few minutes or hours pouring over receipts and numbers were better than paying bank fees.

Jamie kept him talking until his time was up. She wanted to hear more about giving herself a funeral or some kind of memorial service. But Billy didn't know about that. Something about it just felt wrong for Jamie to show up at any event that was to honor her life and set her death on a more permanent record. He told her that it wouldn't be too appealing if the person who it was about just so happened to be sitting in the back row of the church. He told her that it was no better than stealing.

"Funerals," he pointed out, "are for the living. Not the dead."

"No one will even see me. I'll hang in the back."

He laughed. "And like no one is going to come up and talk to *you* about *you!*" He shook his head. "Not a good idea, Jay. If we do anything, and I'm saying IF…you'd have to stay away and be content with that." He gave her a stern face.

The dead girl pouted. "Haven't you ever wanted to attend your own funeral?"

"Doesn't matter," he said, rocking his noggin from side to side. "When I die I won't be here anymore. Just toss me in a box or char me up. I don't care. But I won't give you a memorial service if you're going to sneak in and see what everyone has to say aboutchya. It's just too damned narcissistic for my tastes"

He got up, readying for work. "It's just wrong, is all." He leaned down and planted a kiss on her forehead. It had only been a few short days since he'd cleaned her up and already fresh stubble was growing on top of the dead girl's head. "Put some of that Vaseline on your skin again. I left it sitting out on the bathroom sink. Maybe it'll help."

"I will," she told him as left for the garage.

      With the echo of the closed door firmly falling into the kitchen latch, the silence of the apartment moved around her. Clouds lazily etched themselves across a blue sky. The yard below the balcony was littered with black feathers. Her birds were molting, getting ready for the new season. Jamie could taste its coming on the wind. She also tasted wheat fields and barley, factory storehouses, and bus exhaust. The wind brought the dead girl a menu of sights and places unseen and the scent of the sea. Some winds were damp and heavy, some laden with perfume, and some were as light as desert sand. From her small perch in the city, Jamie imbibed the whole world, and it was such a beautiful day.

XLV.

Autumn came and found the dead girl withering. She, like the leaves were turning brown. When the month of July had come and August loomed in the calendar, Billy rented the other apartment in the duplex for Jamie. He helped his neighbor move out on a Saturday and moved Jamie in that following Sunday morning as church bells rang down the street. Jamie didn't have a whole lot of things to take with her to her new home. Billy could afford the rent on both places, but he couldn't afford to furnish it. So, it was a good thing the girl didn't have any high aspirations of decorating a killer pad. There was a lawn chair, his favorite recliner, and a TV that he'd picked up at a thrift store along with an end table and lamp.

He hooked the cable up by himself, splicing the feed off his line, so that she could enjoy HBO, Cinemax, and a slew of other channels. It definitely wasn't any luxury accommodation, but it was ample enough for the dead girl, and she was thankful. They each had a key, but mostly kept the doors unlocked. Jamie still flittered between both units and Billy was always there to help her sooth her decaying frame. Nature was unkind.

Even though she washed regularly with and without Billy's aid, maggots always seemed to thrive. They especially adored her bullet hole and slashes, eating her, bit by bit. Once Jamie had became more accustomed to the wormy insects always hanging around she started to name them: Ralph and Eddie, Frank, Joe, and Lisa. She'd tell Billy what they had been up to on a particular day. He knew she washed them down the drain on a regular basis, but the same names stuck. Jamie laughed about her maggots, as if they were children, even though Billy never found it funny. He just listened, spending all his time away from the garage with her. Neither one of them knew just how long she really had left before the decay of Mother Nature had its way with her. Or when Horus was going to return and reclaim what was his.

Each day the mechanic came home he half-expected to find her missing, or at least find a note, or some sign that the ancient Egyptian had come back and taken her away. But day after day, the dead girl remained in his presence, and the two apartments became home. She became his world and oddly it felt like it used to, when they were living together, before she had moved out. But her body was a changing canvas of decomposition. There was little they could do to thwart what was happening, so they tried to manage it as best they could and keep her as fresh and limber as possible. Baths and massages with scented lotions had become ritual, and Billy was fast becoming fond of bringing home car fresheners from work. He hung them from the ceiling in her place, and when the weather had turned and the leaves were parachuting from neighboring trees, her side of the duplex was decorated by a cardboard forest.

Billy and Jamie took walks at night when they knew that a fair amount of people were home with their families or in bed, leaving sidewalks vacant and clear. Jamie wasn't always able to handle a stroll around the block. Sometimes, her muscles and joints ached so badly that all she could do was sit still and listen to Billy read to her from the numerous books she was amassing or have him tell her stories from their past.

He always found her in the backyard when he came home, sitting in the lawn chair, as if each day were her last and she didn't want to miss it. Rain and gloomy days never seemed a bother for the dead girl. He found her there. So Jamie was in the backyard when he came home from the memorial service that he and Loni and thrown for her. It had taken some convincing, but Jamie agreed to stay out of it. Billy had told her that Loni was convinced that her vengeful spirit had come back from the beyond to make Tony pay for what he'd done and to lead her away from suffering the same kind of fate. The poor girl felt indebted to her and told everyone at the service how they were the best of friends. Loni had joined a church group and was attending mass regularly. Jamie could scarcely contain her laughter. She wanted a riotous chuckle, imagining it, but feared jarring something loose in her jaw or neck if she let go too wildly.

Billy told her all about the service as he pulled the other lawn chair beside her and took a seat. They talked well into the night. Mostly about who had shown up and who had cried and who had commented on the chosen photo. It was all very touching. Her old boss, Douglas Rand, had brought a huge wreath. Jamie couldn't help but find the whole thing amusing. It just seemed odd to hear how people had remembered her. Time was a distortion of perception, a thin wheel where only glimpses shone through. As leaves fell outside, inside Jamie's apartment bouquets of flowers and the funeral wreaths sat wilting with distinction.

By winter's harsh breath they had formed several routines to maintain Jamie's condition and she had stopped looking out of the window or over her shoulder for Horus to return. They enjoyed many games of Scrabble, Jenga, and Backgammon. They both learned new card games and for Christmas Billy bought his rotting corpse a scarf and set of poker chips. They decorated both apartments together, though Billy did most of the work. The multi-colored lights lent a strange vibe to Jamie's barren rooms and pine-shaped air-fresheners.

He had gotten her some gloves and thick wool socks, and a winter's coat that she didn't like to wear. He was worried that he'd come home one day and find her frozen stiff to the lawn chair in the backyard and that he'd have to carry her in, like a gigantic ice cube, and thaw her out inside the duplex. But the dead girl never froze over, though her touch felt just as icy. Jamie never abandoned her perch either, not a single day, but her winged companions had to move on. As the dead season fell upon the city, Jamie's crows flew south to warmer climates where foraging and carrion were better.

Every now and then one of them would fly back to see her. They'd caw at her from the telephone wires or edges of brick and she'd talk to them from her worn out chair in the yard. They always brought news that placed her in a decent cheer. Snow clung to the damp and dark places of the fenced in yard, littering the dead gray grass with islands of white. Besides Billy, the blackbirds were her only companions. She missed seeing them in full force above her head as the fierce winter nights descended. She had come to rely on their constant vigil and was saddened for days at a time when they had left. Though, she felt it in her bones that they would come back...*one day.*

Her eyesight wasn't what it had once been and she hoped that when the birds did return that she would, at least, be able to see them before the summer winds blew her to dust. As shadowy days shortened and the air blew in fragrant wisps of bitter, frigid mountaintops Ralph and Jake, Erin, Joe, Frank, Eddie, and Lisa stopped ravaging her body, leaving her alone when Billy went off to work. Bits of bone were showing now and Jamie was finding it hard to move at all. Even talking took considerable effort, and this was when she was inside with the heater turned up, as Billy liked to keep it when he was over.

One day as he finished some Chinese takeout, Jamie told him that she loved him. She said that she couldn't leave it unsaid any longer. She wanted him to know how she really felt. She had always loved him, since high school. There had never been any other person that she'd ever loved. It had been, and would always be, him. Jamie explained that she wanted to get it out before her vocal chords had completely rusted and she was rendered speechless, as she feared her course was heading. Her voice was already a mean grate of loose sandpapery rasps. There was no telling how long it would last.

By early spring Jamie had become mute, and her skin and muscles were flat against her bones like a skeleton. Billy had to help her walk from the house to her seat outside. He started to place her there at the beginning of the day, before he left for work, and bringing her back in at night once he'd gotten home. The grass was green again, the sun was high, and butterflies and honeybees, from some far off glade, were making daily stops to the backyard.

Jamie enjoyed their company immensely. After the desolate shoal of winter and all its bleak canopy of neighbors, it did her old bones good to be surrounded by such beauty and life. Even the crows began to come home. Day by day, their dark spots filled the cityscape, outlining buildings with a rich thick edge of black. Billy was happy to see them again, and he had to admit that he'd gotten used to their sullen shapes and frequent caws into their conversations.

He did all the talking now. The dead girl could only nod. On occasions she would write a few things down on a pad of paper that he'd collected for her, along with some pens. He often wondered if she could still hear his prattling, but Jamie always made him feel that she could, or at the least, that she was interested in what he had to say,

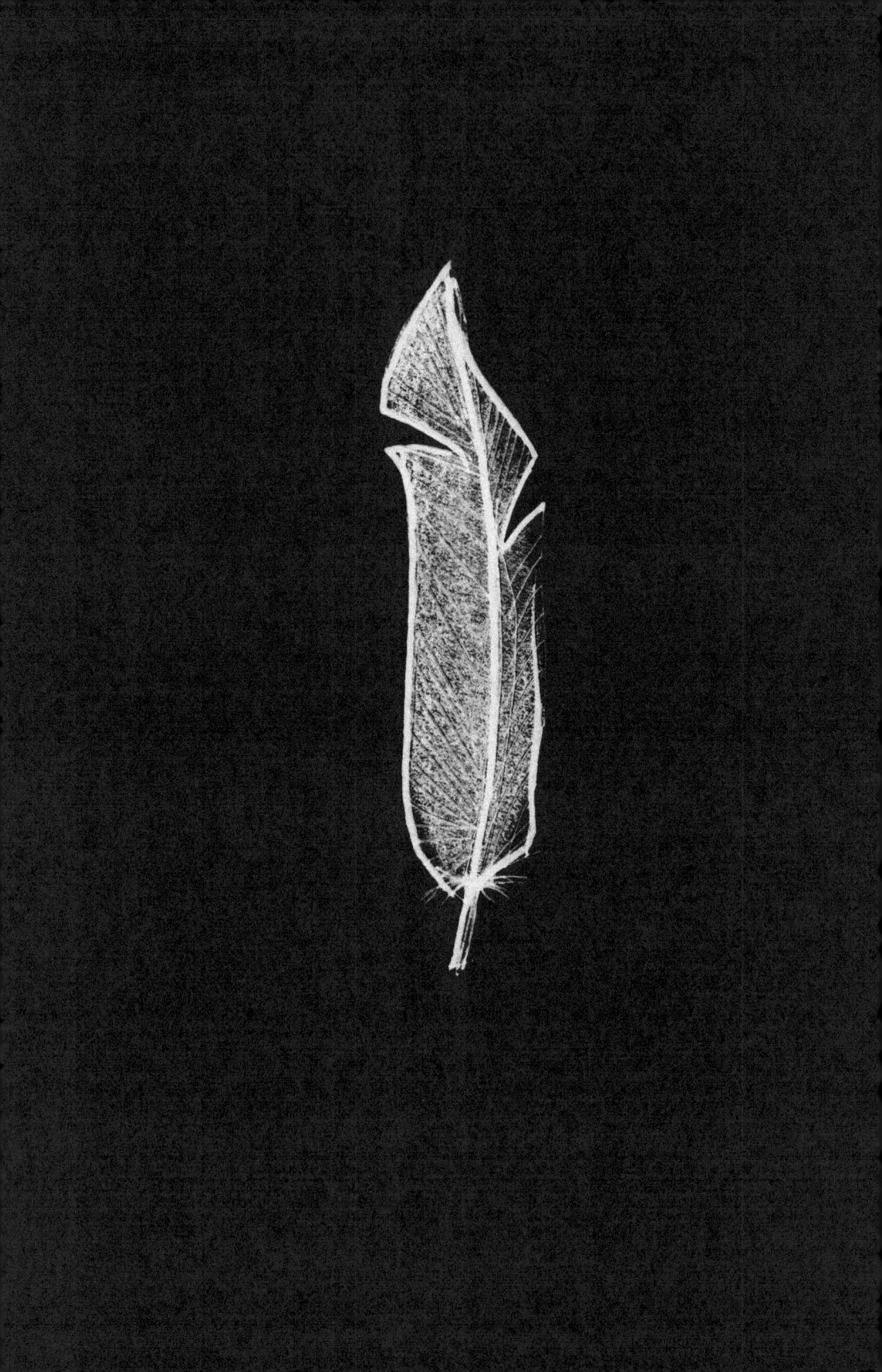

despite the fact that he knew he'd already told her the same story about a month earlier.

As the weather warmed and the rains came and went and summer hung on the horizon of all the advertising, Billy couldn't help but feel anxious every time he came home. He fully expected to walk in and round the corners of the rooms, step out onto the back porch and find her gone. He imagined it so many times that when it finally happened it didn't phase him. And he didn't go looking for her inside her apartment as he once thought he would. There was just something inside of him that ticked. It told him that he wasn't going to find her there anymore, and that it was okay.

For a long time, Billy kept her lawn chair nestled into its weather worn grooves. Even after the straps that held it together had rotted and broken, becoming a fixture in the yard, he seldom cut the grass around it. Before it rotted like its owner he used it, once he had moved all of her stuff back into his place, cleaned the other unit up, and posted an advert for a renter. Billy would sit out there alone, thinking of her. Or with his new neighbor, looking to a skyline not darkened by the flights of crows. For many years after Jamie had vanished, Billy would always turn at a blackbird's caw with the hope of seeing his dead girl one more time. But he never did.

Jamie knew when the blackbirds began to return that she only had a little time left. She felt the call in the dried marrow of her bones, on that last day, as Billy walked her to her perch in the backyard. Even if she could have opened her mouth and let words tumble from her shriveled, taught lips she would not have told him that she was leaving. It would have been too hard for the both of them, and he wouldn't have wanted her to go. The dead girl knew she had to leave and that she had to do it on her own. Billy had done enough for her already. It was immeasurable in her non-beating heart. He had loved and cared for her despite all her fallacies, being there like no other. This last leap into the eternal was meant only for her. So, Jamie just squeezed his arm as he left, like she had done on so many other mornings past.

After Billy was gone, she went back inside and threw on an overcoat, sunglasses, shoes, and a hat. Every movement was a struggle, but she felt the fire of Horus within her, burning with an unearthly energy. It gave her the strength to shut the door behind herself, and head slowly up the street. Jamie followed the crows to the edge of the city. A fruitless patch of opened ground where no roadways or high-rises jutted like hard flowers from the earth, it had been zoned and forgotten about long ago for some buried economical use. To where trees loomed in the distance and the sun shone down with an incredible fiery light, grasses waved gently at the dead girl's approach.

Jamie stripped her carcass of all garments and accessories, letting them lay where they fell. She walked naked through the air and sunlight. Her body was barren, shrunken and emaciated. She looked like a wraith against the blue sky and the billowing clouds that were temples in the heavens. A thousand winged souls encircled her, like they had on one other occasion. They remembered carrying her soul as if it were a pebble plucked from a river in their beaks.

They understood the weight of the dead girl's burden and shouldered some of her plight. They had felt the caliber of her heart and witnessed great fear overcome. From the timbre of their tiny throats to the blinding eye of the sun-filled sky caws erupted like trumpets and drums. It felt loud enough to shake the belly of the city loose. Jamie spread her arms wide, tilted her skull back, and waited for the delicate hand from heaven. The sun grew hotter and burned the air around her to a brilliant flashing white.

When the bright essence had dissolved to the evanescence of a clear natural sky, the dead girl was gone. There was no trace of her except the impression of her foot embedded in a dry patch of earth between some grass, her clothes left casually arrayed, and the blackbirds flying away with the glint of a new jewel held silently in their beaks. A few feathers fell to earth, but no more. They were the only things that landed from that tarnished and painted sky, as their winged masters cawed the quiet bell of the city.

Publisher's Note

Also Available by the Author!

Fiction:

Blood Junky
Love in Vein

NonFiction:

Spoken Word

Vampire News: *volume one*
Tasty Bits For You To Sink Your Fangs Into!

Vampire News: *volume two*
The (*not so*) End Times Edition

Vampire News: *volume three*
Really...Vampires Suck!

Documentary Film:

Committing Poetry in Times of War

Upcoming Books:

Blood in Vein
Firefly's Kiss
Baltimore

More from the author at:

www.crazyduckpress.com
www.studioonthesquare.net
www.kaoskustomfangs.com

Photo: Jacquie Coté

Stavros is a writer, musician, poet, photographer, painter, graphic designer, fangsmith, and award-winning filmmaker. In 2001, he created the Poetry Television Project for public cable access, producing eight volumes of the groundbreaking series, and released the documentary, *Committing Poetry in Times of War*, in 2007. A publisher, he helped to launch The Independent Underground Newspaper, BioGamer Girl, and Unpublished Magazine. He's had a coffeehouse, an international clothing design company; and performed drums at an impromptu concert for Max, the Crystal Skull. Author of the critically acclaimed novels, *Blood Junky* and *Love in Vein*, two of his plays have been brought to the stage, he writes screenplays, and creates photographic illusions that he peddles like a gypsy. A father of two, he lives in America.

Author's Studio Site:
www.StudioOnTheSquare.net

Cool eStore:
www.CrazyDuckPress.com

On Facebook:
https://www.facebook.com/stavros.cockrell
https://www.facebook.com/ogbloodjunky
https://www.facebook.com/ogdeadgirl
https://www.facebook.com/loveinveinmovie
https://www.facebook.com/CrazyDuckPress
https://www.facebook.com/StudioSquared
https://www.facebook.com/KaosKustomFangs

Twitter: @VisualLyricist
Twitter: @CrazyDuckPress

Custom Fangs, Tusks, & Zombie Teeth:
www.kaoskustomfangs.com

Stavros Wishes to Thank:

Special Thanks to The Almighty, My children: One & Story, Mom, Jacquie, Lisa – for all her hard work crunching through pages and listening, to Donna for voicing her interest in the story when no one else would, to the Fathers and Mothers at Our Lady of Kazan Skete for their prayers and guidance; Amy, Crystal, and Paula for their constant support, Tara – for her insightful gifts with words, CH for original visualizations, Grandma for da' love, C. Delaney for some notes, Aaron – for taking the story to the next level, and PB – 'cause in truth… All Thank Yous To Grace Pena!

Live. Love. Create.

Photo: Vivan Chime Concepcion

Aaron is the eldest of three siblings who all happen to pursue art passionately – *drawing, painting, music,* and *sculpting.* Born in the small town of Minglanilla, Cebu province, Philippines, he suspended his Architecture college courses to further develop his drawing and painting skills. Though he earned good scholastic records in formal education, he made a more lasting impression with his artistic skills, and as the years went by, continued to develop progressively, earning a reputation from successive wins at various poster-making contests.

Aaron is a lover of poetry and literature, and can be quite a compulsive bookworm at times. In 2006, he won the regional essay-writing contest where he was pitted against some of the best candidates from the region's prestigious Philippine schools. He is currently an artist for Vapor Comics.

On Facebook:

https://www.facebook.com/Baruct.Vaolswi

https://www.facebook.com/ogdeadgirl

Vapor Comics:
http://vaporcomics.com

Publishing Site & Cool eStore:

www.CrazyDuckPress.com

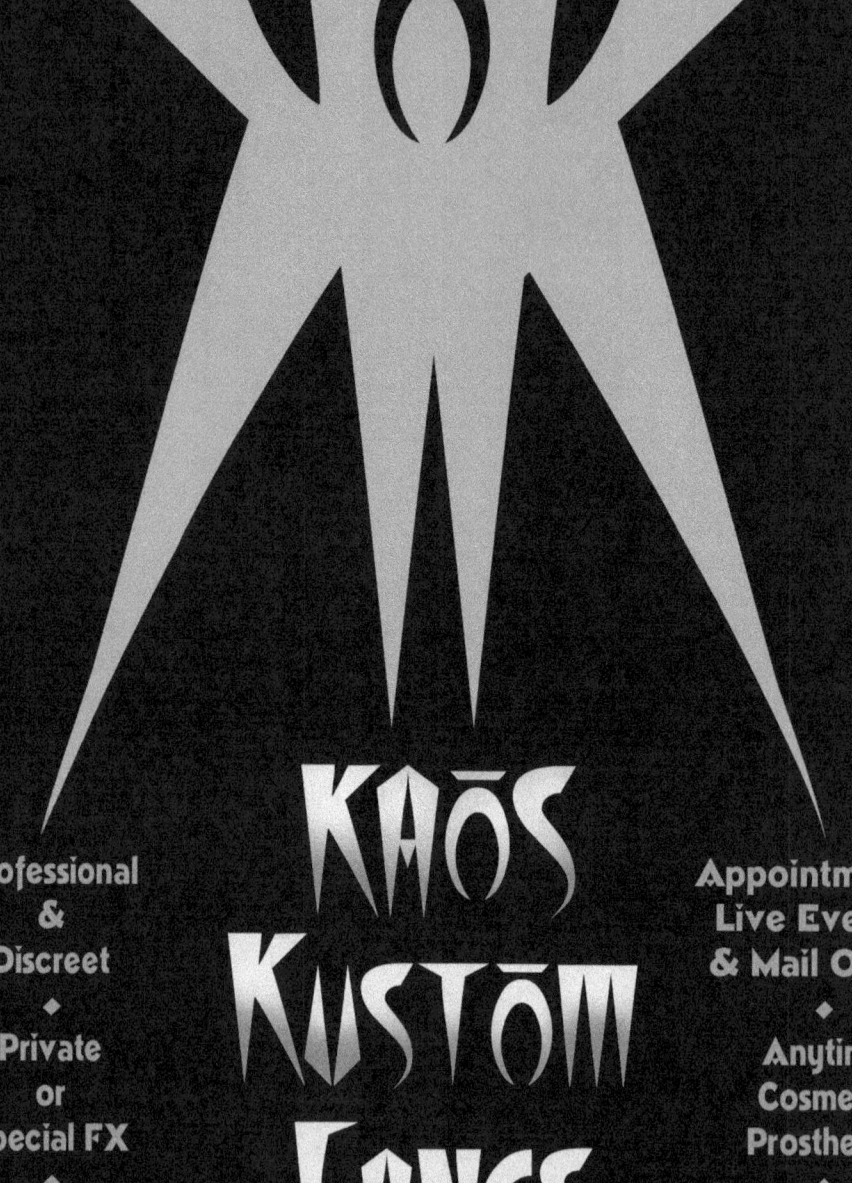

www.ingramcontent.com/pod-product-compliance
Lightning Source LLC
Chambersburg PA
CBHW071233250626
47163CB00001B/161